1295

W9-BSP-435

Hot and Bothered

. . . .

by

ALGONQUIN BOOKS OF CHAPEL HILL
Post Office Box 2225
Chapel Hill, North Carolina 27515-2225

a division of
WORKMAN PUBLISHING
708 Broadway
New York, New York 10014

This is a work of fiction. While, as in all fiction,
the literary perceptions and insights are based on
experience, all names, characters, places, and incidents
are either products of the author's imagination or are
used fictitiously.

Library of Congress Cataloging-in-Publication Data
Downey, Annie.
    Hot and bothered : a novel / by Annie Downey.—1st ed.
        p. cm.
    ISBN-13: 978-1-56512-474-5; ISBN-10: 1-56512-474-X
    1. Divorced mothers—Massachusetts—Fiction.   2. Identity
(Psychology)—Fiction.   I. Title.
PS3604.O942H67 2006
813'.6—dc22   2006045873

10 9 8 7 6 5 4 3 2 1
First Edition

Hot an
Both

. . . .

a novel by *Annie Down*

Published
ALGONQ
Post Off
Chapel

a divisi
WORK
225 V
New

© 2
Pri
P
b

ALGONQUIN BOOKS OF CHAPEL HILL   2006

Hot and Bothered

a novel by

Annie Downey

ALGONQUIN BOOKS OF CHAPEL HILL   2006

Published by
ALGONQUIN BOOKS OF CHAPEL HILL
Post Office Box 2225
Chapel Hill, North Carolina 27515-2225

a division of
WORKMAN PUBLISHING
225 Varick Street
New York, New York 10014

This is a work of fiction. While, as in all fiction,
the literary perceptions and insights are based on
experience, all names, characters, places, and incidents
are either products of the author's imagination or are
used fictitiously.

Library of Congress Cataloging-in-Publication Data
Downey, Annie.
        Hot and bothered : a novel / by Annie Downey.—1st ed.
        p. cm.
        ISBN-13: 978-1-56512-474-5; ISBN-10: 1-56512-474-X
        1. Divorced mothers—Massachusetts—Fiction.   2. Identity
(Psychology)—Fiction.   I. Title.
PS3604.O942H67 2006
813'.6—dc22   2006045873

10 9 8 7 6 5 4 3 2 1
First Edition

To my family

Hot and Bothered

one

A Week from Hell

I feel like an ogre with a rotten tooth. Scream at Lucy. My tooth is getting worse, despite three painkillers. I tell Brendan to turn off the computer. Get into bed sweaty and in pain. Fall asleep with my light on. Suddenly Lucy is standing at the foot of the bed, twirling a pencil like it's a baton. She has that look—pure evil, with her I'll-get-you-back-rotten-mommy eyes—pajama bottoms up to her knees, and long feet flexed like a tigress's. I awake momentarily. Slight drool on my pillow. I shut off the light. Tigress daughter leaps up and runs down the hall to her room. Surely Brendan is still on the computer.

Sunday

I wake with a dreadful start. Go into Lucy's room. Her light is on and I switch it off. Lucy's body is stomach down, arms tucked underneath for warmth. I throw the blanket, which she has kicked off, back over her. Always-brooding son is already up and in the bathroom proudly examining his new hickey. I've yet to extract confession as to who neck-sucker is. Undoubtedly some Hoover-lipped teen with vampire aspirations.

"Brendan, I have to use the bathroom." I knock on the open door. He grunts, then pads away from the mirror, bending his head underneath the doorframe. I'm in denial about just how big he actually is, hence I can still yell and give him much-needed time-outs. I rush past him and squat.

"Shut the door, Mom. You're disgusting," he grumbles, and slams the door to his room. Death music instantly pounds through the walls.

I scream from the toilet, "Turn it down!" But he already has, and my "down" is released into silence.

"I am. Jesus!" he screams back.

"Don't use that tone with me!" I shout and smirk. He groans and bangs drawers shut. I decide to let him vent his anger before serving a lovely breakfast of cheese danish. Pray this will calm him down enough for him to reevaluate his prudish standards of bathroom etiquette and choice of morning sonnet.

I have a flashback to Brendan peeing off the porch, dressed only in cowboy boots and a belt stuffed with plastic swords. My heart seizes up with quiet despair as I realize that during naked swordsmanship era I couldn't wait for him to grow into a quiet sulky teenager with afternoon sleep tendencies. Kick myself for always wanting him to be something else. Decide I need a new attitude.

In the kitchen, the floor is unbearably cold on my bare feet. I try to tiptoe. No go. Still freezing. I open the breadbox; danish has vanished.

"Brendan! For god's sake, we always have danish on Sunday, you know that!" Brendan does not respond. I know it was him and his rabid geek friends who sit around his computer screen downloading crap music and pretending to be hackers with user names like Sledgehammer and Deathslayer. I stomp upstairs and rap on his door. Nothing.

"If I find danish remains in there, you're dead, Mr. Man." Still nothing, so I fling open the door. Brendan is draped on the bed with headphones strapped on his head. The danish container sits atop an altar of stolen eats overflowing in the midget wastebasket.

More like waste cup. I make a mental note to buy him a big metal trashcan, then wave my hands in front of Brendan's face. Not a blink. I observe him. The image of peace and good fortune, very feng shui—listening to hardcore—clothes rumpled, a slight smell of mildew.

He's a replica of his father, and Lucy is the female version. Their blond hair and lanky bodies represent some sort of genetic denial of my dwarf darkness. My fear of Brendan inheriting my four-foot-ten frame and developing a huge complex as he compared himself to his father's six-four was radical overkill. Brendan at fourteen years old is already taller than his father. Lucy is seven and almost my height. I have an acute intuitive sense that she will not be able to get a date taller than her navel after she hits eighth grade. Am now terrified that they both have gigantism gene. And who knows what the divorce has done to them! Have prayed regularly on both these matters.

Brendan shifts. His eyes flicker. He smells the tangible presence of mother and opens his eyes wide, throws up his hands, and says in perfect pitch, despite blasting headphones, "What now?"

I point to the waste cup. He shrugs, showing absolutely no contrition. I pull off his headphones and snarl, "At least say 'Sorry, Mom!'"

"Sorry, Mom," he repeats, deadpan.

I stomp out of the room. Hear him laugh. Stomp around the house for a while. It feels good. I feed Ugly, who inhales the food in one bite then licks the bowl over and over until it's on the far side of the kitchen, pushed against the baseboard. He whines, licks my legs and feet. The smell of doggy breath rises from my now sticky legs. I let Ugly out in the backyard to roam and sniff. Only forty minutes until church. I make a cup of tea with extra honey to lure Lucy out of her customary morning coma, this one intensified by last night's hyperactive meanderings. Ponder leaving them both at home, since Lucy will throw tantrum after tantrum until doughnut time after Mass and Brendan will sit five feet away in a four-foot-long pew carrying a look of total disdain while exhibiting that mark of the devil on his neck. I bring tea up to the slumbering demon, set the cup on her dresser, and bounce up and down on the foot of her bed. Her smooth white-blond hair, framing her peachlike cheeks, jiggles with the bed. Her eyes do not open, yet she growls, "Stop it," then, "Leave me alone!" I continue to bounce but my effort remains fruitless.

Without cheese danish my spirits are down. I stop bouncing. Get up. Drink Lucy's sweet tea. Walk down the hall and tell Brendan I'm off to church alone. He looks at me as if his own prayers have been answered and immediately goes online. I warn him not to use headphones, under penalty of my throwing the computer in a hellish inferno.

"Why not?" he grumps, taking off the headphones.

"In case your sister awakens from slumber, packs a small suitcase, and leaves."

He rolls his eyes. I take the headphones. He rolls his eyes again and I choose to ignore him. Far better this way.

Headphones hidden in my closet, I dress in fetching worn-out fishermen's sweater and stretchy flare pants. I try to look artsy by adding hot pink clogs. Why? Have a certain hidden desire to find a man who cherishes my hot pink clogs—can't explain. I consider waking Lucy—so we can be match-y—since I bought purple clogs with hot pink flowers for her. Think better of it; negative far outweighs positive. I make sure all the doors and windows are locked. Check everything three times, grab my cell phone, and leave.

As I turn left at the top of Granville Road and head toward Harvard Square, I have a feeling akin to Christmas. Can't remember the last time children were at home and I went somewhere without them. Usually I wait until visitation with their father or they are in school to go anywhere. Now I'd like to play hooky and go to a fancy brunch near a very shiny blue swimming pool. Have no idea how to attain hooky ideal.

Mass

I reach the parish and delight in recognizing only a few people. The priest talks about children obeying their parents and parents loving their children unconditionally. I start feeling beyond guilty. Imagine my house on fire. Distract myself from these thoughts by staring unscrupulously at new young male parishioners and their perfectly groomed blond wives, all a foot taller than me. The only other brunette is a heavenly-looking Vietnamese woman. She nods continuously and rubs her perfectly behaved son's head every time the priest says "love" or "child."

I check that my cell phone is on. It is. No calls missed. I resolve never to go to church without precious angel children who sulk so cutely. Think fondly back to Mass two weeks ago when Lucy was lobbing pretend grenades at the priest, whom she had chosen with much deliberation to be head of the mutant army she alone was fighting.

My heart races as I suddenly notice Perfect Guy a few rows in front of me. My hands begin to sweat. Horrible. I slink five pews back, where I am better able to observe, unfettered, his steel-cut buns outlined in rich muslin fabric. As we kneel in prayer, I admire his shoulders beneath his crisp cotton white shirt—very un-autumn. Perfect Guy does not attend after-service doughnut worship, nor does he ever notice me. I, however, have an eye on his pulse. Perfect Guy is unusually light today. A distinct orange-blossom odor emanates from his pores, enveloping me. I don't like it. His darkness is gone. Who is she? I instantly imagine a southern accent, poetic stance, manicured nails, and husky chuckle. Miffed, I decide she is definitely the sort who scratches her boyfriend's back in long sultry swoops in public. I'm envious—always wanted to be a temptress yet mostly end up looking like a pixie.

The service has ended. I do not go in peace. Rather, I breathlessly walk past the first set of double doors, press my fingers into the slimy holy water, and pray Perfect Guy's temptress gets hit by truck. Cross myself.

Pip

Shortcutting it over to Garden Street via Harvard Yard, I hear the muffled ring of my cell phone. I fumble manically in my purse and locate the phone. My hands shake. Am sure someone has broken into the house and is holding the children at gunpoint. "Hello," I manage.

Pip, my best and only friend, says in a raspy morning voice, "So was that perfect guy you can't shut up about at church this morning?"

"Yes," I say meekly, knowing what she is going to ask next, having vowed this past Friday that I would introduce myself to Perfect Guy.

"Did you go and speak to him?" I don't answer. Instead, I twirl my hair with my free hand.

"You didn't even say 'Hi,' did you?" I remain mute. "I knew it!" Pip says, and hangs up.

I throw the phone in my bag. My rotten tooth, which has been under control all morning, starts to throb. I root around in my bag for painkillers. Have forgotten them. I bring miserable pixie self home like a little black rain cloud.

Back Home

Home again, home again, jiggedy-jig—little black cloud breaks into sunshine. My radiant son has made a huge feast of pancakes. Demon Princess is still a-snooze, but I don't think about her bedtime seven hours from now. I listen to folk music on public radio and put my feet up on the kitchen table. Relish this tranquil moment of single motherhood. Thanks to the divorce settlement in my favor, I am "displaced homemaker" with no "job skills." Lovely.

Later That Evening

The phone rings just as I am settling into "my time," which consists of a large bowl of popcorn, some licorice, and a television program about sex and single women who don't have children. Totally my kind of fantasy. Am highly addicted. The kids are quiet. I suspect they're playing some violent computer game instead of going to bed. Don't care, as long as I can put my whole being into the show.

The phone stops ringing, then starts again. I think it entirely possible my mother has plummeted to her death after parachuting from a plane; I pick up. It is my rat of an ex-husband. Am thrown into vile mood.

"You always interrupt my show," I fume. "It's this passive-aggressive tendency of yours."

"What show?" Ex-Rat asks innocently.

"The show I watched every Sunday night for the last four years of our marriage!" I yell.

"What the hell are you talking about? What show?" he yells back.

"Never mind," I say sullenly. "You never even noticed me the last four years of our marriage, so it is not shocking that you don't remember my favorite show."

"It is not like you noticed me either," he says.

"Oh, sorry, I think I was too busy cooking dinner for you every night, making your lunch, washing and ironing your clothes, all while you screwed everyone in the neighborhood." I gather speed. "Actually, this is probably why you don't remember my favorite show, you were probably at the office catching up on some paperwork—didn't that usually go on until two in the morning?" I am dizzy with rancor.

"Let's not go there," Ex-Rat says.

"Why? Am I being too honest? Was it better to simply believe I didn't have a clue? That I was your dumb wife at home?" I dig.

"Just stop," Ex-Rat demands.

"I knew every one. Every single one. Each and every time," I say.

Finished with my rant, I feel wonderful. Calm and peaceful. I remember that the yard looks like a hayfield. "By the way, the lawn needs mowing," I say airily and hang up. Don't want to miss one more second of precious dialogue. I chomp my popcorn, eyes glued to the tube.

Computer

My show ends. Bloated and satisfied, I trod down to Brendan's room, having found Lucy's empty. They are fixated on the computer screen. Brownie crumbs are all over the floor. It's after ten on a school night. I explode.

"That does it!" I scream. They jump. I walk over and pull out all the cords. Lucy starts biting me with her demonic brownie-stained teeth.

"Oh, that *really* does it," I say more evenly now. She keeps biting. I open the window, chuck out the mouse and keyboard. They land on the porch roof. Lucy and Brendan become silent and turn white. I heft the monitor down the stairs, adrenal glands pumping. Ugly barks at me. Walking out into backyard, I dump the monitor on top of the trash can, then go back upstairs. The children are in bed. Lights off. Not a peep.

I sit in bed and try to thaw. Think of the cost of a new computer. Pray it doesn't rain. Have sinking feeling that I am becoming my mother. Wonder if I need meds. At least I'll have something to talk about other than Ex-Rat during tomorrow's therapy session. Joy.

Driving to School

The alarm wakes me. It's still dark. I hate October mornings before setting the clocks back. I remember it's my day to volunteer at the senior center. Groan. I really went too far with this Perfect Guy thing, having volunteered for every church activity in vain hope of bumping into him. Never have. Am now stuck doing all these dreadful honorable things. I toss my feet over the side of the bed, on top of Ugly, who grumps. I climb off the other side of the bed, walk down the hall, knock on Brendan's door, which is ajar. I hear the toilet flush. I go and dress Lucy in her school clothes. Half-dragging her downstairs, I direct her to the couch, where she falls back asleep. I make lunches and two toast-and-egg breakfast sandwiches, then shove the lunches into an old tote bag with the library logo. Discover missing overdue books inside.

"That's where they were!" I say out loud, truly delighted.

Brendan comes downstairs. "You know that I have a jazz band meeting this morning, right? I have to be at school by 7:15."

I nod vaguely. Have no memory of a jazz band meeting. Now I will have to drop off Brendan first. The high school is in the opposite direction of Lucy's elementary school and the senior center is closer to Brendan's. Grrrrrr! I place the egg sandwiches in his hands. Sprint upstairs and dress myself in yesterday's church outfit, which is still on the floor in a heap. I tug a brush through my hair and call for Ugly, who groans as he lifts his old body from the floor. I put out Ugly's food and water on the back porch and direct a sleepwalking Lucy from couch to car. Precious peachy-keen Lucy stirs; her eyes open and close.

I start the car, carefully backing down the driveway. Fallen leaves from my out-of-control yard are slowly creeping out and beyond to the neighbors' better maintained properties. I make a mental note to purchase a rake, since ours is now a nub with a broken handle thanks to Brendan using it to whack a soccer ball against the side of the house.

We drive up Granville Road, then into a wealthier area next to our neighborhood where it's too quiet—no one is out, no kids dragging backpacks behind them, no dogs loose and sniffing, no homeless pushing grocery carts full of bottles. This section of Huron Village is safe and snug as a museum with its vast houses and circular driveways, its quiet groundskeepers, who move in and out like ghosts, snipping and clipping, painting and scrubbing, until everything gleams, dead, unmoving.

I turn on the radio, since my old Volvo wagon is not equipped with modern audio technology, and find the oldies station. Cat Stevens is playing and I turn the volume way up and begin singing—"Morning has broken! Like the first morning . . ."—disrupting the unnatural quiet of this place. Brendan starts making fake puking noises and takes out his iPod. I stop, turning down the music as I reach the intersection near Cambridge Common where cars halt at the traffic light. The dashboard clock reads 6:59 a.m. Yes! We'll make it to Brendan's school on time! Watching the college students bike through the park on stylish three-speeds, the leaves beautiful reds and golds, drifting, I release a breath. Suddenly I feel an amazing sense of control over my environment. Am feeling quite good about myself, actually. Like I have my life together. An excellent start to the week. I look in other car windows to see if anyone is staring enviously at me. No one is. Pity.

Drop-Off No. 1

At school, I drop off Brendan (minus visible hickey, thanks to my insistence on a turtleneck) with sax in hip new carrying case slung over one shoulder, backpack on the other. His fists are hard in his pockets, head down, ever so slight backhand wave without turning around. I realize he has forgotten his lunch, so I beep the horn, and lean my whole upper body out the window, holding the lunch bag. Red in the face, Brendan grabs it from me as I try to kiss and pat his retreating figure. End up kissing his stomach. He literally jumps back as if scalded and runs to join his classmates.

"He hates when you kiss him, so why do you keep trying to do it?" Lucy says, opening her window and chucking her uneaten sandwich out of it. I pretend not to notice her sandwich mutiny and smile pleasantly while scoping out drop-off line to see if any perfect parents in their gleaming SUVs are looking on in utter horror that I have raised a nasty litterbug. Luckily, all are busy reapplying lipstick in rearview mirrors or talking rapidly on cell phones. I turn off the engine, putting the key in my pocket in case Demon Princess tries to lock me out of the car, and quickly leap out to grab egg bits and toast, which I then stuff in the driver's door pocket.

I remind myself to remind myself to get rid of carnage at the nearest receptacle. Sure to forget. I hand Demon Princess a protein bar made exclusively for women. Seeing that it's covered in chocolate, she eats it. Hope it balances future raging hormones.

Drop-Off No. 2

Late for Lucy's drop-off, I screech into the parking lot, barely missing the crossing guard, and leave the car, still running, in a fire lane. Anxiety huge—like, huge. Am positive we've missed sharing circle time, Lucy's favorite school activity in the whole wide world at the moment. When we reach Lucy's classroom, her classmates are lined up inside the door with their slicked-back hair and scrubbed faces. I try to comprehend, while catching my breath, why this is. Then a shark-like gravitational pull causes me turn to the far corner of the room: Ex-Rat is standing next to the teacher's desk with an envelope. A false smile on his tight face, he waves the envelope at me.

"Thought you might have forgotten that it's picture day," Ex-Rat says, still flapping the envelope back and forth. Lucy runs over to hug and kiss her father, who dips, enfolds her, and says, "Hey, pooch!"

I wrap my arms tight around me, tap my clog on the floor. I miss him deep, like quicksand. He is still everything—graceful ease, molten honey, whatever it is that makes women swoon. I try to gather wits, instead gather rage, since it's more readily available. I need air and walk toward the door, then turn. His hair falls over his brow and he pushes it back impatiently. How I miss . . . just that. I cannot breathe. Must flee down the hallway.

I'm almost to the exit when I hear sneakers squeak and Lucy yell, "Mommy, you forgot to hug me good-bye!" She strides over haughtily and stops, hands on hips. Her eyes betray her. They brim with tears. Guilt fills me. I hug her, sharply aware of her warmth, the smell and texture of her hair.

"Sorry, bug," I say softly. She pushes me away and wipes her tears. "Better?" I ask, and she nods her head, smiles lopsided, embarrassed, and skips back down the hall to where Ex-Rat stands by the classroom door with his accusatory envelope. He smiles and waves. I pretend not to notice. Hate him for being so adult and organized. I should face the dismal truth: I forget most things. I turn and open the door, my heart clenched like a fist.

Off to the Senior Center

Am having a delicious fantasy—a favorite diversion while driving. Typical en route daydreams consist of me as a famous singer wearing thigh-high boots on stage while over a million fans hold up lighters. Not today, though. Today it goes like this: I buy a big truck with a double cab. Color: red. It has a CD player and airbags. I load only the essentials. Which means everything. I pick up the kids from school, buy snacks for the road, and we hit the highway, driving north. Once we cross the state line, I call Ex-Rat on my cell phone. His fiancée answers (per usual). When he is on, I say, "I just wanted to tell you the kids and I are moving out-of-state."

"When," he says in his bored voice that means he doesn't believe I will actually ever do it.

"Right now," I say, pushing End and tossing the phone out the big truck window.

Wake-Up Call

Persistent ringing wakes me from my fantasy daze. Am sure Brendan left his Nintendo DS on. Or is it one of Lucy's chronic-need keychain pets? Realizing the true source, I search my bag for the cell phone and my car almost hits an old man walking across street. I panic, grab the emergency brake and slam to a stop going about fifteen miles an hour. My chest hurts from the seatbelt. Thank god the car's too old to have air bags!

It's my mother. "Hi, darling!" she chirps, as the man starts rapping on the passenger-side window, motioning me to roll it down. He is not that old after all and he is rather angry — in fact, extremely pissed off.

"Hi, Mom," I say, as the rapping changes to thuds on the roof.

"What the hell is that racket?" my mother asks.

"A guy I almost hit."

"Oh, my god, is he OK?"

"Almost. Not *did*." Spittle now covers the window and windshield; he is on a rant about cell phones in cars.

"Then get the hell out of there — go — put pedal to the metal!" she yells.

"What if I run him over?" I say, anxiety mounting to the point of white knuckles.

"Self-defense! Is anyone watching?" she adds, descending into legal paranoia. I look around and see only about a hundred or so people, being as it's after 9 a.m. in the center of the Harvard-Radcliffe mecca. Cars start beeping behind me. Am fortunate I didn't get rear-ended.

The almost-hit man has stopped beating on my car and is now chatting with a woman who is carrying a potted plant. He walks over to the sidewalk and they embrace; the plant bangs against his back. I immediately lurch forward. Chest thumping, I weave and buck, then remember to release the emergency brake. I hang up on my mother, of course. The whole incident is her fault.

Decide never to use the cell phone while driving ever, ever, ever again.

Phone rings. I pick up.

"Where are you? Class is starting right now," Pip says. I hear bad music in the background.

"It's Monday, I'm volunteering at the senior center today, remember?" I tell her.

"That's right, forgot. God, you're so pathetic—if you're going to volunteer for crap just so you can *not* say hello to this supposed perfect guy, at least sign up for something fun. Shit, I really wanted to chat and have a sauna after Chow Box or Tee Bow or whatever the fuck it's called."

Pip hangs up. I hate wireless technology. I throw the phone into the backseat and vow to cancel service ASAP.

Fine Arts

In front of the senior center—or rather, senior mansion—I park and lock the car, then walk up the big white steps. I place a finger on the buzzer and the door instantly opens. A middle-aged woman with a sour expression asks, "May I help you?"

"I'm here to help with arts and crafts," I say, pulling down my oversize sweater.

"Oh, yes, you're our Monday volunteer from the church," she sniffs. "I have to warn you there's a horrible stomach flu going around the center. I'm not sure you'll find many seniors up for the *fine arts.*"

I think about bringing home a horrible stomach flu. It takes one second.

"I'll come back next week," I say.

"Why don't you call ahead and see if the bug is still going around? Things just seem to linger forever here," she says dryly.

"It's just that I have children," I add hastily.

"Yes, yes, I completely understand," she says, but slams the door shut.

I feel like a total cad. Ponder knocking again and asking if I can help change soiled sheets. Think better of it and head down the street to look for a coffee shop. Find none. Quite disconcerting. Could have sworn there was a coffee shop on this corner. I backtrack toward the senior center parking lot by way of Sumner Road and come upon an enormous pile of leaves in front of an elegant three-story house with a beautiful apple tree, browning fruit scattered on the ground, bees abuzz. I walk over to the leaves, wanting desperately to jump in. The acrid smell of overripe apples reminds me of Vermont and childhood visits to my grandparents' farm. I take off my clogs and place bare toes on the edge of the pile.

A shout: "You may enjoy them as you like. Just keep them sorted, neat and all. My son worked so hard this morning raking them into that mountain of a pile for my grandson to jump in after school." I turn to see an older woman walking up behind me, an Irish setter pup beside her. She looks like some Queen of Beantown, the very essence of Boston Brahmin, with her regal walk, wool tweed, and silk scarf tied around her neck. She unleashes the dog and he runs round and round us like a maniac. "How I despise that creature—he pulled and twisted my arm all the way home. And picking up his waste," she shudders. I think of Ugly in my backyard, too old to do anything but eat. He won't even go for walks anymore.

"I could walk the dog for you," I hear myself say. (Really must discuss meds with therapist!) "I mean for money," *Jesus,* I think. *Shit.* She looks at me disparagingly. I must sound like total loon. "I own a dog-walking business," I lie, fearing she'll call the police and have me committed.

"It is my grandson's dog," she says.

"I see," I say.

"Come in and have tea, and we'll discuss it."

Shit and double shit, I think. "Well, I really must—"

"No, I insist on hearing all about this dog-walking business of yours." She marches up the steps, reaches in her purse for the key, unlocks the door, flings it open, and says, "Follow me."

Tea

The house is similar to Ms. Who's in *A Wrinkle in Time*—or what I imagine that house to look like. The pile of leaves outside is apparently the only thing gathered and contained. Socks and underwear are draped over chairs. Hammers, nails, and a circular saw rest on the kitchen counter, along with Weetabix, boxed milk, and a large jar of oozing honey. Dust lingers in the air. A collection of moth-eaten scarves hangs on a menacing goblin hook. Newspapers are stacked in towering lopsided piles across the floor, alongside boxes full of empty soup cans. There are cartoons glued to the wall. I stop and examine them more closely: frogs playing squash.

"Those are from Glidden's *Let-Please* series," Queen Bean explains. "My son is simply rabid for anything squash. I personally prefer Glidden's portraits—particularly his self-portraits." She eyes me. "Like my son, Glidden was a tremendous squash player, *you know,* and quite handsome."

"Oh," I say, and twirl my hair.

The kitchen table is crammed with stuff: an old shortwave radio, mountains of library books, an ancient typewriter. I tap idly on a key before I can stop myself, then blush. "He's a writer," she says.

"Who?" I say.

"My son." She plugs in an electric teakettle.

"Oh, how nice," I say, removing a stack of newspapers from a chair and sitting down.

"It *is* nice," she says, then looks at me hard. "Are you happy with your lot in life as a dog walker?"

"Yes, very," I say.

Post-Tea

I'm now an official Monday, Wednesday, Friday dog walker. Much better than getting stomach flu. I get ten dollars a walk—plus tea.

Waiting for Therapy

Frank Sinatra plays softly, creating a moblike atmosphere. I wonder if this is a new tactic to heighten anxiety of waiting patients. Clearly, I'm becoming a wee bit paranoid—will discuss this in my therapy session, along with the meds. I peruse the new age book with an arrow-toting naked male on the cover. It gets me every time in here, whether or not I'm ovulating. My therapist won't let me borrow it because I keep "forgetting" to return her sex-therapy book, which she lent me a few months ago. Truth is I don't know where the heck it is; Brendan must be hiding it somewhere. I've asked my therapist if I can pay for it or replace it but she insists I have to "claim my inner adult" and find the book. I think she's on to me.

I notice that the office secretary looks sheepish, not her usual open, smile-ridden self. My therapist swooshes into the reception area, being very "swoosh" with her long, thick, curly hair, peasant blouse with frilly cuffs, and swirl skirt. A man follows her out of her office. He looks flushed and disheveled.

My therapist addresses him with a scrumptious smile. "Same time next week?" The man nods lasciviously and quickly leaves. My therapist bends over the secretary's moon-shaped cubicle, her breasts spilling forth. I notice the hair on the back of her head is tangled in knots. She whispers something into her secretary's ear.

The secretary coughs. Long, choking coughs.

My therapist twirls and swooshes over to me. Teeth aglow, she is like the great mother, ready to gobble me up.

"Shall we?" she asks. I can't move. I am chained to my seat.

Therapy

I huddle close to the heater, as far away from the swoosh goddess as possible. Her breasts have become Plath's Persephone. I think of her poor husband, whose photo sits on her desk. Hate my therapist and her golden-globe breasts. Am certain she and the man I saw leaving her office are having an affair. She has that look: selfish, satisfied, and smiling. Memories of Ex-Rat's extramarital affairs release a torrent of anger within me.

"I quit!" I yell.

"Quit what?" my therapist asks, smiling indulgently.

"I quit therapy," I practically scream, all the while hoping she'll tell me I can't.

"OK," she says, still smiling. Quite infuriating.

Embarrassed by my childlike tantrum, I run out of the room and past the secretary. I come to a standstill right outside the door of waiting room. No one follows, and I sigh and proceed down the stairs.

Garbage Bin

Once outside the building, I decide I have made an excellent decision. Feel immensely proud of myself. Am true infidelity survivor! I will no longer allow that type of immoral behavior to create toxicity in my life. I remember I vowed to cancel my cell phone service and, as I walk past a garbage bin on the sidewalk, I stop and think. Decide it would be much easier to just throw the wretched thing away. I grab the cell out of my bag and stuff it down into bin. Remember I didn't turn phone off. Fetch it back out. Turn the phone off. Stuff it back down. Instantly experience a high. Wonderful. Strange, seems ridding oneself of technology by way of a trash receptacle is extremely satisfying. Far better feeling than meds could induce, surely.

One Minute Later

Dread the thought of finding a new therapist.

Library

I hand over a crumpled twenty-dollar bill. Must pay late fees on loads of books never read. The librarian takes my money and informs me that I still have a balance due. I have a brain surge and ask her if there are any volunteer positions available. Apparently I am compelled to apply everywhere today! I believe it entirely possible, though, that Perfect Guy from church is a library lover. He looks the type. This way, I could bump into him as a volunteer and I would be carrying a huge stack of books, looking divinely smart. I could intentionally drop them. We'd bend to pick them up and our eyes would meet. Very romantic.

Also, a great way to make sure that borrowed books are brought back on time.

The clerk lifts her monobrow and her anorexic shoulders become even more concave.

"Yes, but it's not as glamorous as people tend to imagine when they inquire about volunteer opportunities here at the library," she warns. "It's a lot of hours spent in the basement sorting donated books for our annual fundraiser."

"I see," I say, handing her a check for the rest of my late fees. Am totally defeated. No chance of bumping into Perfect Guy in the basement.

"I hope you do," she says with a short, tight smile.

I totter into the children's section and comfort myself with *Are You There, God? It's Me, Margaret.* Feeling better, I fantasize about starting a kids' puppet theater in the library. See myself just so: running around, blowing kisses and sewing tidbits on Frog and Toad costumes as armies of single dads gather at my feet. They smile eagerly. The children call me Ms. Poppins and beg to be my special helpers. I giggle daintily and use words like *tinkle* instead of *pee*. When the wicked-witch clerk happens by, children scream at the sight and climb in my lap. I arch waxed brows in her direction and with quiet concern and sympathy croon, "I'm sorry to have to say this, but you must leave. They're so upset."

"I understand," she says.

"I hope you do." I hug children closer and shake my head.

At this point in the fantasy Perfect Guy walks in and falls madly in love with me.

A Different Clerk

Still in character, I wait in line to check out my new stack of books. Wish I had a carpetbag. The woman in front of me is baring all to different librarian from the one I now hate. This one is male, young—*and cute*. I pucker my lips and pinch my cheeks.

"That's what he did, the little bastard—in the middle of the day—knowing I was out, creeping in and stealing the TV, which I never watched—I read, I have a brain—not like the twin shit-for-brains he just hooked up with, she's like a newly hatched egg, he could be her father, for Christ's sake—wait till she grows a set of tits and realizes he is walking birth control." I consider changing Ex-Rat's nickname to Shit-for-Brains or Walking Birth Control. I think better of it—too hard to remember.

I'm now in love with this rippling male librarian, who listens attentively to old and crazy dumped bookworm. After about twenty minutes of recounting her life drama, she walks away, still muttering.

"What a nut, huh!" I say with a winning smile.

"That nut happens to be my mother."

Well, he definitely won't be placing an "I Spy" ad in the personals: Seeking horrible mother-hating bitch checking out *The Princess and the Pea.*

Tuesday

I get finishing touches on my root canal. Take large, numbing pill. Make Brendan put the computer back together, since I cannot move from the couch.

No Life

"I'm totally fucking stressed. I'm going to go scope out the new meditation center. It's become the rage. My coworkers can't shut up about it. See you there after work. Around five-thirty," Pip says, and hangs up. She is totally rude. Really! Like I can just drop everything. I have no clue where this meditation center is. It could be in downtown Boston and traffic will be murder during rush hour. I call Pip back at work, get the recorded greeting for the Boston Bruins, and punch in her extension.

"Pip McSweeny, media relations," Pip says very professionally. I can see her in her spiffy business outfit. Eight phones glued to her ear. Thousands of ex-boyfriends calling her for free tickets. Having a best friend who is successful and gorgeous is not a big boon to my self-esteem.

"Where is the meditation center?" I ask.

"Oh, it's you," Pip says. "The goddamn press has been ringing here all fucking morning," she adds, making me feel even more insignificant and pathetic.

"Where is the meditation center?" I ask again and she gives me the address.

"Oh, it's in Cambridge," I say. Now I can't use traffic as an excuse not to go. I think of another. "There's no way I can meet you at 5:30 p.m. I have to pick up the kids and make dinner."

"Nice try. You don't have the kids tonight—it's Friday," Pip says. I should know better than to try to fool a media relations expert. Pip knows bullshit when she hears it.

Meditation Center

At the meditation center, we wait in a long line of high-powered people wearing suits. We're required to check all cell phones, laptops, and Palm Pilots. This being my first time at a meditation center, I proudly show the check-in person my handbag, which is devoid of technology. I offer a most serene look. Surely I must be a natural guru. Pip throws her satchel of computer-enhanced devices on the counter. I shake my head.

"Don't mind her. She has no life," Pip apologizes to the check-in person. I follow her dismally to the changing area, even though I have no clothes to change into. Pip gives me her thong leotard.

"I'm not wearing that! It has been up your—you know what," I whisper.

"I washed it. What are you going to wear? Your granny pants and sweater?" Pip asks, slicking back her perfect short chestnut-colored hair and applying more make-up to her ivory skin. She slides her perfect body into a one-piece yoga suit.

"I have on stretchy pants. They're kind of meditation-like," I point out.

"They're fucking maternity pants," she says, looking over her shoulder at the mirror to get a better view of her butt.

"These are not maternity pants," I say defensively. "They're just stretchy."

Pip snorts, shrugs, grabs her special little meditation pillow, and leaves the changing room. I ditch my clogs and trot after her.

We enter the room of silence, which is worse than a library. More like a morgue. People sit with idiotic expressions on their faces and their hands on their knees. Pip dumps her pillow on the floor and sits down. I sit on the hard floor next to her and try to mimic the positions of other meditators. I can't concentrate or keep my eyes closed. My butt is becoming numb. I shift my body to more of squatting position.

"You look like you're about to take a shit. Sit down," Pip whispers, pulling at my sweater. I plop back down. Am desperate. I rap on Pip's shoulder. She gives me dirty look.

"This is really boring," I whisper in her ear.

"That's the point," Pip says.

A Beautiful Body

"So are you going to walk your ass over and introduce yourself to Perfect Guy this Sunday?" Pip says, raising her eyebrows and peeling off her one-piece in the changing room.

"I will," I say, taking off my sweater to cool down.

"Don't do that," Pip says.

"What?" I ask.

"Lie. You're really bad at it."

"I think he has a girlfriend," I say.

"You don't know that!"

"Well why wouldn't he? He's *perfect*. Besides, why would he take a slightest interest in a stay-at-home single mother with two kids?" I say miserably.

"Well, maybe if you stopped dressing in maternity wear and flaunted that beautiful body of yours, he would notice you and you wouldn't *have to* introduce yourself."

"You really think I have a beautiful body?" I ask timidly. Pip rarely dishes out compliments.

"Yes," Pip says firmly, "though I agree with you about the kid part. Maybe you can ship them away to some tiny island in the middle of the ocean or something."

"Pip!"

"Just kidding," Pip says, though I know she's not. Pip loathes children. She convinced her gynecologist to tie her tubes in her early twenties. "Now let's go shopping and buy some clothes that will show your waist. This way even if you *don't* introduce yourself to the guy at Mass on Sunday, at least you won't look like you're pregnant."

"Thank you so much for your unbridled concern."

"Don't mention it," Pip says lightly. "And by the way, if you want a date, you may want to take off your fucking wedding ring."

Shopping

I am now the proud owner of thong panties, a push-up bra, a micro-mini and a tight-fitting see-through shirt.

"But I can't wear them until spring," I say, as we walk out of the store.

"What are you talking about?" Pip asks.

"The clothes, I mean, I can't wear a mini and a see-through shirt in forty-degree weather. I'll be freezing."

"Are you joking? How can you go wrong with hard nipples in a transparent shirt?" Pip says, looking at me like I am the dumbest woman alive.

"You want to go to the bookstore?" I ask. Going to the bookstore in the evening is my absolute favorite thing to do—actually, the only thing I do on weekend nights when the kids aren't with me.

"I can't. I'm meeting Martin," Pip says importantly. She loves reminding people that she has a boyfriend. This is due to the fact that she was a late bloomer and spent the entirety of college a virgin. So I really can't begrudge her for it. Pip looks at her diamond-studded Rolex. "Shit. I've gotta run. I'm already late. Call you tomorrow," Pip says, giving me quick peck. I stand there with my bag and watch her dash down the street on her stiletto heels gripping her little black shiny purse—looking all grown up with somewhere to go.

Fan Club

Carrying my bag of hard-nipple goods and a double vanilla latte, I enter the bookstore and see Perfect Guy immediately. He's standing in front of the Readers' Choice Twenty-third Book Pick with a pencil behind his ear. Love, love pencils behind ears! He is also wearing a yellow anorak with blue-and-white striped fabric inside the hood. His black hair is wild and reckless, his skin flushed, five o'clock shadow on his upper lip and chin. He takes the little pencil from behind his ear, chews on it while he looks more pensively at the page and then places it back behind his ear. It's a very private gesture and completely lovable.

I position myself in front of Readers' Choice Seventy-sixth Book Pick on other side of the store and haphazardly take the book off its pedestal with one hand. I pretend to be immersed in the blurbs on the back cover while furtively peering at Perfect Guy. Suddenly a gaggle of girls, all sipping from paper cups with white lids like mine, position themselves directly in my Perfect Guy line of vision. One of them whispers loudly, "Oh, my god! There's Professor B!"

"Where?" the others ask in unison, scanning the bookstore hysterically. The girl points him out.

"Oh, I'd so love to *do him*," a little red-haired girl croons.

"Who wouldn't? Every girl in our class wants him."

"Professors have no business being that hot. It's far too distracting. How are we supposed to absorb a lecture on history when all we can imagine is him *naked*?" says a very smart-looking girl in a wool cap and glasses. They all nod. "He's single-handedly ruining my GPA," she adds. They all stand there sipping and staring.

I notice there are a few other women around my age listening attentively to the girls' conversation and then stealing glances at Perfect Guy. They are also pretending to read books. However, unlike me, they are not wearing maternity clothes. I suddenly feel like an insignificant frumpy member of a very large Perfect Guy fan club.

Perfect Guy (who is in a true reading frenzy) is oblivious to his groupies, which makes him even more alluring.

"I'm going to go over and say something to him," the little red-haired girl announces.

"Good luck. I tried to seduce him last week and he didn't even notice. He still gave me a 62 on the last exam," the smart girl says.

"Go ask him if he's single," says another girl, pushing the red-haired girl in his direction.

We all watch with breathless anticipation as she walks timidly toward Perfect Guy, then turns and looks back at her pals. "Go!" they urge.

The little red-haired girl takes a few more steps when she is intercepted by a bookstore employee. "Miss! You need to take that beverage outside!" The rest of us look at each other guiltily, trying to hide our coffees. Too late. "You, you, you," a pause, "and *you,*" the clerk says, pointing to me. "Outside with those."

Empty Nest

I unlock the front door and put down my bag. I hear Ugly stretch, moan, and shake as he slowly makes his way into the foyer. I bend down to greet him.

"Hey, big guy. Did you miss me?" Ugly wags his tail and nuzzles me. I rub his rough fur and the grandfather clock chimes, echoing through the quiet of the house.

two

A Week of Mixed Feelings

After spending most of the weekend cutting my front lawn, since Ex-Rat refused to mow it, insisting that I needed to "build independence skills" and do it myself, I am cheered by the prospect of picking up the children and having a life again. Must say, mowing was particularly trying, since the mower kept grinding to a halt and dying because the grass was up to my armpits. Unfortunately I don't own a scythe and had to use shrub clippers. Horrible. I would have assigned Brendan to yard duty; however, Lucy would have demanded to be included in the blade-related chore. Idea was entirely unsettling.

Brendan has an away game and I must hurry if we are to make it. I jet over to Lucy's school. With Demon face, Lucy stomps out of the double doors and down the steps, then flings open the car door and chucks her backpack into the back seat.

"Did you have a nice day at school, honey?" I broach.

"You forgot to put Mr. Beetle in my backpack for sharing circle!" Lucy screams at me. I vaguely recall seeing some kind of Kafkaesque insect in a baby jar with a pierced lid resting on Lucy's night stand. I smack my forehead.

Football Game

I notice Ex-Rat-Mobile in the football parent lineup. Brendan, towering over his friends, is already suited up for the game. He notices me, along with everyone else, by my honking ability. I am a good honker.

"What are you doing here?" he asks, as if I'm some stranger off the street trying to kidnap him.

"I'm driving you to your away game so Lucy and I can watch. We've never been to one of your away games and since the season . . ."

"There are no more away games," he interrupts before I can finish. "Our last game was last Thursday. Today is the touch-football game—parents against kids. Dad is already here, see, and he said he'd give me a ride home after the game, so you don't have to worry. I tried calling you on your cell phone but it was off, so I left a message on the machine at home."

"What field is it at?" I ask, obviously having missed yet another crucial element of my child's schedule.

"Home field." He turns his eyes heavenward.

"I would love to play, thanks for asking, no, no, I'll just throw on my old gym clothes that are in the car," I say.

"Mom, quit guilt-tripping. Dad saw it in the parent newsletter and wigged out. He bought himself all brand-new gear—he is really into it—and plus, only the dads play anyway. The moms watch."

"It's touch football. How bad can it be?"

"They'll never let you play," he says.

"Because I'm a woman?" I fume, defending whole female race.

"Maybe because you might get really hurt."

I shut off the engine and open the car door. Lucy climbs over my seat and I grab her before she makes a mad dash for Ex-Rat in the parking lot. Only she doesn't, instead becoming mesmerized by her brother's begging technique. "Please, please, please don't play—it gets really aggressive—like totally aggressive—you have no idea—it's no joke, Mom—it's hard-core—people don't play nice."

"All right, all right," I say, as Ex-Rat starts walking over. He is the image of vitality in tight football pants and loose mesh shirt over shoulder pads. It's all too much. How can anyone continue to be so good-looking after it has been determined that he is a slimebag? I shove Lucy back into her seat, slam my car door, and restart the engine.

"Whatever. Have fun. Ask Dad to buy you some dinner after the game." I zoom out of the parking lot, anticipating a torrent from Demon. I'm wrong. She is quietly blowing on the window and then writing her name in the fog of her own breath. I turn on the heater, the temperature having suddenly dropped, and wait for warmth.

A Realization

Why is it that by late afternoon I feel like a potato? My energy just sinks. The phone is ringing when I step through the door, and I let the machine pick up. It's Ex-Rat telling me to come down and watch the game. He is a pillar of generosity, after rubbing my nose consistently for weeks in my parenting incompetence. His voice is like fluffy icing. How nice it would be, I think, not to love him even the slightest bit, to feel absolutely nothing anymore. No ice-pick chest, no lunacy, no intense desire to have him hug me, hold me, still me. I consider if dating might help. Yes, I think it would. Decide to start dating immediately.

Corner Market

Rain has begun. I grab Ugly's leash and bundle up Lucy in a lined raincoat and frog boots. I put on my own rain gear and we all head out to the corner gourmet market for a newspaper. I buy all area papers, three Italian cookies, a peanut-butter dog bone for Ugly, and a pack of blue Trident gum. I have developed a blue Trident addiction. I go through at least a half-pack a day. Gum snapping adds sassiness to my hot pink clogs. Hot pink clogs, I notice, are fraying around edging. Must order more hot pink clogs, pronto. Lucy splashes in new puddles on our way back from the store. I think of lots of muddy men and a little football. Should have gone. May have gotten a date out of it, instead of looking through personals. What's not to love about big, sweaty, muddy men? I ask self. Get no inner response. Really must find someone to mate with.

Ordering Clogs

Major crisis. Hot pink clogs have been "discontinued" or, as phone order lady put it more gently after hearing my terrified response of "WHAT? YOU CAN'T POSSIBLY BE SERIOUS!" they were "let go of to make room for a new color."

"What new color?" I ask, in freak curiosity, as one would ask to watch one's own crotch being stitched after birthing a ten-pound baby.

"Lilac," she whispers.

"Purple," I admonish.

"Yes, it will be coming out in our new winter catalog," again in a whisper.

"Oh, god, I have to have hot pink," I say, now hyperventilating. "Please say you still have some hot pink."

"Let me check." There is tapping and clicking on the line. "Yes, we still have some sizes in stock. What size do you want?"

"Size 5, oh please, tell me you have size 5." I hold my breath.

"Yes," she says.

"How many pairs are left?" I ask.

"Eleven pairs, actually. Lucky you're size 5. We're all out of most other sizes," she says cheerfully.

"I'll take them all." I am beside myself with greed.

"Will you be paying by credit card?" she asks, nonplussed.

"Yes." I try to add up the total. Can't fathom. Mail order lady crisply states it. I feel hot all over and need to confess to someone. I hang up, and find Lucy.

"I just bought eleven pairs of hot pink clogs," I spill. She gives me an owlish look. "Eleven is my lucky number," she tells me.

Definitely a sign. I feel much better. Crisis averted.

Panties

Pip calls as I am perusing personals. She is at a lingerie shop buying underwear. She is always buying red or black frilly undergarments. This is to go with her closet full of S&M goodies. Pip is never without real sex or cybersex. Such are the benefits of being highly perverted. Her boyfriend, Martin, is the "passive" in their "open relationship." A fragile vegan, Martin has pasty white skin and has shaved his head because he is going bald at the tender age of twenty-six. Pip, fourteen years his senior, looks younger, thanks to her no-carb, meat-filled diet. Pip is big on strong breath mints to cover her "meat breath," her carnivorous nature being Martin's one complaint. She talks to me between slurping mint-sucking breaths—she must have just wolfed down a T-bone.

"So—*ssup*—what's up?—*ssup*." I hear her rummaging through the panty racks.

"I'm looking at personal ads," I say, proud to have something to talk about other than picking up Lucy and making dinner.

"If you just had worn that new outfit to Mass, *like I told you to do,* you might not be *desperately* searching the personal ads for a date. *Ssup.*"

"He wasn't at Mass last Sunday, anyway, and I'm not *desperately* searching—"

"Shit, it's silk." I am interrupted by her exclaiming. "*Ssup*—what time is it?" Martin refuses to touch silk for the same reason he doesn't eat honey. Vegan boy does not like earth's creatures messed with. He works very hard to establish his chi while being spanked.

"After 4 p.m.," I say, and then look at the clock. "Four-forty-eight, to be exact."

"I've gotta go. I have to meet Martin at some vegan potluck. Wish me luck." When she hangs up, I realize we established no connection and wonder if most of our recent conversations are like that now that Martin is in the picture. They are. Lately we have nothing to talk about other than panties, her sex life, and my lack thereof.

Personal of the Week

I open the newspaper and the first personal I read makes me reevaluate mating route:

> SWM, 1954 standard stick, slight rust, a little room in trunk for the right kind of baggage, ready to spot a sweet automatic with nice headlights that has kept herself roadworthy. Test drive first, possible road trip later.

I want to vomit. Others are similar. Seems men like to represent themselves à la Ford, Chrysler, and Chevy. Another popular motif is to list one's athletic proclivities. For example:

> SWM, 40 yr., likes rock climbing, sky diving, scuba diving, kayaking, running, biking, hiking, basketball, soccer, downhill and cross-country skiing, baseball, football, wrestling, and hockey. Seeks female 18–21 with similar interests. Love of all sports a must.

Finally I find a personal that is somewhat normal and circle it:

> SWM, 31 yr., good job, good genes, and just want to have a good laugh. Seeks female around my age who might not place

an ad herself but might respond to one, to have dinner with and maybe see a flick.

I fixate for a while on the word *flick,* making up sentences: "Will you flick off that switch?" "Did you just flick that booger?" Decide I shouldn't be so picky. It's the personals, for god's sake, everyone is irregular. I pick up the phone, dial the 900 number, but slam down the receiver as soon as the recorded voice becomes serious, warning that I must be eighteen or older and I will be charged for the call starting now. Am nearing forty yet feel much younger than eighteen. Good thing I hung up.

The Crone

My very upset son does not say hello. He runs up to his room and slams the door. Ex-Rat rings the doorbell. He is ruddy-cheeked, eyes bright, wearing his gray sweat suit from college. It's soaked at the shoulders. I am able to observe him dispassionately and objectively only when he is agitated. Why this is, I don't know, yet I take in his image: the goose bumps on his neck; the stubble on his face; thick, full lips; curly blond hair descending in a short ponytail.

"Hi," he says tensely.

"Hi," I say back.

"The dads won. I think Brendan is a little upset with me. I made the mistake of making a joke about it at dinner. Can you make sure the phones are plugged in so I can call him later when he cools off?" Remembering last night's phone treachery, I make no comment. "Well . . ." He fidgets, waiting for me to release him of his duty.

I close the door without saying good-bye. I never say good-bye, and suddenly I am fully aware of what this means and ready to face it head-on. I open the door. He is almost to his car.

"Good-bye!" I yell. He turns around, startled. There is a young girl in the passenger seat. She is all doe. I think of the dumped book-worm in the library and my heart turns over.

Ex-Rat reddens but says flatly, "She's a friend of Brendan's." I take a few steps outside the door. The neck biter is a beautiful Asian girl. Tiny like me. She gives me a shy smile and raises her slender wrist, on which hangs a small gold chain. I feel rising jealousy that my son is willing to reveal his girlfriend to Ex-Rat and not me. Then I am distinctly concerned about Ex-Rat alone in the car with a breathtaking nebula.

"I'll drive her home," I say, beckoning Ex-Rat to me. His agitation increases: He knows my thought processes.

"Her parents are my next-door neighbors so it was easier to drop Brendan off first," he states curtly. "I guess I'll be over to mow the lawn tomorrow afternoon. The weather is supposed to be better," he adds, inspecting my haphazard clipping of the front yard.

"The lawn mower was broken," I lie defensively. "It wouldn't start."

"Sure," he says, releasing a long martyr sigh and then hops in the driver's seat with a smug grin. He loves it when he has successfully set me up for failure.

Brendan's girlfriend's shy smile persists; its essence seems of a deeper nature. I feel like a crone. Standing in the rain and darkness, I wrap my sweater more tightly around me. The front steps are a mountain of loneliness.

Homework

Brendan has not come out of his room. Lucy and I go over her spelling words. The eerie emptiness of this fall night keeps us both focused. The phone rings and I yell to Brendan to answer it, which he doesn't. The machine picks up but there's no message, just a click. I know it is Brendan's beautiful girlfriend and not Ex-Rat. I want to know her name. I want to go shopping for feather boas and nail polish with her. I imagine us together, floating about town, drinking hot chocolate and window-shopping. I'm desperate for her to like me. Why didn't she get out of the car and say hello? What kind of girl doesn't say hello to her boyfriend's mother? Does she realize how rude that is? Then a change in perspective as I entertain the idea that they might be having sex. After all, she lives right next door to Ex-Rat. The word *intercourse* settles itself inside my skull. Like a flashing yellow light. *Intercourse. Intercourse.*

I pray to stop thinking about it. It doesn't work. I know they are. I know by the click of the answering machine, by her shy smile, by the way she didn't get out of the car. Mothers can sense these things. But we also have a strong denial instinct. Mine kicks in, and I go to the sink and fill my tiny cup with water. I walk back and forth from the kitchen sink, watering plants, singing bits from *Fiddler on the Roof.*

Lucy pours rice on the floor. Purposefully. She gives me a look. Piercing. Brave. "I saw that," I say, clutching my little cup.

"So," is all she says and goes to get the broom.

First Day on the Job

It's raining icy buckets. I'm en route to my dog-walking job, suited up in a fishmonger raincoat with steel clips and big black rubber boots my mother bought for me at the farm-supply center, her favorite place to shop.

My mother is always prepared for the worst, ever since my father left her for another man. When she comes to visit, she unloads zillions of bags and two coolers filled with organic wheat-free sundries. In 1999, she bought an acre's worth of electric fencing in case the millennium brought hordes of crazed city dwellers to her humble abode in the suburbs outside of Boston. "It just shocks them; it doesn't kill them," she said with a look of utter PC satisfaction.

She was truly impossible as a mother, until Ex-Rat dumped me. Now she has become a valuable man-hating resource.

Ugly, whom I've brought along as a calming presence for the manic puppy, whines in the backseat. I park the car on the street. Queen Bean dashes out and into the rain, covering her head with a newspaper. "Let me move my car out of the drive, you'll get a ticket if you park on the street without a sticker," she yells. We trade parking spots.

Inside, she shakes her head. A crown of raindrops sits atop her hair, having failed to penetrate its armor. "I tried to straighten up a bit," she says.

"I see," I say. The sink is the only thing without a pile.

"It's just that he's so busy teaching and writing his books. He's quite swept up in everything." She picks up a puppy-peed-on newspaper.

"He teaches as well?" I ask.

"Yes, he is a professor at *Harvard*." She arches her brows, then says, "I was thinking, perhaps, since it is such a horrid day, you might clean a bit and then take the dog for a short walk." I am shocked. She gathers speed before I can protest. "Of course, I'd pay you. It's just that I'm not able to keep up, I live over fifteen minutes away, and I have my bridge club," she says shrilly, with importance.

"You don't live here?" I ask.

"Me? Don't be absurd, my son is a grown man! I live on Beacon Hill!"

"Oh," I say, and then think, *Figures*.

"My son and grandson live here. I'm just seeing to it that my son gets his life sorted out—"

"Sorted?" I interrupt.

"His wife died two years ago from breast cancer."

"Oh, I'm so sorry," I say. And I am. I feel sick to my stomach. I imagine my own children motherless and being raised by some child bride of Ex-Rat.

"Since his wife's passing, my son has been trying to manage on his own without any sort of domestic help and as you can see things are just falling apart—"

"My dog is in the car. I need to go get him—" I interrupt.

"Are you coming right back?" she asks, voice rising.

"Yes," I assure her. I have a massive codependent urge to tidy up her poor widow son's entire life.

"Oh, thank god," she says and plugs in the electric teakettle.

A Package

My father calls as I am hot-gluing orange felt for Lucy's Halloween costume.

"Hi, pet! I shipped Lucy's costume UPS. Did you get it?" My father refuses to leave his own neighborhood. He mails everything. He lives over in the South End, so there is really no shipping involved. I picture a little brown truck screeching from his house to my house in about fifteen minutes.

"Yes."

"Wasn't it perfect?"

"Yes," I lie. What he sent looked to be something Cinderella would wear to the Oscars if she were on speed: a tiny strapless number covered in rhinestones and feathers. My father, a costume designer for the theater, is currently working on a very earthy production and using a lot of natural fibers, which he detests. In fact, he finds the whole organic movement in bad taste. I've excused his overzealous attempt at a Halloween costume as a desperate cry for help. He's probably watching talk shows on TV nonstop and cooking up gourmet food like a maniac. He always does this when forced to use browns.

"I just love the *twenties* sense of style. I could just see Lucy in that little flapper headband with that gorgeous white blond hair of hers," my father says. I'm semirelieved by this comment. I had thought said headband was a garter belt and the whole ensemble some representation of a Vegas showgirl. I do not tell him that I took one look at it and threw it into the trash compactor, sensing Lucy would likely want to add wings and demand to go to school in the tiny number, probably even refusing to wear underwear because it would "show." Too taxing to contemplate.

I keep glue-gunning felt. The costume is starting to look like a gourd instead of a pumpkin. My father turns the TV on loud in the background and I hear Dr. Phil's calling card: "Is it working for you?"

"Call you back," my father says breathlessly.

Trick or Treat

We walk from house to house, our fingers frozen, teeth chattering. Ex-Rat suggested driving in his heated road hog, but I demand traditional suffering. Our breath comes in little puffs. Ex-Rat holds Lucy's felt candy bag and jumps furiously up and down to keep warm. He's wearing only his hip leather jacket, which stiffens and starts to squeak as we head to the fairy house.

The fairy house is light pink with little moss-green shutters. On Halloween every year it is covered with white Christmas lights. Sparkly gauze fabric billows out, down, and around the porch front. Pumpkins spray-painted rainbow colors line the steps, with "Peace" written on them in silver marker. This year, there is a sea of white and pink mums with fake butterflies hanging from the porch ceiling. I worship this house. It makes my spirit soar with gladness. I leap up the steps. Lucy follows, yelling, "Fairy house, fairy house, I'm a pumpkin this year!"

Ex-Rat, afraid of being turned back into the rodent that he is, remains on the sidewalk. Two very old ladies dressed in fairy costumes answer Pumpkin with a camera flash and some fairy dust. They coo, "Little pumpkin, sweet little pumpkin, now you will be safe from ghouls and bad witches that would turn you into pumpkin pie." They dance about Lucy, wings aflutter. I dance, too. Fairy dust collects on my eyelashes. "I love this," I say. "I just love this so much."

The Closet

The kids are with Ex-Rat for the weekend and I have no idea what to do with myself. I walk around the house, checking things: doors, windows, stove. Feel like Woody Allen's mother. I make tea and drink it to the ticking of the clock in the empty kitchen. Everything gleams sterile. I wonder if it's possible to make the house any smaller and messier. It needs a lived-in look, not the current obsessive-compulsive vibe, which makes me feel like an unwelcome guest in my own house. It's all due to the neat-freak gene I inherited from my father, and to a New York decorator hired by Ex-Rat.

The decorator turned out to be a model-chic babe who put her soul into pretending to be his wife while I watched. The kitchen's restaurant-like steel, exposed brick, and large framed black-and-white photographs of erotically charged produce are all her invention.

"Men love kitchens," the decorator said. "A lot of women laugh when I say that, but I'm totally serious, they get totally turned on by the thought of a woman cooking. Maybe we should paint the walls this dusky rose color? Give it some feminine warmth. Men *love* rose. It reminds them of the soft recesses of a woman's body." She let me in on this carnal knowledge at eight in the morning, after I'd been through twelve hours of straight-out nursing followed by twenty-five minutes of sleep, as I banged pots around wearing a puked-on old hospital gown with a sanitary napkin the size of a truck between my thighs.

I finish my tea, check the stove again. Then again. Then I head upstairs, like an old junkie, knowing where I am going, full of shame as I already regret the tomorrow of it. Inside Ex-Rat's old closet, the stuff he left behind is still neatly folded on shelves or hung. I reach for my favorite T-shirt, which is kelly green and so threadbare that there are patches where I can see through it to the flesh of my fingertips. I hold it up to my face and inhale his scent. There is a shoebox full of notes from our first couple of years of marriage, when we were all love and lived in a shitty one-bedroom apartment. My old, scratchy cursive: "Honey pie, went to store to get lemons, pucker up bad boy—be back lickity split. me OXOXO." "Brendan is teething, heading to co-op for clove oil—will get that chocolate that you love." "Went to the Laundromat—can you put diapers out for horribly mean diaper service man? I'll love you forever and ever. Smooch."

I drag the comforter and a pillow from the bed, wrap myself, cocoonlike, and read on about happy years of errands.

Second Realization

I think about donating contents of the closet—including myself—to the fine arts museum and calling it "No Life: A Permanent Installation."

I drift off to sleep in the closet.

My Mother

The phone rings and I make a mad dash for it. On the way I bang my hip hard on the dresser and scream, "Shit!" After a deep breath I say, "Bonjour," in an overly serene voice.

"What?" my mother asks.

"Oh, it's you," I say.

"Yes, it's me. Don't sound so excited."

"I won't," I respond.

"You're so cranky every time I call lately," she rasps. "You need St.

John's wort. I think you have a touch of depression or the start of Seasonal Affective Disorder. Are you still seeing your shrink?"

"I dumped my shrink weeks and weeks ago, remember? And I happen to be a wee bit cranky only because it's after midnight," I say. "What's wrong?" She never calls this late.

"You know that man I met at my retreat last weekend—the very tall one who was into yoga—and I said we had nice chemistry?" she asks.

"Yes." How could I forget? She calls daily to discuss.

"Well, Rain—the woman I told you about, with the mole and really huge breasts?"

"Yes," I say.

"She says he's not even bisexual, that he's a hundred percent gay. I think she is full of shit and just jealous. Besides, I have developed sixth sense about the whole gay male thing since your father—"

"Mom," I interrupt.

"Yes?"

"I really can't handle this much intensity right now," I say. "I can barely manage my own problems."

"Well, what do you think?" she presses. "Do you think I'm right?"

I am becoming irate with my self-absorbed mother, who only wants to talk about her own ridiculous issues. "They're all gay, Mom. Remember I read that survey that said 99.9 percent of men have had a homosexual experience? At least he's honest about it," I say. Pure spite.

"I'm going to try Margo again," she says. "She's been online all night."

I hang up. It's now one in the morning. I am certain my mother is doing a juice fast to slim for pending yoga-inspired intercourse and can't sleep. I lock the door, take a shower, and feel immensely sorry for the whole single female race.

First Frost

The backyard is like spun sugar. My breath hangs heavy in the cold air. I carry Ugly down the stairs, knowing his arthritic back legs will give out on the slippery steps. He is half my size and I am in fuzzy pig slippers. I slip and almost kill us both as we land sideways on the frozen ground. I cut my lip with my tooth and scrape my elbow. Ugly gets up, shakes, then licks my face. More startled than hurt, I start to cry. Ugly licks my tears and starts to pee and then looks at me with his rather ashamed and sad old doggy eyes.

Temptress Outfit

Thank god it's Sunday and I can go to church. Something to do. The house is unbearably empty. I hope Perfect Guy is there. Leaving Ugly sleeping on the couch, I go upstairs and get dressed in one of my recently purchased outfits. Pip would be proud. I put on the micromini with cable knit tights, leg warmers, and my brand-new hot pink clogs. Decide against see-through shirt. Hard nipples are really too much for church. Instead, I stick my favorite barrettes in my hair. I look very un-church-like, a temptress instead of a praying pixie. Feel delicious. Pip was right, this new outfit is sure to woo Perfect Guy. I take off my wedding ring.

Perfect Guy

I arrive late and Mass has already started. I open the door quietly, scan parishioners for Perfect Guy, and see him all the way up front. He is wearing a lovely cord coat with elbow patches. Too cute. There is no pew open in front of him in which to show off my mini. Cursing myself for being late, I tiptoe to my seat and take off my coat. Churchy groomed wives observe my temptress outfit in shock, pursing their lips and whispering to their husbands. Suddenly I feel like a prostitute instead of a temptress. I try to pull down my skirt. No go. I wrap my coat around my waist and pray for the courage to introduce myself to Perfect Guy. Still praying when the service comes to end and parishioners begin exiting, I unwind my coat from my waist, continuing to kneel in prayer until I see Perfect Guy coming up the aisle. I cut right in front of him, doing my best sashay and flip my hair seductively as I walk past the first set of double doors. Nonchalantly, I drop my coat, then bend to pick it up.

The second set of doors opens to reveal a high sun, which blinds me. I've stopped wearing sunglasses since I saw Mini-Me in *Austin Powers;* now I feel nauseated whenever I think of little people (myself included) in hip shades.

"Henry! How wonderful it is to see you. It's been eons!" A male voice booms from the sidewalk. I scrunch my eyes and see a small professorial-looking man wearing wire-rimmed glasses approach the steps.

"Yes, it has!" Perfect Guy booms back from behind me. I'm dying to turn, but cannot look so blatantly at him, my shyness unearthed by such near perfection. He is like this noonday sun: So brightly lit that it's impossible to stare directly at the source. I stumble down the steps holding my coat and cross the street to my favorite coffee shop so I can gaze out the window at him while waiting in line for my mocha.

From inside, I watch him chatting away, with his huge adorable smile, then see him gesture toward the café. He and the professor start walking toward me, myself, and I. There is no bathroom in which to escape. I press up against the young man in front of me in line. He has a nervous twitch and is examining a booger on his finger. I am forced to back away. Perfect Guy sidles up behind me. His breath grazes the back of my neck. I am beyond myself as close encounters of every imagined kind shoot deep into my sex-starved psyche. It's almost my turn to order so I try to prepare: blank, blank, blank, yes, definitely blank—brain no longer functioning. Finally I come to and overhear their conversation in midstream.

". . . he was Boston Irish, you know, that's why I was at Mass this morning. I'm doing some research," Perfect Guy says. The coffee shop has the surreal feeling of movie set.

"Oh! That's what you were doing there! You had me scared for a minute. Thought you'd left Protestantism behind! We're a rare few in these parts, you know!" the Professor chortles.

I have been schlepping to church for a Protestant! My devout Catholic Grammy would disown my little-miniskirted behind if she ever got wind of it. I'm thinking just this when I hear the Professor ask, "So how's that woman you're seeing, what is her name again?"

"Oh, yes, Kate. She's a little harried. She is in the middle of an interview process. It's been hell on her nerves."

"She's a doctor, right?"

"Yes. She's interviewing for an emergency department position at Boston Hospital."

"She seemed like a bright lady. I'm sure she'll get the position."

I surrender. Not only is he not single, he has a doctor for a girl-friend. I now have raging appetite for sugar and large doses of fat; don't care if Perfect Guy hears my Catholic peasant order.

"May I please have one of those mocha jobs with double choco-late and extra whipped cream?" I sound like some coffee-porn star. I blush.

"Skim milk?"

"No, whole," I whisper. The blond counter girl with massive breasts and a butterfly tattoo yells my order to her also blond big-boobed coworker. They both give me Daisy Duke smiles and peer over the counter.

"You have no idea how refreshing it is to hear a word other than 'skim,'" Booby No. 1 says warmly.

"Yeah," adds Booby No. 2.

"People don't realize the chocolate mixture we use to make our mochas has tons of fat already in it, so skim milk really doesn't make a whole heck of a lot of difference," Booby No. 1 continues.

"Yeah," Booby No. 2 says again.

Booby No. 1 is definitely the communicator. It's clear why she's the one behind the cash register. The Professor interrupts our highly intellectual discussion about fat and coffee by barking, "Well, girls, you better fatten this one up, she couldn't weigh more than fifty pounds soaking wet!" then adds, "Look at her feet, they're like a child's—so tiny." Booby No. 1 hands me my frothy obscene drink with whipped cream dripping down the sides, reminding me somehow of spoiled sex.

"Be careful now, you mustn't get burned, it's very hot." Booby No. 1 purrs, reinforcing my sense of toddlerhood. Shall chuck my barrettes into burning fire, grow out bob to elegant bun, wear eight-inch stack-heeled shoes, and pluck my brows to dagger points.

I burn my mouth on the first sip, then head for the door. Perfect Guy rushes over and opens it for me. I announce, like the toddler I am, "I am capable of opening doors myself!"

"I know," he says, looking directly at me, "but this gives me an opportunity—"

"An opportunity for what?" I interject. Whipped cream drips down arm and I try to steady my scalding coffee.

"To say I really like your clogs." And the door shuts with a bang.

Phone Call to Pip

After changing out of hussy outfit and putting my wedding band back on, I call Pip.

"He 'really likes' my clogs," I say, when Pip picks up the phone.

"Who?" Pip asks.

"Perfect Guy," I say.

"Holy shit, did you actually say 'Hi' to the fucking guy?"

"No," I say.

"Then how do you know he likes your clogs?"

"Because after I found out he's Protestant and has a doctor

girlfriend, he was kind enough to open the door and tell me he really likes my hot pink clogs."

"Get out!" she laughs. "How can he be Protestant and go to a Catholic church?"

"He's doing some research," I say.

"You're kidding?"

"I'm not," I snap.

"What is he researching? How to be a good Catholic and still get laid?"

"That isn't funny!"

"Come on, it's funny."

"It's not funny in the least." I begin to sniffle.

"Oh, cheer up. Come over and hang out with Martin and me. We're watching a movie on DVD." I think about sitting on the couch in between their "open relationship." Would rather jump off a bridge.

Domestic Bliss

Queen Bean is preparing pigs in a blanket. She unfurls Pillsbury dough and wraps it around cocktail wienies. She is the image of domestic bliss in a fresh fifties apron that reads TO HECK WITH HOUSEWORK! She sips her sloe gin. I can tell she's pleased with my progress. There's a Dumpster now taking up a good portion of the driveway. My eyes are bloodshot from dusting. I feel like a coal miner. Still, there's something hugely satisfying about organizing an anonymous life. Gets me out of post–Perfect Guy funk.

"Care for a cocktail?" Queen Bean slurs.

"I better not; I'm almost finished downstairs," I say.

"Have you gotten to the third floor at all today?"

"Not yet."

"Well, then," she says, good humor gone, shoving little piggies into the oven.

Moonboy

Later, when I come downstairs, a boy has appeared in the kitchen. He's the color of coffee and looks about Lucy's age. He quietly hangs up his coat and backpack and slides into a chair. He is facing away from me, but I can see his finger tracing a line in the grain of wood on the countertop.

"He's adopted—from *India*," Queen Bean quickly explains in a low voice. She turns away from me and looks hard at the boy. The tension is immediate. "You always sneak around like a ghost," she chastises him. "I hate it. I really do."

I can smell his hair. It smells of earth and goodness. He flops his head around and turns toward me, though he does not look at me immediately. It is a slow acknowledgment. Yet it comes. His eyes are like gentle moons.

three

A Week in the Country

I watch the plane as it leaves the ground, at first floating just inches above the runway, then rapidly ascending. I imagine Lucy pumping her skinny arm, yelling, "Bye, Mommy!"

"Bye, bug," I softly respond. My heart has sunk to my bowels and I run to the bathroom. This is my first Thanksgiving without the children.

The Turkey

In the car I find a box wrapped in blue construction paper. Inside is a card with a big turkey drawn in careful detail, its hindmost feathers colored in bright neon crayon. A Xeroxed message is glued on the inside: "Have a Turkey of a Day!" Also a school photo of Lucy. Her hair is plastered against her forehead. She oversmiles. I smile back at the photo. On the outside of the box something is written and I recognize Brendan's left-handed scrawl: "Don't flip out." The words soothe me. Must reconsider male intuition.

Traffic Thoughts

In the first grade I made a picture of a big rainbow and wrote under it, "Women hold up half the sky." My mother has had it hanging in her kitchen for over thirty years. It was her proudest moment as a mother when the teacher handed it to her, with a "humff," at a parent-teacher conference. Once, when I was visiting my mother, her friend Margo was tapping her nails on the counter as she waited for my mother to find some Sweet Herb to put in her green tea (Margo has "the diabetes," as she calls her condition). Her nails were painted blue, with little jewels embedded in each tip. I was fixated on her hands and wasn't paying attention to their conversation until Margo stopped abruptly, pointed to my picture, and said, "Which half? I hope not the one with the hole in it. You know, the ozone thingy."

Knee Deep

Queen Bean is in a disastrous mood when I arrive, as promised but late, to do a "light clean" before I leave for Thanksgiving at my Grammy's. The light clean is to stem the tide that is sure to sweep the house while I'm away.

I've yet to meet the owner of the house. Very creepy but thrilling as well. I don't even know what he looks like—the house is void of photos. I'm sure they are in the third-floor bedroom that is always locked. My fantasies include these: He is really a JFK-looking senator in the midst of a presidential campaign and is hiding the product of an illicit affair by making his Boston Bean mama play full-time granny to love child; when the senator and I finally meet, he falls madly in love with me and moons about, trying to get my attention, but I ignore him with look of disdain—as I dust and mop—until I finally agree to be his wife. We have a fabulous wedding on Beacon Hill and invite Ex-Rat.

The second fantasy, of course, is that he is William Hurt, and his wife is in the locked bedroom on the third floor with the nurse, and I am Jane Eyre.

The third scenario is that he is a weasely-looking sportswriter.

I've tried to imagine him as a sexy sportswriter but cannot. I believe this fantasy has to do with the coffee-splattered magazine clippings about every sport imaginable—squash, hockey, football, baseball—that are stacked by the typewriter on the kitchen table.

Queen Bean fixes me with a look, as I have managed to stare blankly at her for five minutes. "The basement has flooded," she says, with sharp irritation.

"Oh," I respond neutrally.

"And he's been at it all morning," she says.

"Dear god," I blurt out, imagining her mysterious son having raucous sex.

"I'm lucky a plumber could be found on such short notice," she continues, "so I shouldn't complain. However, between the banging and the sucking my nerves have called it a day. Unfortunately this is *not* the worst news. I just got off the phone with my son and he informed me he is not going to make it back in time for Thanksgiving. He left his wallet containing all his identification in some cab and they won't let him board the plane. Now he's stuck in some god-forsaken airport in god knows where—all because of some silly book tour!" She begins to pace.

"Oh, my god," I say.

"Oh, my god is right! I've already made plans to spend Thanksgiving with my friend Ellen from my bridge club! And Ellen detests children of any kind—so bringing my grandson would be out of the question. I haven't a clue what I'm going to do! I can't very well change plans *now*." She stops pacing and snaps her fingers, "Maybe my grandson could come along with you for the holiday?" She laughs and says lightly, "I don't know what I'm thinking! That's impossible, seeing as you are going to your grandmother's."

I am dumbstruck.

"I'll bring him to my Grammy's if he would like to come," I hear myself say. "He is more than welcome."

"Well, that's very generous. I think I'll take you up on that offer.

Of course you'll be paid for your inconvenience," she says, with a full smile.

"I think that's up to your grandson and what he would like to do," I say.

"Oh, I'm sure he'll love the idea! What's not to love about Thanksgiving in Vermont? It's a win-win situation if you ask me—my grandson will have the opportunity to spend some time in the country and I'll spend the day with my friend Ellen as planned," she says brightly.

A plumber comes thudding up the stairs and opens the door to the kitchen. He is an elderly Hispanic man carrying a red tool box.

"Hi," I say. He nods and hands a bill to Queen Bean and then leaves.

"Well, they don't know a word of English but they certainly know their math," she snorts, looking at the bill.

"That is . . . an awful thing to say," I falter.

Queen Bean looks at me in surprise, "Oh dear, I didn't mean *all* domestic help, only the ones who don't speak English." She pats my hand. I grind my teeth to keep from screaming. "I have to say I am delighted that my grandson will be spending Thanksgiving with you instead of some stranger."

"He doesn't even know me," I say, my outrage now bubbling over.

"Don't be ridiculous," she says, with a warning tone, her eyes narrowing.

Limbo

Five fifteen p.m. and it's already dark. Headlights careen past my window. Moonboy and Ugly are silent. They have both chosen to sit in the backseat. Moonboy is holding an unopened coloring book and crayons I bought for him at the drugstore on our way out of town. The coloring book is full of pictures of butterflies. He obviously does not like the subject or the materials. I ask him about school. He either nods or shakes his head in response to my questions.

"Do you like your school?"

Nod.

"Do you play any sports?"

Shake.

"Do you have a lot of friends at school?"

No nod or shake.

I stop asking questions. I feel like we're in a spaceship. Too quiet. Right about now, Demon Princess would be out of control, kicking the back of my seat, asking every minute when will we be there, while Brendan says over and over, "You just asked, you freak." I miss their noise. Ugly doesn't; he has a look of doggy bliss instead of his typical stressed-out car whine. He's become quite an old party poop.

Arrival

Vermont is hopping. Yuppies have invaded. SUVs with mini TVs congeal into traffic jams on dirt roads.

Moonboy and Ugly are sleeping. The lights of Grammy's house are visible from the road. Glowing plastic statues of Mary, Joseph, and the three wise men standing over an empty manger have already been placed at end of the drive. A sign by the mailbox reads: "Put Jesus Back in Christmas."

When we pull up to the house, Grammy is standing on the porch. Even though she is eighty-four, she has the vitality of some-one half her age. Must be from all the farming and praying she does. Grammy yells, "I saw you coming up the road!" Moonboy stirs.

"Shhh!" I put my finger to my lips, and point to the backseat.

"I thought the kids weren't with you," she mouths, tiptoeing to-ward the car.

"They're not," I mouth back. She looks in the backseat.

"At least this one sleeps," she says. Moonboy surfaces and looks Grammy over. "Did you have a nice trip?" she asks him. He nods. "Not a complainer, either, that's good." She continues to observe at him and he stares back. "Well, *Iron Chef* is about to start and I don't want to miss it. I'll put your Uncle Cain and his trollop wife to some use by having them come out here and help you with your suitcases." I feel instant pity for Uncle Cain, who is forever damned for being the first of her children to go off to college and promptly embrace the world of sin—sex, drugs, and rock-and-roll were far more alluring than spreading manure. She walks back toward the house, then nods toward Moonboy, "He's got your staring problem. I'd nip that in the bud if I were you."

Moonshadow

Moonboy glides silently behind me as we make our way up the stairs to the attic room. Ugly is with his hot-dog friends by the wood stove. The attic window is already open to release saunalike heat. Over each of the two beds is a crucifix. There are small bedside tables with tiny lamps, rosary beads, and holy water in little bottles with the image of the Virgin Mary on the front labels. Grammy believes these surroundings will stop unwed kin from fornicating like rabid wolves.

Moonboy tries to get in bed with his clothes on, but I find a pair of crusty pajamas in his valise and show him to the bathroom. I hand him a new toothbrush, bought along with art supplies at the drugstore, and shut the door. He is quick about it, unlike Demon Princess, who would linger until screamed at. He slides into bed and closes his eyes.

"Goodnight," I say.

Silence.

For a moment I feel his stillness. His purposeful quietness and careful observation.

I shut off the lights. The darkness is all that passes between us.

Thanksgiving Day

When the rooster crows, I run to the bathroom and get dressed in the now-freezing attic. Moonboy wakes and I lay out his clothes at the end of the bed. I hand him a towel and tell him to take a shower. His tranquil face blossoms into terror and he shakes his head. "Should we go and collect eggs instead?" I say, with a smile. He smiles back. It's a beautiful smile. It could break your heart.

Farm Chores

Uncle Abel has already done the milking and put the cows out to pasture. He nods to us in his shit-covered boots. "Well," is all he says, by way of greeting. Moonboy takes to him instantly, sensing a kindred spirit, and doesn't wait to smile at him. Abel is not the smiling type, though, so it's wasted. Abel lives on the farm and is my Gram and Grampa's favorite son because he never questioned Vermont farming tradition, unlike his older brother Cain. Abel hands us used egg cartons, and we go collect eggs in the chicken coop while Abel stomps loudly, shooing the chickens out of their warm nests.

Moonboy follows Abel to the pigpen as I take the eggs into the house. Grampa is loading wood on top of the cinders. The smell of smoke hangs thick in air. Ugly rises slowly and wags his tail when he sees me. His hot-dog groupies run underneath his legs, excited that he is up and about. I put food in his dish and bring it out to the front porch. As I place the kibble down, I find that Grammy has already filled a salad bowl with what looks to be the butt of a pig. Ugly skitters over before I can grab it. He drags the rump roast down the front steps, growling between clenched jaws at his four-legged buddies, and disappears around the corner of the house.

It's amazing what Ugly is still capable of, given the right circumstances.

More Arrivals

Uncle Abel and Moonboy sit on the couch, watching football. Ugly farts by the woodstove. Grammy has roasted the bird and puts it on its back to retain juices. When I question where she learned such a clever culinary trick, she waves her cigarette in the air. "Cooking Channel," she says.

Uncle Cain is smoking weed with his trollop wife behind the barn when my brother, Derek, arrives in his Hummer. The men have been waiting all day for this. It's my brother's girlfriends that are the big draw. They act as though a real-life Dallas cheerleader has come to cheer just for them. Usually this isn't far off, considering that these babes are always doing everything and anything to make us happy. It's their nature, given that they're all airline stewardesses.

My brother is a commercial pilot. He is short and has a gay father. His way of assuring everyone he's not gay is to show no signs of having an intellect and to consistently screw different women and then talk about it loudly. I don't judge him. Between a raging man-hating women's-lib mother and a father who showed up for high school baseball games with peevish men wearing their eyeglasses on gold chains around their necks, I believe it is his way of rebelling.

Following right behind my brother are my mother and Margo. Margo has never had children, so she always comes to our holiday festivities. Margo is in her late fifties, extremely overweight, has dyed red hair, and wears bright, tight-fitting rayon outfits. My mother, the complete opposite, is svelte with long, dark hair that is going naturally gray at the temples. She is the image of Mother Earth in loose Flax clothing. The only thing they have in common is that they are close in age and divorced. I guess this is enough, because they do everything together, from online dating to grocery shopping.

Derek walks over and hugs me. "So are Mom and Margo shacked

up yet or what?" he whispers into my ear. He lifts his sunglasses and gives me a wink. His girlfriend tilts her head to one side and smiles as she shakes my hand.

"Hi, hi, hi, your brother has told me so much about you, I just couldn't wait to meet you, give me a hug, I feel like I already know you, god, you're so petite! Like a little bird." She gives me a polite hug, but her boobs smash against my face.

My brother launches into a deep, private conversation with Uncle Cain, whose eyes are nearly shut. I hear Derek loudly whisper, "This one is out of control, totally out of control, like a wildcat." Uncle Cain drools slightly.

Grampa comes in from milking, takes a gander at my brother's new gal, removes his hat and says, "Well, hello there." Derek's girlfriend's face is all dimples as Grampa takes her elbow and escorts her to his keg of homemade ale.

Late Arrivals

My mother's sisters live in town. They know everyone in the county because they are nurses and also sell baked goods at the local farmer's market. This tends to make them late for family gatherings, since somebody is always showing up at their doorstep with an order for eighteen pies or to ask them to attend the birth of their first great-grandchild. They never say no. They can't. They're almost saints.

Today they arrive four hours after they said they would, which is early by their standards. Their huge station wagon with fake-wood side paneling roars up the driveway and screeches to a stop. My aunts are small people, like the rest of my family, so you can barely see them over the dashboard, which is covered in Beanie Babies. The antenna is loaded with little smiley-face flags. The fenders are hidden by bumper stickers with slogans such as, DO UNTO OTHERS AS YOU WOULD HAVE THEM DO UNTO YOU. SIGNED, GOD, and DENIAL IS NOT A RIVER IN EGYPT.

They both hop out of the wagon and run to the back of the car as if their pants are on fire. Aunt Mary checks the tires and screams, "Everything is right as rain!" Then she jumps up and down and lights a cigarette.

Aunt Eve yells, "Thanks be to God! I didn't see that freaking pothole until we were on it. Scared the crap out of me!" She lights a cigarette, too. They stand there puffing.

"Well," Aunt Mary says to me, "are you gonna stand there gawking or help us with these pies?"

These almost-saints speak their mind.

Fixins

"So, Missy, your divorce finally come through or what?" Aunt Mary asks as she spears some turkey from off the platter and passes the plate to my mother, who looks at it, grimaces, and passes it onto Margo without taking any.

"I already *told* you it did," my mother says to Aunt Mary and grabs the untouched plate of tofu from the table.

"I'm not asking you, though, am I? I want to hear about it from her," she says, eyes waiting patiently.

"Yes," I acknowledge.

"When?" Aunt Mary says.

"A couple of months ago," I mumble. Uncle Abel fills Moonboy's plate.

"Took long enough. So Mister High and Mighty has the kids this Thanksgiving?" Aunt Eve asks.

"Yes," I say.

"I've never heard such bullshit," Aunt Mary comments.

Grammy scolds, "Mary, watch your tongue."

Aunt Mary waves the comment away with a flick of her fork. "He never took one drop of interest in those kids until taking them might mean less child support that he had to pay."

"I heard he still has to pay a crapload," says Uncle Cain.

"What man takes his children away from their mother on Thanksgiving?" Grampa spews. He is red in the face from about a gallon of ale. I am transfixed; he's usually quiet about emotional issues.

"Calm down, old man," Uncle Abel says.

Everyone goes quiet.

Grammy breaks the silence. "Maybe having them more will make him realize how hard she worked."

"He'll *never* know how hard she worked," my mother says, about to burst. "They're practically grown. He waited until they were out of diapers, I'll give him credit for that."

"What man leaves his wife and children?" Grampa bellows, then starts coughing. Uncle Cain pounds his back.

"He's a patriarchal asshole!" My mother is screaming now. Grampa has stopped coughing and is making motions toward his throat. Aunt Mary bangs through chairs to get at him and then heaves him up from behind, lifting him off his chair. A no-longer-creamed onion pops out of his mouth and lands smack in the middle of his butternut squash. Grampa takes a deep breath and starts coughing again.

"Cain, pounding is the worst thing you can possibly do!" Aunt Eve yells, pounding her own fist on the table.

"That was intense!" still-stoned Trollop Wife says.

"We forgot to say grace!" Grammy exclaims in horror.

"The food is delicious. Thank you for having me as your guest," Moonboy suddenly addresses Grammy.

"Where did *he* come from?" Uncle Cain asks, noticing Moonboy for the first time.

"I suppose from someplace where they teach people manners!" Grammy says. She throws her napkin on the table, heads to the hallway, and hollers up the stairs to my brother and his girlfriend, "I hear you up there, and if you don't get your fanny down here in two shakes I'm going to cut your balls off and feed them to the pig!" Back at the table, she says to Grampa, with her finger about two inches from his nose, "That's what you get for not saying the Lord's Prayer before stuffing your face."

Grampa turns a darker shade of red. We all stiffen. Derek and his girlfriend tiptoe to their seats. We bow our heads in prayer.

Thought

During the Lord's Prayer, I think of my children at another table far away. I wonder how I got here, alone, without a husband, without my children. How does one accept such emptiness? I look at my mother, her mouth set in angry lines.

Pie

Pie is as soothing as a kiss. A balm for all my inner wounds. I hope that if and when I get to heaven, I can eat pie every day.

A Phone Call

The bedroom door opens. I am only half awake. Grammy walks over to my bed and shoves the phone in my face. "You tell whoever the hell it is that it's 11:38 p.m.," she hisses, slamming the door on her way out.

"Hello," I say.

"I'm sorry to whomever I'm disturbing by calling so late," comes a strange male's voice. I'm now wide awake and terrified.

"Did the plane crash? Are they hurt? Was it a car accident?"

"No, why on earth would it be anything so awful?" says the man.

"Then what happened?" I whisper loudly.

"Nothing has happened," he says.

"Is this the police?" I ask, almost shouting now.

"No!"

"The airline?"

"No!"

"Does this have anything to do with my children?" I see the whites of Moonboy's eyes in the dark.

"*Your* children?" he asks.

"Brendan and Lucy," I say.

"No."

"Oh, thank god." I lie back down on the pillow.

Then I guess who it is. "Do you realize what time it is?" I ask, very ticked.

"By my watch it's nearly twelve," he says.

"Exactly!" I hang up. What kind of father waits till midnight to chat about how his son's Thanksgiving went with some stranger? A weasel. A weasel whom I now despise.

A Favor

Queen Bean calls the next morning with the "tiresome" news that her son has been requested to continue on with his book tour, now that his wallet and briefcase have been found. It turns out her son left them in the airport restroom, not a cab, and they were sitting in the airport security office the entire time. Now he needs his mother to drop everything to take "the boy" for the remainder of the weekend and into next week. This sullies her bridge festivities. Her son's publisher couldn't be more thoughtless, blah, blah, blah. I can see where she's going with all this, considering I'm supposed to drive Moonboy to the tiny state airport in half an hour to be delivered back to her doorstep.

"Could you keep him?" She says this resentfully. She hates to ask for anything.

The Bath

After three days of hanging out on a farm with Abel and the animals, Moonboy's lovely earthen scent has been rendered to cow dung. After much deliberation, Grammy is the one who braves it. She strips Moonboy down to his underwear and throws him in the tub. He flails like a cat. "Might as well get them underwear clean as well," she says, as she dumps a bucket of water on his head. Moonboy screams. "My Abel is just the same. Can't stand getting his head wet. It's because he had a difficult birth. The doctor had to use high forceps with Abel. I didn't feel a thing, but Abel had a head like a banana and was all bruised."

The water instantly runs dark brown. Lint and hair float to the surface. Moonboy keeps screaming but Grammy tells him, "It has to be done, you can't go to church smelling like you've been smelling." She lathers him up, dumps more water on him. I hand her the shampoo and she lifts Moonboy's matted dark hair off his shoulders and then grabs me hard by the wrist. On back of Moonboy's neck there is a birthmark in the shape of a cross.

A Marked Difference

Grammy has decided not to tell the "filler" priest about the mark. She feels a bit uneasy about it. Who is she to say it's a sign from God? She tells me this, in shaky excitement, as she combs Moonboy's hair to a rich silkiness, trims his toenails, and rubs his feet and hands with my mother's homemade comfrey cream. It's like Mary tending Jesus. I go to the dryer for his pajamas and when I return, she's whispering, "In the name of the Father, the Son, and the Holy Spirit . . ." Moonboy is back in the empty tub, and she's holding a huge green wine bottle.

"What are you doing? Pouring wine on him?"

Moonboy is gripping the sides of the tub, ready to bolt.

"It's not wine, it's holy water," she says.

"What is it doing in a wine bottle?" I ask. It has a white label with HOLY WATER, LOURDES written in black marker.

"Betsy from Addison County Homemakers brought it back as a gift from her trip," she says. I imagine Betsy dipping used wine bottles in some holy-water fountain and then sticking them into her little black shopping cart on wheels. "What are you doing with it?" I ask Grammy, who is looking very nervous.

"You know what I'm doing," she whispers. And I do. She's baptizing Moonboy. "Just in case," she adds.

"Just in case of what?" I ask.

"Just shut the door and mind your own beeswax," she whispers firmly. I place the clean PJs on the toilet and close the bathroom door behind me. I feel as though I just caught Grammy stealing. Decide to pretend I didn't see.

The Little Church in Town

The filler priest is telling a joke. The joke is about how Jesus carries his cross into a cross shop and tells the clerk behind the counter he needs a new one since his is worn out. Jesus looks and looks and finally eyes one that is perfect. The clerk says, "But that's the one you came in with." The parish gives a polite laugh. They miss their old priest, who left under "medical duress" due to pending liver failure.

"This one doesn't drink," Grammy tells me. "And he's no good at telling jokes."

"Hey, that guy is rubbernecking you." Aunt Eve points to a gorgeous and tall mountain of a man. Mountain Man blushes.

"He's Brendan's height," my mother says.

"Look at the body on him, holy mother of god, what a hunk-a-chunka," Aunt Mary says shamelessly.

Grammy shushes her.

"Haven't ever seen him around town. Must be visiting," Aunt Eve whispers.

"He's probably married. The good-looking ones always are," Aunt Mary says.

"That doesn't stop any of them," my mother states grimly.

Grammy puts her finger to her lips and gives us the look of death. We all kneel, except for Moonboy, who has finally found some interest in glitter crayons and butterflies.

The Diner

The town diner still lets you smoke. A big plus for the aunts. My mother and Margo refuse to join us in the "death chamber" and they head home, happy to get an early start. My eyes begin tearing and my throat closes as soon as we sit down in the back, by the TV. Abel and Grampa take our coats and pull out our seats. Love this about them. Very old-fashioned and just plain nice. Moonboy is highly cheered by the paper placemat with a maze on it. His butterfly coloring book falls to the floor.

The waitress, a shy girl with soft eyes and a fragile smile, takes our order. Aunt Eve attended her birth.

"Oh, my god," Aunt Mary says. "This is my reward for going to church at eight in the morning." The tall Mountain Man from church is taking off his long-sleeve wool shirt, revealing a tight-fitting long-underwear top. My thighs quiver. He walks over to an old man sitting alone at a booth.

"Must be Maynard's grandson," Grammy says.

"Is he the grandson who set the barn on fire?" Aunt Eve asks.

"Maynard only has one grandson, Eve, so of course he's the one." Aunt Mary lets out a long breath.

I spent all my summers on the farm when I was growing up and I remember when Maynard's barn burned down. I was fifteen that summer and hadn't even a hint of breasts. Aunt Mary bought me a training bra anyway and I wore that thing day and night.

"Even if he *is* a pyro, he is one fine specimen," Aunt Mary marvels, then gets up and walks over to their table and we watch her nodding and chatting away. Eventually she sits down with them and asks Ellen, the waitress, to bring her coffee over there. Aunt Eve goes over to join them. When our breakfast arrives, they're still talking and laughing. The men eat their lumberjack breakfasts silently, Moonboy picks at his. I put jam on my toast and let it sit. The table is boring without my aunts. Grammy shouts to them that their breakfast will get cold. They finally extricate themselves and come back.

"He's single and he's some kind of tour guide in Alaska. We gave him your number," Aunt Mary says to me and grins.

"You what?" I ask, incredulous.

"He's a hunk, so shut your trap and be thankful," Aunt Mary says. "He asked all about you. He remembered your name and everything."

"He says you two used to swim together down at the river," Aunt Eve adds. I have a dim recollection of a weird boy showing off on the rope swing. Aunt Eve taps my left hand. "You might want to take off *that ring*."

"Now you'll have something to fantasize about while driving home to your empty house," Aunt Mary says.

"She has her kids, she doesn't need anyone to fantasize about," Grammy says to Mary.

"Kids don't warm the cockles," Aunt Mary moons.

I look over at Mountain Man. He catches my eye and smiles—a really nice smile.

He has beautiful white teeth. His eyes sparkle with warmth. "What's his name?" I ask.

"Mason," Aunt Eve says.

I love that name.

Grampa Remembers

"By the way, a fella called about the boy the other day," Grampa says, pointing to Moonboy across the table.

"What day?" I ask.

Grampa scratches the top of his bald head. After much deliberation he says, "It must have been the day you drove up."

"The day before Thanksgiving?" I ask.

"Yup." Grampa nods. "I think he called that day, too."

"That day *too*?" I say. "It's the same day, Grampa."

"Oh, I don't know! Now you've got me confused. He called a bunch of times," Grampa says, standing up and putting on his hat. "A Nervous Nelly if you ask me. I told him not to worry. His son was having a fine time."

"Thanks for telling me," I say, remembering that I hung up on the Nervous Nelly. I start to twirl my hair.

"No trouble at all," Grampa says proudly.

"I'm surprised he even remembered to tell you," Grammy says. "He usually doesn't even remember his own name."

Back in Boston

I drop Moonboy at Queen Bean's condo on Beacon Hill. Potpourri in an autumn spice scent fills my nostrils. It feels like the inside of Aphrodite's shell. A number of women sit around the dining room table, holding cards and drinking martinis. There's no food in sight, save for glass fruits arranged from largest to smallest on a faux fireplace mantle. Queen Bean is clearly not pleased that we have arrived on time. She escorts Moonboy to the living room and turns on the television. "Well, we'll settle up tomorrow then, shall we?" Queen Bean says.

"I won't be coming tomorrow. My children are flying in mid-morning."

"Children?" she asks, aghast.

"My children," I repeat.

"I didn't know you had children," she sputters.

The Empty Nest

The light bulb on the porch has burned out and now the house is mercilessly dark. I walk up to the front door, instead of the garage door, so in case I am attacked, I can scream and run into the street faster. Ugly stays in the car, sensing my fear. No one jumps out of the bushes and I open the door, pushing it hard since there is junk mail piled behind it. I turn on all the lights and go back to the car to collect my bag and Ugly.

There are no new messages on the answering machine, so I replay the old ones. Question my existence. Pinch myself. Turn on the radio, and then turn it off. I microwave some popcorn, grab a bag of licorice from the cabinet, and go into the living room, forcing Ugly to come with me. Luckily, favorite Sunday single-gals sex comedy is all about their being miserable with being single and afraid of dying alone. At least I'm not the only one.

Speechless

I clutch the phone because I can't believe he is calling me. Yes, yes, yes! "I hope this isn't too weird," he says. "Your aunts gave me your number."

I cannot find my vocal cords.

"I mean, well, I saw you at church, and, well, I guess you know that already, that I saw you, it was pretty hard to miss, and then your aunts said I should call you, or rather, that you might like a call from me . . ."

He is groping. I feel a rising panic. Must say something. "Oh," is what I say.

"OK," Mason says. "I'm going to be up front, well, honest, I guess, I've had a crush on you ever since I was ten. I still remember you in a little pink polka-dot bathing suit—and, well, all I wanted to be was sixteen that summer when I first laid eyes on you, but instead I was a measly little kid doing spastic jumps off a stupid rope swing. When I saw you at church, I couldn't believe my luck."

"Oh," I repeat.

The line is silent for a very long moment. "Well, listen, um, I'm sorry I called, I don't know what I was thinking . . ." His voice trails off and he hangs up.

"Wait!" I tell the dial tone.

Wonder how I could be such a dork.

Decide I hate myself.

four

A Week of Self-Loathing

I'm going to put up Christmas decorations early this year but have mistakenly packed away all the trimmings in the garage for a possible spring yard sale. I happen upon this realization after spending a good chunk of the morning tearing apart the basement and attic. Have no idea where, in the huge pile of cat-piss-smelling stuffed garbage bags, my frilly frollies lay. I imagine little squeaky voices calling to me: "Please find us! We will miss shining prettily and making children happy!" This is a tactic left over from childhood that spurs me on to find useless objects. The smell of car fumes mixed with cat piss is making me sick and I vow never to leave the garage door open for days at a time because I am too lazy to shut it. "But where will all the homeless little kitties sleep?" the squeaky voices ask.

A Foul Smell

In the afternoon, at Evil Weasel's house, I'm sorting mismatched socks in the laundry room when the doorbell rings. The mailman hands me a long, narrow package. There is flowery script on the wrinkled brown paper. As I sign for it, the mailman nods, and says too brightly, "Thanks!" The package smells foul. Even Ugly and Manic Pup are disgusted. I shake it and squeeze it. It's solid but claylike. I put it on the table. The odor of rotten liverwurst lingers on my hands. What kind of idiot would mail a perishable that can achieve such rankness?

The Bedroom

Evil Weasel's bedroom is unlocked today and it's not as I imagined. There is no bed layered in dust. No nightgown folded atop a pillow. No hand mirror or brush. No ancient Chanel lipstick in classic red on the vanity. No evening gowns in the closet. No ticket stubs to the *Nutcracker* or dried flowers.

There is this: a twin bed, very unmade; stacks of books and papers in various piles; photos stuck to the wall with tacks; many nasty half-drunk cups of coffee, and a brand-new computer. The photographs interest me, but on closer inspection they are also a bummer—old and blurred, all of men and women playing squash.

Very boring. Very boring indeed.

This represents neither the JFK lookalike nor William Hurt. My hopes are dashed completely.

A Run-In

The package contents are revealed: Queen Bean is back from having her talons painted and is sitting at the table eating sweetbreads. She grumbles as Moonboy wraps himself around Manic Pup just as the sound of the front door opening causes both dogs to howl. In walks Perfect Guy!

Now I recall where I saw the name *Henry C. Bannister.* Hundreds of times on letters and just this morning on the foul-smelling package.

"Hello, little man. Hello, Mother. Well, I do believe I have had the pleasure of meeting these clogs before." He looks at my feet. I soak him in. His crooked nose. His piercing eyes, now seemingly distracted by deep thought. Messy black hair. Vast cheekbones.

Dimpled chin. Rueful smile. I moan inwardly, careful not to open my mouth. I twirl my hair rapidly as he tries to remember. "But where, where, where . . . Oh, outside, no, inside the coffee shop!" He snaps his fingers and gives me another gorgeous smile.

"I'm Henry, by the way. We haven't officially met," he says to me, shoving on reading glasses and picking up the mail from the table.

"What the hell is that smell?" he asks.

"Sweetbreads from your Aunt Emily," Queen Bean answers.

"I told her my cholesterol was up."

"Don't be silly, your cholesterol is fine," she says.

"That's not the point," Henry sniffs and loosens his tie. His fingers are very long, with fine, broad nails. "Have you eaten?" he asks.

"Me?" I ask.

"Yes."

"Why, no, it's still early."

"Mmm, it is, isn't it, yet I'm sort of hungry, even after smelling those sweetbreads. Would you like to go out for dim sum, or maybe some sushi?" he asks.

"It looks as though I am no longer needed. I'm going home," Queen Bean huffs. Henry rolls his eyes. Moonboy smiles.

"Mother, you are welcome to join us," he says.

"No, no, it's almost cocktail hour—must hurry." She walks quickly out the door.

I stand awkwardly in the kitchen. Moonboy points at me and says, "That's how cranes sleep."

Henry says, "How about it? Game?"

The thought of waltzing around the city with a famous local author is too delightful to turn down, even if he is a Protestant Evil Weasel. I hope we run into Ex-Rat.

"Mmm, OK," I say, acting cool. "Can Ugly stay here by the fireplace?"

"Of course." He runs upstairs to change and comes clunking back down in a red plaid flannel shirt and paint-speckled khakis.

I feel overdressed in jeans and a baby-doll T-shirt. He looks me up and down. It is very rude, but I like it. He adjusts his glasses and then takes them off. "I want to let you know I'm sorry for calling you so late on Thanksgiving—I normally wouldn't do such a thing." He is frantically wiping his glasses on his shirt. "When I found out my mother had asked you to take my son for the holiday, instead of her taking my son to the club as planned, I panicked. Since you didn't leave a cell phone number, I called your grandparents' house immediately in order to try to rectify the situation—but you hadn't arrived yet—so I left my number and waited for you to call me back—"

"I don't have a cell phone, and my Grampa forgot to give me the message—I mean messages—he's over eighty years old, you see, and so he forgets everything—I mean, I do too—so maybe it's not his age—maybe it's genetic or something—" I stop before I tell him my whole life story.

"Oh, I see, I didn't realize—" he pauses. "Regardless, I've been meaning to return some kindness for the nice Thanksgiving you provided for my son." He walks over to me and removes the barrette from my hair. I am astonished but don't move. He fumbles in his pocket and takes out a beautiful bobby pin with a silver seahorse on it. "It was my wife's. I know she would want you to have it. It's really a gift from her." He places it gently in my hair. "My wife loved seahorses. It's the male of the species, you know, who gives birth," he says. I touch the delicate tail.

"Thank you," I say, looking up at Henry. There is something so gentle and earnest in his eyes. So like his son's.

"No. Thank *you*," Henry says.

Empty Fridge

As we grab our coats, Henry says with sudden gaiety, "I know! Instead of going to some restaurant, I'll make fondue! I just bought a fondue pot! It has little skewers and everything! OK with you?"

Henry heads into the kitchen. Moonboy and I tag behind. "We are going to bedazzle our guest with culinary genius," Henry says to Moonboy, who looks at his father doubtfully, then at me, and shakes his head. I laugh. We watch as Henry opens a brand new cookbook. The cover reads *Fondue 1, 2, 3!* He flips through its thick picture-book pages. "Here it is, Basic Cheese Fondue in fifteen minutes! That even looks like our pot!" He shows us the picture, points to the fondue pot on the kitchen counter. He scans the recipe, "We need cheese." Before I can stop him, Henry looks in the refrigerator, which is empty and gleaming. Henry holds the fridge door open with a stunned look, "There's nothing in it!"

"I know, I cleaned it," I say, twirling my hair.

"Right," Henry says, and pulls open produce bins. They're empty as well.

"I threw out everything that was past its expiration date," I explain. "There's a market around the corner. I'll just run and get some cheese."

"No, no. I'll go. You're the guest."

"Let's all go," I suggest.

Library Park

Moonboy zigzags across the sidewalk in front of us, pretending to herd chickens. Henry and I stroll, watching him.

"I think you have a farmer in the making," I say.

"He doesn't stop talking about your Uncle Abel and all the animals."

"Really?" I can't imagine Moonboy saying more than a sentence or two.

"At night, after reading stories, I get him to open up by playing a game with him in which I try to guess what he is thinking. I'm always wrong, of course—so then he has to correct me." Henry winks. "He's like his mother that way, quiet. It's not a bad thing. It's not a sad quiet, but more like he's observing."

I want to ask him about his wife but don't. Instead I ask, "Why aren't there any family photos in your house?"

"I came home one day and my mother had taken them all down and hid them somewhere. She thought it would be best."

"That's—"

"Horrible," Henry interrupts. "It was. I suppose she thought it would help me move on." He smiles weakly and adds, "Though my son does see his grandparents on his mother's side quite often. In the summer he visits them in Philadelphia for a whole month. They've been a tremendous help, making sure he knows what a wonderful person she was and about her long battle with breast cancer—you know—when I couldn't even mention her name without breaking down. There are plenty of photographs of her there, at their house, in Philly."

We walk to the end of the block in silence.

"Do you like parks?" Henry asks me. I nod. "Have you ever been to Library Park?" I shake my head. "The park has these cat benches—they're interesting. If you're not starving yet, maybe we could go take a quick peek at them on the way to the market?"

"As long as it is a quick peek, I need to pick up my kids in an hour or so," I lie, knowing that I am supposed to be at Ex-Rat's house this very moment.

"Oh, I didn't realize, we should have invited them along."

"No, no, it was too last minute, my ex-husband has them to-day—he'll probably take them out to eat." *I hope,* I think to myself.

"So you are divorced?" he asks, pointing to my wedding ring, obviously confused. I put my hand in my pocket.

"Yes, just recently," I say. "Mmm, well, I mean, it has been a year since we separated, so I guess that is not so recently, if you look at it like that . . ." I mumble, sounding, I'm sure, like an idiot, "but the *actual* divorce was just finalized a few months ago." I take my hand out of my pocket and twirl my hair, stop, and put my hand back in my pocket again.

"A year," he says eyeing my ring again, "well . . . what a shame." He pauses, "How are you getting on? Forget I said that, it was a dumb thing to ask, since you're still wearing the ring." His face is comically askew.

"Oh! I'm fine—*really* I am." I pause, sighing loudly. "It's just that men hit on me *all the time,* so I wear my wedding ring to keep the masses at bay," I joke, trying to make light. It works. Henry's face splits into a grin. I put my hand to my mouth, "I can't believe I just said that. I must sound like a *complete* show-off."

"Mmmm . . ."

"I do, don't I?"

"A total egomaniac," he teases.

"I'm really humble once you get to know me," I say.

"Sure," Henry laughs and then runs ahead and steers Moonboy toward the library. We walk around the outside of the building and into the park. Henry dusts off one of the crazy-colored cat benches and motions for Moonboy and me to sit. We all squeeze onto the bench, which is cold and hard and not at all comfortable. Big, fat, wet flakes of snow begin to fall, clinging to our lashes.

"I don't think you're supposed to sit on these benches in the winter," Henry says.

"I think you're right," I say.

Marzipan

The market is dense with foreign packaging: cookies, crackers, and cereal display colorful European seals. I spy a rack holding nothing but colorful fruit-shaped marzipan. I press a cellophane package up to my nose and sniff its glorious almond scent. "Yummy!" I say aloud. I notice Henry is staring at me from the other side of the rack with a serious look. I stop sniffing. Feel like a marzipan pervert.

"Are you seeing anyone special?" Henry asks.

I snort. An awful snort. I can't think what is worse, the snort or the sniffing, so I pretend I didn't do either. I don't want to sound like a true dateless wonder, so I twirl my hair and say casually, "Sort of."

"Sort of?"

"Mmmm, well, we *just barely* started seeing each other."

"Oh, I see. It must have been hard to choose someone special with all those men throwing themselves at your feet," Henry smiles and steps closer to me.

"It was." I drift, his near proximity causing my skin to tingle.

An inhumanly gorgeous female holding a bottle of imported seltzer strides down the aisle toward us. "Henry Bannister?"

"Yes?" Henry asks cautiously.

"Bonnie Winslow, I live two doors down from you, in the white colonial. Our boys go to the same school," she says.

"Oh—right," Henry stumbles.

"I *just* finished reading your new book! *It was an amazing read!*" she cries, as if climaxing.

"Thank you, you're very kind," Henry says.

"You modest thing, you!" she chides, giving his shoulder a playful push. "You really should give a reading at the school. All the Montessori mommies are *just dying* to meet you! And your bookstore readings are always *so* crowded."

"Errr, yes, well, we'll have to see—"

"Who's this?" the woman asks, finally noticing me. Her eyes narrow.

"She's . . ." Henry begins.

Afraid he is going to say "cleaning lady," I interrupt. "I'm the dog walker," I say. Unfortunately this sounds just as bad.

"Oh! I've been looking for someone to walk my Goldendoodles—Max and Tucker! How much do you charge?" she asks.

"It's really just a hobby," I say.

"A hobby?" The woman laughs a high, tinkly laugh—the kind to which I've always aspired. Instead, of course, I'm a snorter—a snorter with a marzipan-sniffing problem and a dog-walking hobby.

"She's joking," Henry says to the woman. "She's actually taking time out of her busy schedule to take care of my son. I don't know what I would have done without her on this last book tour."

"Oh! So she's your personal assistant!" the woman says. "I have one, too! Aren't they just the thing to have in a pinch?"

Turns out, flitting around town with a stud-muffin local author is not as delightful as I imagined. I pick up a package of marzipan and head for the counter. Moonboy appears with various blocks of cheese in a red market basket and a fifty-dollar bill given to him by his father. We pay for our items. I pick up the grocery bag from the counter, shift it onto my hip, and take Moonboy's hand. I call over to Henry, "We'll meet you at the house."

"Wait—" Henry says, and starts walking toward us but the woman grabs his arm.

"We'll meet you back at the house," I repeat.

Moonboy and Me

On the way home, I had to stop, release Moonboy's hand, and switch the grocery bag to my other hip. I take his hand in mine again.

"Your hand is nice and warm," Moonboy says happily, his nose crinkling, his dimples showing.

"So is yours." I tilt my head back and look up at the snow drifting down through the glow of street lights. I think how good it feels to be needed—wanted even—by this magical little boy.

First One Home

"Hey," Henry says, running backward past us.

"You caught up," I say, raising my brows in surprise.

"I left the store right after you two did. Rather, I *fled* from the store." Henry smiles.

"You did?" I say.

"Yes. But I decided to hang back."

"Why?"

"I don't know," Henry shrugs. "I guess it was nice to watch you two walking together. It felt like Christmas or something." Henry takes the grocery bag from me and yells, "First one home is a rotten egg!" Moonboy lets go of my hand and races past his father.

"The second one has to eat it!" I call after them.

Watching the Pot

After fifteen minutes, the cheese has not melted. Henry checks the flame under the fondue pot. "I don't understand why it's not working. The flame is still lit."

"Maybe we should just eat the marzipan I bought," I say.

"I bet you were hoping I'd fail at this fondue thing all along. I saw how you sniffed that package."

"I can't help that I like to sniff yummy things!"

"Yummy things?" Henry laughs.

"Yes—yummy things," I say. Henry leans over to me and sniffs.

"What are you doing?"

"Sniffing something funny," he says, just as the phone rings loudly. I jump and Henry runs to answer it. "Oh, hi, Kate." As soon as he says her name, I remember he has a girlfriend and that his girlfriend is a doctor. I sigh and realize I have left the kids with Ex-Rat way beyond the appointed pick-up time. I go rouse Ugly, kiss Moonboy good-bye, and wave to Henry.

"Just a sec," Henry says into the phone. He puts his hand over the receiver. He looks at me, "You don't have to leave. I'll be off the phone in a minute."

"I really do *have* to get going. I've stayed later than I should have."

"OK, then, I guess I'll see you tomorrow? Maybe the fondue will be ready by then. Sorry about dinner." He smiles, and then puts the phone back up to his ear.

Ex-Rat's Fiancée

Tiffany is at his house. She's all legs. Like a spider. I say hello first. She nods but says nothing. She surveys me as one would a kumquat. Ex-Rat is sullen. The children do not speak. I suspect they are waiting for me to have a freak-out. I surprise myself by not giving a crap.

Ex-Rat stands there with a forlorn look.

"I'm sorry I'm so late. Hope I haven't messed up your plans tonight," I say. "Maybe I can grab the kids for you one day this weekend."

Tiffany speaks: "Unfortunately we will not be able to book reservations at Mistral for another week at least."

I swallow.

"We tried your cell but it kept going instantly to voice mail," Ex-Rat says to me.

"Umm," I say, thinking of my cell phone in the garbage outside my ex-therapist's office.

"You lost it—didn't you?" he accuses.

"No, I didn't lose it. I cancelled my cell phone service."

"Well, it would have been great if you could have informed me," Ex-Rat says.

"Sorry, I didn't know you had made reservations for dinner. It's a weeknight."

"Since we never have a weekend in which we *don't* have the children, weeknights are the only time James and I can go out and have a romantic evening," Tiffany states dryly.

I ask the kids if they've eaten.

"No," Brendan says angrily.

"We were waiting for you," Lucy says, with tense little shoulders.

"We didn't know when you would show up," Ex-Rat says. "I have nothing in the apartment." He begins raising his voice. Tiffany smugly smiles.

"Why didn't you order a pizza?" I ask, my voice rising too.

"We thought you would be here hours ago!" Ex-Rat now yells.

The kids retreat into the hallway and put on their coats and shoes. I follow, stuffing Lucy's hands into her mittens and jamming her hat onto her head, then herding the kids out the door, their backpacks banging against the frame. Ex-Rat grabs the handle and opens the door wider.

When the children are safely out of earshot, I turn to Ex-Rat and say under my breath but clearly enough so he hears, "I cannot believe you asked that *thing* in there to marry you." I stare openly at his face, which holds no shame, just grim satisfaction that I am angry and miserable once more.

Standstill

Sitting in the parking lot with my head pressed against the Volvo's steering wheel, I can't move. For six months after Ex-Rat left me I couldn't leave the house. I was too afraid. I feel the same way now. Why did I go in there? Why didn't I just wait outside for the kids like I usually do? I was in such a great mood.

"Mom," Brendan says, shaking me gently. "Start the car." I lift my head up and look momentarily at Ex-Rat and his fiancée Tiffany's apartment complex. When I turn to Brendan, I see his face is drained of color. "Mom, start the car," he repeats.

"Yes. OK," I say, and stick the key into the ignition. In the mirror, I catch Lucy sucking her thumb and my stomach turns. She hasn't done that in so long—since Ex-Rat and I first separated. I stop thinking, flip on the headlights, turn on the radio and sit up straight, then buckle my seat belt and make sure the kids are fastened in. "So what do you two feel like for dinner?" I ask.

Lucy takes her thumb out of her mouth. "Chinese!" she says.

"Are you cool with that?" I ask Brendan.

"I'm *down* with that," Brendan corrects me, smiling just enough to let me know that he's all right.

Happy Family

I am drinking sweet coffee and staring at the varied Chinese dishes on the menu. I tell Brendan to order Happy Family, but instead he orders lo mein. Lucy wants just white rice. I am too tired to argue with her, so I nod and grab some cash from my roll. "Holy crap, Mom, where did you get all that dough?" Brendan gasps. I look at the roll. I hadn't noticed how large it had become. "How much is there?" Brendan asks.

"I don't know. Count it," I say, handing the roll over to Brendan. Luckily the joint is empty. We are sitting in a nasty corner table under a fluorescent light. I discreetly open a bag from my favorite bun shop in Chinatown. I love their coffee and long braided rolls with raisins (I'm starving, as I never actually had dinner and I left my marzipan at Henry's house). I munch while Brendan tallies. He's still at it when the short, beefy owner sets our order in front of us. Guiltily, I slide the bun under the table and Brendan covers the wad of bills. He looks at us suspiciously.

"Good to have *tall* hard-working son," he says, pointing to Brendan. I nod and smile and hold off chewing the piece of bun in my mouth. He stands there waiting. After a while he walks away, confused and annoyed.

"You have two thousand and fifty-eight dollars!" Brendan exclaims.

"Now you can buy me an XBox!" Lucy yells.

"Mom, it is so not cool to be walking around with this much flow," Brendan says sternly. I agree. I'd thought it was about five hundred. He carefully rolls it back up and puts the rubber band around it again.

"I had no idea dog walking could be so lucrative," I smile. My whole mood has changed. Delighted with myself.

• • •

A Goodby

I wake, reach down, and touch Ugly's fur. Hear no nasal breath. He is gone.

I dial Ex-Rat's home phone. "Ugly isn't breathing," I say, when he picks up.

"I'm sorry," he says, and clears his throat. "I'll be right over." He hangs up, but I cannot let go of the receiver. It blares its angry disconnected cry.

A Wind Blows

Ex-Rat's little blond ponytail bobs up and down as he loads Ugly into the backseat of his brand-new Mercedes. The hairstyle looks too young for him in the morning light and I see now that his face has shifted, a slight loosening of the flesh. The children get in on either side of Ugly. They touch the sheet, delicately placing their fingers in the creases. Ex-Rat puts out his hand, leading me to the passenger-side door. He arranges my skirt and sweater so they won't catch in the door.

I am amazed at Ex-Rat's gentleness. His old James self. It stabs me in slow piercing waves. Thaw, I tell myself. Let it out. Breathe. Cry. Something. We are all quiet. He places his hand on mine between shifting the gears. I sense the children's eyes on us and move my hand away. He bites his lower lip, turns on the radio, turns off the radio. I laugh weirdly and abruptly, like a cough then clench my jaw and look out the window.

Ugly is gone. Our Ugly.

The Vet's Office

Doug, Ugly's longtime vet, is standing at the door when we pull up to his office. An old buddy of Ex-Rat's, Doug's a runner and is almost anorexic-looking. All his movements seem startled. This morning, however, he is slow and measured. We discuss Ugly's pending cremation and he asks if we are certain it is OK to move forward with this. Also, have we said our final good-byes? I want it to be tomorrow or yesterday. Whichever. Just not today.

A Message

"It would be really helpful if the next time you decided to take the day off, you could give us some notice." There is a click. Everyone looks toward answering machine.

"Who was that?" Ex-Rat asks.

"Queen Bean," I say. I just want him to leave. Having welcomed himself into the house after Ugly's quick cremation, his sappy kindness is creating discomfort for Brendan, Lucy, and me. He turns pink at my remark.

"That's Mommy's dog-walking boss," Lucy says, shoving pennies around on the kitchen table.

"You have a job?" asks Ex-Rat, surprised.

"She's had it for months. She cleans, cooks, walks the dog, and takes care of this freaky Indian kid. She's made over two thousand dollars," Brendan says, dully. He is leaning the chair back, with his arms wrapped around its back.

"Sit properly in the chair," I say to him.

"She used to bring Ugly with her," Lucy says, "even though Ugly smelled really bad."

"Can we go to school now?" Brendan asks, uneasy with his own emotions.

"How about a cup of coffee after we drop the kids at school?" Ex-Rat asks.

"How about not?" I'd like to smugly say but hold my tongue. His solicitousness hurts me as much as when he is a jerk. I say, "Maybe." The thought of us sitting across from each other in a public setting feels like the anticipation of a blind date. How did he become such a strange hybrid to me? A murky shady character, almost.

We all gather our things. I want to take my car and suggest Ex-Rat follow.

He forces a smile and says, "There's no need to take two vehicles, I'm happy to go in yours."

I sigh aloud. He shoves his hands in his pockets. "Let's go, then," I say, with rising impatience. We all exit. It's like a play. The door is quietly shut and the set is dark and empty. The characters lingering ghosts.

Coffee

We are in the same coffee shop where Henry first noticed my clogs. Boobies No. 1 and No. 2 are not working today; instead two cute college boys with pageboy haircuts are behind the register. Ex-Rat goes to the counter and orders. The only seats available—barstools—are too high. I have to climb up to sit down and my feet don't reach the footrest. I think of an article I recently read about a midget who had all his furniture scaled down to his size. Bet he felt very grown up sitting in that furniture. Bet he was able to make very important decisions.

Two women are chatting at the next table. They stop talking and raise their eyebrows when Ex-Rat walks by carrying two large coffees. He smiles affirmation in their direction.

I forgot how much I don't miss that.

"I put cream and sugar in it, like you like." He is very serious and intent. I squirm. Can't wait to get back to my empty house and disperse the contents of his closet. "I want to share something that's a little on the awkward side," he says. Instantly, I toss aside closet thoughts and sense an anxiety attack surfacing.

"Perhaps this is not the best moment—" I say. He cuts me off.

"I have started attending a sex addicts group."

I assume the expression of a marshmallow.

Sensing my confusion, he continues, "For individuals who suffer from sexual addiction."

"Suffer?" I whisper.

He grimaces. "I know my addiction caused you serious pain. Part of the program is making amends."

I am growing pale with fury. I jump off my barstool, spilling my coffee. The pool descends off the table in a stream.

"Listen, I just—"

"Ugly is dead, you self-centered moron," I say. "I don't need your emotional baggage delivered FedEx on my overwhelmed lap." I shake my head and try to walk away, but my sweater catches on a chair and it pulls down hard against the back of my legs. Ex-Rat tries to help. I wave him away, unsnag myself, and continue walking. I marvel at my witty word usage despite the pain of huge welts forming on the back of my thighs.

Ugly

I cross the street to my church, which is empty inside. I light a candle and say a prayer for Ugly, then sit in a pew and try to cry, conjuring up all sorts of dreadful images of past Ex-Rat stunts. Nothing comes. When I finally do cry, it is because I panic for a moment that it is past eleven o'clock and I haven't fed Ugly or taken him for a walk, and I remember I don't have to because he is dead. It is always the day-to-day grind that gets you, the everyday annoying stuff.

. . . .

five

A Week of Merriment

We are watching *How the Grinch Stole Christmas* for the third time today. Lucy insists I view it with her again while we both sit under her fluffy purple fake-fur blanket. We chomp on Pringles. Rather, she chomps on Pringles and I eat the crumbs from the bottom of the can. I haven't changed my pajamas for more than a week. My hair is greasy with leave-in conditioner—during episodes of depression I tend to fixate on beauty products.

I have let Ex-Rat take over. He shops, cooks, and cleans—then goes home to his own apartment and his new fiancée. Tiffany is not a dog lover and apparently not all that understanding of my mourning process. But Ex-Rat is happily making sexual addiction amends. He glows with newfound purity and light. I think he has switched meds as well. I have become a docile puppet. Wonder where my rage has fled? A small Pacific island? A Wal-Mart under construction? I miss my rage. Wish it would stop in for a visit so I could at least clean the house.

"Rewind! Rewind!" Lucy screams the minute the movie ends. I hit the remote. "Faster! Faster!" she yells at the machine. Brendan strolls by with his pants hanging past his butt. He backs up and surveys our scene.

"Jesus, she is being a spoiled brat! She should go to bed. That's the zillionth time she's watched that stupid movie. And what is that crap in your hair? You look like a greaseball."

"It is only the third time she has watched the movie and I have leave-in conditioner in my hair, I'm going to wash it later when I take a bath," I say, yawning.

"You're always taking baths," he snaps. "You should buy stock in the water company."

"Too bad the water company is a public work," I say, swigging back the remaining contents of the Pringles can.

"You're pathetic," he says under his breath, and leaves the room.

"What did you say?" I call after him. He looks back in shameful surprise.

"Not you, but the situation is pathetic," he says bravely.

"How do you mean?" I say.

"You haven't left the house in two weeks. All you do is take baths. Dad comes in and out like he lives here. It's creepy. You're going to lose that dog-walking job, and it seemed like you liked it, even though the boy is kind of weird. They call and you don't even come to the phone. They're worried about you. The dad thinks it's something he did. He seems really nice. You should at least call him so he doesn't think it's his fault or something. I mean, if you're not going back to work there."

"I will tomorrow," I say emptily.

"Yeah, right, whatever." As Brendan walks away I push PLAY on the remote. Demon Princess sighs happily and I tuck her in on the couch, then go upstairs to take a bath. Halfway up the stairs I realize that tomorrow is Christmas Eve.

A Hang-Up

"What the fuck is wrong with you lately?" Pip yells in my ear. "You don't even fucking call me to call me back. I've called every day, every fucking goddamn day, to tell you I've been fucking dumped right before Christmas for a nineteen-year-old vegan shithead. That he's in love with her and you don't even fucking call me," Pip continues to scream.

"Ugly is dead," I say.

"Ugly was a dog. I am your friend."

"Ugly was my friend," is my response.

She hangs up. One of us had to do it. At least it wasn't me.

Back to Life

Everyone is asleep and I am packing. I pack presents in purple foil. Stockings filled with chocolate. Two pairs of hot pink clogs. An assortment of red nail polish. Little pinafore dresses in red and black with matching plaid tights for Lucy. Striped long underwear and wool socks for Brendan. A snow tube. Candy canes.

I load all the stuff in the back of the Volvo and then, having no room left, heft the storage container onto the roof rack. Don't ask how I do this. I feel like the Grinch—green and reckless. If I could hitchhike, I'd do it. I'm flying up, up, up. Invincible. Alive. I throw in three moth-eaten sheepskins, in case the car breaks down in a blizzard. This makes me think I also need a flashlight and a compass. Got it.

A Phone Call Returned

"I just wanted to let you know that I am taking a long vacation because Ugly died," I tell Henry's answering machine. "I may or may not be back. It's up in the air."

"Hello! Is that you?" Henry's voice interrupts. "Hello? Are you there?"

"I'm here but I'm not here. I refuse to live in this house a moment longer," I say.

"That can't be good, can it, since it is your place of residence?"

"No, it isn't good," I agree.

"Well, what's to be done about it?" he asks.

"Leave, I suppose. I'm packing right now. We'll leave tonight. After all, this is *his* house. *He* belongs here, not me. He belongs with the erotic produce."

"*Who* belongs to the erotic produce?"

I ignore him and plow on. "He belongs to the would-have, could-have, should-haves of this place; the erotic vegetables are just a metaphor of my life, untouched, unplucked, unsevered, left alone in my kitchen—rather, *his* kitchen. Anyway, I can't stand living in the city." Saying this aloud, I recognize it as my creed, my final understanding of how out of touch I've been with myself. It is my river escaping. I am finally speaking my truth. It burns with special brightness.

"You can't dislike living in the city. It has everything." Henry sounds incredulous.

"It does not have pastures of green, cows, forests," I say.

"True, but there are parks, big parks with ponds and wooded areas," he points out.

"It's a planned architectural landscape; it's false nature. Thoreau would not be happy taking a stroll in such containment." I am on a roll.

"I think you're wrong. I think he would appreciate the fact that we took care to have such green spaces within our city," he argues.

"I'm a true country woman, a wood nymph."

"I think you just need a change, and moving to the country represents that. What are the children going to do if you up and move them to East Bumlick? How can you tear them away from everything they know?" he asks in earnest.

"TV and the computer? They'll have that in the country." I'm beginning to feel pissy. He is blowing my ideology.

"No, I mean their father, their friends, school, sports. Brendan seems very into his school and sports," he says.

"How do you know that?" I ask, now very upset.

"We've talked on the phone quite a bit. He's been planning a very nice surprise for you this Christmas. It would be a shame to ruin it by moving on Christmas Eve," he says evenly.

I guess: a puppy. A new Ugly but not Ugly. Hate the very thought of it but love Brendan who in his unbalanced-hormones way is trying to care for me. Trying to stir me from my mourning slumber. Now that I am on fire with the idea of motion and packing, though, I don't want to stop for some non-Ugly pup.

"Shit," I say aloud.

"He's worried about you. He thought it would help," he says.

I twirl my hair. Twirl. Twirl. Twirl. "It won't," I say.

"Will moving?" he says. Henry sighs. I sigh.

I think about unpacking the car. Wonder if we can just sit behind it like a Christmas tree and open presents from the hatch. It *is* green, my Volvo. Dark green at that. We could string lights around it. That way as soon as I receive the pup, we can all hop in the car and flee the state.

Christmas Eve

I've just woken from a lovely nap. My son and daughter are eating frozen kids' meals in front of the Playstation game on TV, having found an unwrapped Harry Potter game that I dropped on one of my trips upstairs to the closet while unpacking the car. I curse Henry for ruining my plan to forever leave this house and its erotic produce.

I down a steamy cup of instant coffee and go out to the garage. Find the ladder and drag it into the kitchen. Take down the photographs of the carrot, mango, and peach. The kitchen looks hard and bitchy with bare walls. I smile. Feel delicious. I make another cup of coffee. And another. I call my mother.

"She lives!" my mother shrieks.

"I guess," I say.

"All set for tomorrow? We descend on you midafternoon," she chimes.

"What are you talking about?" I inquire timidly.

"I got your e-mail and I told Grammy. Abel and Grampa are staying on the farm, you know *them*. Cain is going to his in-laws' for Christmas, but everyone else is a show. Though I don't know how chipper your brother will be, since his airline is making him fly the red-eye to L.A. on Christmas Eve."

I quickly gather my wits and grasp this information. Want to kill Brendan. "Thawing the meat now," I say.

"God, I hope it's organic," she says severely.

"Of course it's organic," I say, even though it isn't.

"I'm bringing the works, my usual." I imagine her minivan fully loaded with mini carrots. Her farting the whole way down.

"I'm bringing a special friend," she says. "Margo is annoyed I'm bringing him with us but I don't give a rat's ass. His name is Mark. He's the yoga guy I was telling you about."

"The gay guy?" I ask.

"He's not gay," she spits. I giggle and it feels so good I could cry. So I do.

"Are you on the Pill again?" she asks. "I told you it causes breast cancer."

"I'm not having sex. Why would I be on the Pill?"

"Well, maybe that's your problem. Or maybe it's all the sugar and coffee you ingest."

I giggle again. Feel a manic roar rising in my chest. A guffaw. A scream. I want to bang pots around.

"I want a husband," I say.

"You had one. Why go through that again? It's the sugar, I'm telling you," she says with authority.

"Or lack thereof," I say.

We bark our good-byes. I take out a bag of confectioner's sugar and open it. Sugar dust fills my nostrils. My head clears. I stop fussing around and get to work.

Mistletoe

Ex-Rat arrives with mistletoe and hangs it in the front hall. "Anyone for a smooch?" he smiles dumbly. Brendan chooses to take out the trash instead. I don't look up from my bowl of cookie dough. But Lucy is hot to trot. She gallops over. I hear the smack. She's quite a smoocher.

I call Pip. "What do you want?" she sneers. She has caller ID.

"Stop being a bitch and come over and help me make cookies," I say.

"OK," she says and hangs up.

I make a real pot of coffee, then go to the freezer in the garage and take out frozen summer beans, rhubarb, bananas, pearl onions, and butternut squash. Bless myself for being a Type Squirrel personality.

"What happened to the photos?" Ex-Rat asks when I return to the kitchen.

"I took them down to give them to you as an early Christmas present." Am thrilled with my quick thinking. His face is glum. "You've done so much work these past couple of weeks," I say, "I wanted to give you something. I know how much you loved them."

"You never liked those photos," he says, leaning against the counter and looking up at the ceiling. "Not that I can blame you. I'm sorry." For the first time I feel he *is* sorry. I hand him some cookie dough and he holds it in his palm like delicate china. Am I delicate? I wonder. I am. I am very fragile.

• • •

Pink Pleasure

"Well, isn't this the very image of a successful divorce," Pip says, as she plops her bag full of facial creams and cold cuts on the kitchen counter, about two inches from my perfectly rolled-out dough disk. Ex-Rat lays cutout stars, bells, and moons carefully on the cookie sheets. He bastes them lightly with egg yolk and heavy cream, then dusts them with pink sugar left over from Lucy's Powerpuff Girls birthday cupcakes last year.

"So how does it feel being a total scum bucket asshole for over a decade and then sprinkling pink pleasure on your ex-wife's sweet abundance?" Pip drawls. She is tanked. Totally blasted. Ex-Rat has a fairly good handle on just-dumped turbulent vixens and suavely brushes her off with a chuckle and a toss of his golden locks. "It is fucking amazing that this dick is here to include himself in the festivities," Pip says. Having expertly applied makeup despite being on the verge of blacking out, she smacks her lips and snaps her compact mirror shut.

"Would either of you care to smoke some weed?" Ex-Rat asks smoothly, putting aside the cookie sheets. He and Pip step outside. I thank him inwardly. When Pip comes back in, she starts eating raw cookie dough. Between the pot and the first fat and sugar to hit her body in years, she soon passes out, head pressed against the counter, legs dangling from the stool.

The Wrapping

Pip snores on my bed. Lucy made us move her upstairs because she was afraid Santa would get scared and not come down the chimney. Pip weighs only about eighty pounds, so we managed.

Ex-Rat and I are in his old closet, wrapping presents. It is intimate. The scissors go missing again and again in the storm of paper and tape, and our hands touch, arms bump. I feel a bit of a contact high. He takes off his sweater. His arms are tan, with soft gold hairs. He bites his lip, as he folds down a flap and tapes it, then looks at me and scrunches his eyes, smiles. He kisses me. I back away from him and bang my head on the shelf. No go: again he plants his huge, soft lips on mine. They quiver and dance. I forgot how good kissing him felt. My body leaps to a decision: it claws at him. Rips and tears. Pulls his hair from its band. He lays me down amid the crinkle of paper. Pulls up my skirt and pulls down my white cotton underwear. Whips off his pants and pushes his hips between my thighs.

"I've missed you so much," he murmurs softly.

I grasp his hair, and pray to all above for mercy. Even knowing the dawning of its ending, I can't let go. I submit to my want. It feels good. Too good.

After It's Over

I cannot look at him. He is humming "The Healing Has Begun" by Van Morrison. Years ago when he bought the tape, we listened to it in his beat-up blue pickup on the way to his first demolition job. I was pregnant with Brendan but didn't know it. A panic, like a fierce fire, hits me: I could be pregnant now. The fear grows. So much so, I become queasy. I go to the bathroom and rest my head on the toilet seat. Ex-Rat knocks on the bathroom door, and lets himself in. He sits down on the floor next to me and begins to rub my back. I push his arm away.

"What did I do?" he says in a surprised tone.

"Everything," I say, and start crying in low sharp moans.

"Shit," he says, and tries to hug me. I push and struggle away but he holds firm. I lie in his arms, uncomfortably, and he strokes my hair. I miss my life. I miss my life. I miss my life. It echoes in my ghostlike pit—this hole of need still not filled.

Christmas Day

Ex-Rat is asleep on the couch looking like a cowboy, all tossed and rustic. The kids are not up. Leave it to Lucy to be the only seven-year-old to sleep through Christmas morning. There is a hang-up on my answering machine. I know it's Ex-Rat's fiancée and feel sorry for her in a way I used to feel sorry for myself. Part of me wants to call Tiffany back and tell her not to worry, that I don't have designs on her man, that it was just a one-nighter.

Pip is very much awake and alive, albeit with a roaring hangover. Her head is cradled in her hands, mascara smeared under her eyes. She looks at me in pure unmerriment.

"I told that hyena of a woman that her husband-to-be had a hard-on as big as a house for you last night and you both were presently sleeping cutely together on the floor and I couldn't stand to disrupt such a delightful vision," she says, with a slightly pained yet satisfied grin. "Now she keeps calling back and hanging up, so I decided not to answer."

"I need coffee," I say, lips sticking together.

"Of course you do, you hedonist. I'm ashamed to be your friend. I see now why you don't take that wedding band off."

"Oh, do shut up. How can you even stand to hear yourself talk after how disgustingly drunk you were last night?" Am tickled to be called a hedonist. Pip is awash in newfound jealousy now that I've reached absolute bottom.

"I've worked up to a high pain threshold," she says, serious and proud. "I bet that vegan shithead cries if you talk dirty in her ear. It will never last with them, I just have to weather it out." She bangs her mug on the counter. I feel it is probably not the best to fess my fears that I may have gotten pregnant from last night's indulgent behavior. This, however, reminds me it is Christmas—Jesus's birth-day—and I try to fill myself with warmth and gladness.

"Merry Christmas, Pip, this is our sixteenth Christmas together," I say.

"Yippee do-da fucking day," Pip says, and hugs me. "Look at us bitches—you fucking Ex-Rat and me not fucking anyone," she says, wiping at her eyes and smudging the mascara further on her face.

I put the slightly frozen roast in the oven.

"That's the only hunk of meat I'll be having this Christmas," Pip pouts. She turns on the radio, finds a country station, and then yells up the stairs, "Hey, stupids, it's Christmas, get up already." She listens for kidlike noises. "I don't think they heard me," she says, and pops an Advil.

"No," I say, "you better go up the stairs and yell 'Hey, stupids' a little louder."

So she does. I hear Brendan tell her he can't hear her since he is deaf from her snoring. Lucy screams, "*You're* stupid!" Pip yelps. Lucy must have bitten or kicked her.

I put the Baby Jesus in the manger.

The Puppy

The doorbell rings. Ex-Rat answers it, since I am indisposed, trying to shove a douche bag of seltzer up my crotch. Aunt Mary once told me that in the old days, before contraceptives, women used carbonated beverages to prevent pregnancy.

A silence throughout the house urges me to hurry. Then, a little puppy yip. I quickly dispose of all antipregnancy equipment in the bathtub. I shove my feet into fluffy piggy slippers and slowly open the door. I peer out into the downstairs hall.

"Merry Christmas!" everyone yells, and Henry releases a lovely malamute puppy who sits down where he is placed and barks.

"It is a he," Henry says tentatively, smiling at my piggy slippers. "I wondered what other foot apparel you owned besides pink clogs."

His eyes are the clearest blue. Moonboy is next to him, hugging his leg and smiling at me.

"Well?" Brendan says, thrilled with himself.

"Thank you so much, thank you, he is lovely," I say. As I go to pick him up, Lucy intercedes and grabs the pup. She shoves a bonnet on his head, which he shakes off.

"I want to name him," Lucy says viciously and stares me down.

"Well, I don't . . ." I start but Lucy trots off with the puppy. Brendan throws up his hands. Henry shoves his hands in his pockets. Ex-Rat glares at Henry. Moonboy hugs his father's leg tighter. Pip slurps a mint loudly. It is dreadful.

"His name is Darling!" Lucy screams down the stairs, then slams her door.

"Good name for a male malamute," Henry says. "Very masculine." I realize I am standing under the mistletoe and move a bit to the side. Henry notices and turns red.

"So who hatched this plan?" Ex-Rat grumbles.

"Er, ah, Brendan called me some time back," says Henry, "after I had left a number of messages about his mother's whereabouts and we came to the joint conclusion that ah, well, that it might help to introduce some new energy into the house, since, well, um, ah, well, anyway, we won't go into that." He has pulled his hands out of his pockets and is gesturing nervously, in large swooping motions.

"How do you know my wife?" Ex-Rat asks Henry.

"She's no longer your wife, Dad," Brendan says. "You asked her for a divorce over a year ago." I feel his anger curve its way around the foyer.

Henry intercedes. "Brendan, let's go find out how the puppy is getting on. I suspect it's about time to take him outside."

Brendan leads Henry and Moonboy upstairs. Pip trails a few steps behind them, eyeing Henry's buns. "Oh, my—*ssssuupp,*" she says. "And just when I stopped believing in Santa Claus."

I shall ignore her forever.

Ex-Rat disappears. I locate him in the kitchen. "What the hell was that all about?" I ask. He shrugs and runs his hand through his hair.

"You have a crush. It's cute in a slightly pathetic way," he whispers too brightly.

"I don't have a crush on him. Not that it's any of your business if I did."

"It's obvious you're interested in him," Ex-Rat keeps pressing.

"I am not!" I hurl back at him, truly agitated.

"Jesus, just admit it," Ex-Rat snaps.

"Admit what?" I seethe.

"Admit you like him."

"I repeat: I do not like him! I take care of his son. I walk his dog. Clean his house. Other than that, I barely know the guy." My voice has not yet returned to its normal octave.

"Then why is he here on Christmas-fucking-day?" Ex-Rat hisses, spit flying out of his mouth.

"I don't know, why don't you ask our son?" I say and slam the pot on the stove. Then I notice Pip and Henry standing in the kitchen doorway. I gather from their expressions that they have overheard the tail end of my conversation with Ex-Rat. Henry looks down at the floor. His hands are once again in his pockets. In this moment he must be the most handsome man since Gatsby. I swallow air.

Family Descends

Pip is on her fifth Jack Daniel's. Ex-Rat on his fourth. Lucy and Moonboy are wired on Shirley Temples. I drink warm sake to calm my nerves, inhaling little cup after little cup. Henry sits in the corner, withdrawn and not drinking. Someone presses forever on the doorbell. I finally waltz across the room, carrying a squash-covered wooden spoon. One of my piggy slippers falls off. Henry picks it up and follows me, since we are expecting Queen Bean to arrive any moment. I open the door and am confronted with a large-nosed alien in yoga pants. He is carrying a red cooler. Before I have a chance to ask this strange creature who and what he is, Henry reaches around me and grabs cooler from Yoga Alien's straining arms.

"Your mom and Margo are bringing up the rear in a sec," Yoga Alien says to me in a high, feminine voice. Obviously this is my mother's new beau. I have an urgent need to vanish into thin air.

"I really must get dressed," I say abruptly, and as I turn to go, I touch Henry's arm. He flinches, from which I intuit that he is desperate to leave but too much of a gentleman to say so.

Getting Dressed

I'm having a clothes breakdown. End up wearing a purple velour maternityesque frock that shrank in the wash and is now much too short. I add stripy tights and my hot pink clogs, then go locate Lucy and Moonboy. They are swapping Lifesavers and playing with headless Barbies.

Lucy surveys my outfit and says, "You look silly." Moonboy shakes his head. "You look like a human Teletubby," she adds impishly.

My mother appears. "Oh, there you are! I thought you were changing."

"I did," I say.

"Oh," she says. I brush past her and go back downstairs, leaving her to smother Lucy with kisses. Henry is still wearing his distant expression but is now cornered by Pip, who is extolling the power of protein. Yoga Alien is emptying a gallon jug of spring water into the pressure cooker that he brought in from my mother's car. Ex-Rat is busy with e-mail, sloshing his drink over the laptop keyboard. I bend over and introduce myself to Darling. Ex-Rat slurs, "I see London . . ." I stand up.

The doorbell rings again. It's my brother. With a new babe. But this one is severe looking, not at all his usual type. She has small breasts and her glasses are perched on the end of her nose. Derek hugs me, crushes me against his chest, and whispers, "I found her."

The Roast

I now know what the waiting room of Hell looks like.

Queen Bean has arrived, bringing paté and minced pies, and in under an hour she and Pip are great pals. Pip, perched on the counter, revealing her cleavage, smooches Henry in giddy hilarity. Queen Bean barks out a husky laugh, conferring her blessing on Pip's prostitute-like kisses. Henry blushes hot, smiles self-consciously. The crook looks at me and I feel like calling his girlfriend.

I have no crackers or ice cream.

Margo paints her nails as my mother massages Yoga Alien on the dining room table. He grunts and breathes, as though he is giving birth to a turnip. I despise his yoga pants as much as I despise my mother for bringing him.

Brendan is bouncing a ball against the wall in the kitchen. Lucy is pressing frozen peas between Moonboy's toes. I have unplugged them and they are paying me back. The bastards.

No one has set the table or creamed the onions or taken the meat out of the oven. My brother's "one" surveys the holiday mayhem while Derek loads the blender with ice cubes and drink mix and hits HI. The noise is intolerable.

"This is great," I scowl. "Just great."

"The dog pissed all over my socks!" Ex-Rat shouts.

And my scowl turns to a grin as I pat my legs and call, "Come here, Darling!"

A Surprise Guest

No word from the aunts and Grammy, who are over an hour late—typical behavior for Mary and Eve—and I'm starting to get ticked-off. I'm about to call the farm when the doorbell rings. Angrily, I yank open the door.

There stands Mason, in all his big-frame glory, a lumberjack wearing a black wool cap and a bulky plaid vest holding a mandolin case. Remembering how I screwed up our phone call after seeing him this past Thanksgiving, I want to crawl back in time and never answer the door again.

"Thought you could use a visitor," Aunt Mary says, carrying a tower of pastries, her voice dripping sharp honey, as she shimmies past Mason and inside.

"Mmmm," is all Aunt Eve says from behind another pile of baked goods. Why I bothered making cookies, I have no idea.

"Wasn't my doing," Grammy says and also scoots by me.

"Hey," is all he says, but smiles low and luscious like a movie star mountain man. The aunts follow Grammy and they all disappear into the kitchen. Mason reaches toward my face with his free hand and his huge fingers brush my cheek. "Some flour," he says, then, "It's OK, I don't bite." I open the door wider and he takes off his hat. His hair sticks up in adorable fashion. He deliberately puts his hand on my side, steps sideways into the foyer, puts down his mandolin, then takes off his boots, one of which is wrapped in duct tape. Removing a Swiss Army knife and a pitch pipe from his back pocket, he places them in his boots. He smoothes down his hair but it remains sticking up due to an endearing cowlick.

"It's nice to be warm," he says. "My truck has no heat."

"Long drive?" I ask, sounding dumb and nervous.

"Ten days," he says, matter-of-fact.

"Ten!" I exclaim.

"I couldn't book a flight out of Alaska on such short notice and I didn't want to fly standby on a holiday."

Aunt Mary is now lurking within earshot, holding a frozen cocktail built for someone twice her size. "I told him he could stay with you a few days," she chirps, "since it's such a long drive back." I shoot her a look. She stares right back and mouths silently, "You lucky bitch."

As she waltzes back into the kitchen, I see her prepare to light a cigarette—an absolute taboo in the house—and I want to tackle her but am distracted by Mason, who is now hanging up his vest and fleece, revealing a lovely white long underwear top underneath, a perfect complement to his rugged work pants.

"What can I do to help?" he asks.

Mountain Air

Having completely ignored Pip's body thrusting, Mason has lit a fire in the fireplace; set the table with Moonboy and Demon Princess; sliced the roast; washed all the dirty predinner dishes in the sink; made a perfect cup of coffee and handed it to me, sensing my sake-induced lull; and taught Brendan how to tie five different knots, which for some reason unbeknownst to me, Brendan finds fascinating. Ex-Rat and Henry stand aside looking dim in comparison and wince noticeably when Queen Bean croons, "What *can't* he do?"

The smell of spruce permeates the house. Mason is a towering balsam, a strapping man. I want to place my feet on top of his and let him dance me around the kitchen. I lick my lips and smack my chops. I swirl around and smile lots. Seltzer seeps from my womb, adding to the dampness of my underwear. The aunts look on with knowing satisfaction.

Dinner Is Served

My brother's frozen confections fill globe glasses on the tabletop: pink, green, and red. There are condiments and large slabs of meat, which Pip eyes ravenously. Yoga Alien heaps burned dal onto his plate. Tiny potatoes roll to and fro on the kids' plates as they stab at them with butter knives. I do not find this even the slightest bit annoying. My barrette has moved into my line of vision and my ears feel dull. My coffee having been replaced with strawberry succulence, I sip and swoon. I ask my brother if there is alcohol in my drink, since I cannot taste any. He removes his sunglasses and winks. "Lots," he says. His new girlfriend's mouth twitches, the first hint of a smile I've seen. My brother kisses her.

My mother adds, "I put some Rescue Remedy in there as well, and a little kava kava. It looked like you needed it." This explains why my tongue is now numb.

Ex-Rat is trying to argue with Henry about cricket. Ex-Rat knows nothing about cricket. Henry has stopped engaging and is furtively observing Mason—until he notices me noticing him noticing Mason. Pip moves closer to Henry, nudging her plate along with her. Henry must abhor this peasant feast, I think, again sensing his desire to leave. He is probably wishing he was sipping cordials with other WASPS in some book-lined room—anything besides arguing with a demolition man about cricket.

Suddenly the conversation veers to What do you do for a living? Terror wraps itself coldly around me. I can't bear to look like a non-working loser in front of Mason. I push away my pink globe—frozen confection not a plus. I am suddenly freezing and my teeth chatter. *Where is my cardigan?* I wonder.

The aunts launch right into whooping cough, bedsores, ripped vaginas, and peach pie. My mother chimes in with comments about energy healing and her massage practice. Yoga Alien goes on at length about transcending one's soul in a heated room. Margo shows us her freshly painted nails. My brother spews pilot-speak about storms and gravity. When his girlfriend finds a way to connect all this to something about tax fraud under the Reagan administration, everyone goes silent.

It sinks in that we may have a live IRS agent at our Christmas table. Queen Bean, who is seated at the head of the table, slams down her drink and spews, "He was an actor, for Christ's sake. What do you expect?" Silence again while all parse this, and then slowly the conversational mayhem resumes. Grammy pulls a travel-size bottle of holy water from her handbag and passes it around. Ex-Rat starts talking about his recent big job, the beauty of its collapse—all inward.

Pip interrupts him with a rant about the Boston Bruins. Henry looks like he is about to climb on top of her with excitement. "You work for the Boston Bruins! I love hockey. I haven't missed a Harvard game all season. Do you go to the Harvard games?" Pip nods demurely, even though I know full well she has never been to a Harvard game in her life.

She asks Henry, "And what do you do?"

"Nothing as interesting as working for the Boston Bruins," he says.

"Let me guess. You're a professor?" Pip says with a vexing smile.

"Yes," he admits.

"Sciences?" asks my brother's girlfriend, whose interest is piqued.

"Um, no—history." He looks at his watch. I find this endearing.

"You are also a writer, aren't you?" Mason asks. "Didn't you write that recent account of the Boston Tea Party? It was very good. And you look just like your picture on the jacket."

"Amazing," Queen Bean cackles. "Tell us, Mason, what is it that you do with yourself in Alaska?"

"I lead private hiking and kayaking tours," Mason says.

"Cool," Brendan says.

"Do a lot of *women* go on these private tours?" Pip asks, smirking darkly. I want to kick her.

"Nah, it's mostly men." Mason looks at me, and adds pointedly, "It can get rather lonely."

At this moment, Henry knocks over his water glass.

And just to make sure no one has forgotten me in this wondrous discussion of professional accomplishments, Lucy chirps, "My mom used to be a dog walker, now she's just a mommy again, ever since Ugly died."

I remember where my cardigan is and run to fetch it. My cardigan is in the closet. Definitely in the closet. Deep in the closet.

Ex-Rat's Departure

I roll up the sleeves of my sweater and begin to clear the table. The aunts bolt up from their seats and scurry to pick up dessert plates. Inside the kitchen they place the dishes on the counter and Aunt Mary asks, "What do you think of him?"

"Do you mean Mason?" I question.

"No, the Pope, of course she means Mason!" says Aunt Eve.

"So what do you think?" Aunt Mary actually rubs her hands together.

"I think I'd like to lick every inch of his body," I say, gregarious and loud. Drunk. And all of a sudden Ex-Rat pushes open the door. The aunts laugh and go back out to the dining room.

"So you want to lick every inch of his body, huh?" Ex-Rat asks. I ignore him and dump the dirty coffee cups I am holding into the sink. "Jesus! We heard everything you guys were saying in here. Be thankful all the kids went upstairs after they ate their dessert or I'd—"

"You'd what?" I dare him to say anything more.

Instead he says, "It's a fucking circus in here. How many guys are you seeing, anyway?"

"You're one to talk," I say, trying collect my dignity by pointing out what a louse he is. He grabs his coat and laptop and leaves in a fury, slamming the front door, heading back yonder, I suppose, to his fiancée, who, to her credit, has not called since lunchtime. I hope she dumps him.

Henry's Departure

Lucy sniffs Moonboy before he leaves and says, breathing heavily, "You smell delicious!" Moonboy smiles wide. Henry rubs Lucy's head affectionately and Brendan gives him a tight handshake while holding Darling. "Thanks for helping me with everything," Brendan says.

"My pleasure," Henry says.

Lucy grabs Darling out of Brendan's arms and dashes up the stairs. Brendan chases after her. I try to say good-bye to Henry, but something in his eyes leaves me bashfully chewing my lip. Henry opens the front door and asks Moonboy to go wait in the car, then quietly shuts the door behind his son.

"Thank you ever so much for inviting me—someone you hardly even know—as opposed to someone you would like to lick," Henry begins.

"Shhh!" I put my finger to my lips. I have no interest in his recapping my own drunken slurrings—twice was bad enough. What an unfortunate thing to have said about Henry earlier. And Ex-Rat was right, everyone at the table did overhear me talking so vulgarly in the kitchen with the aunts—including Mason. I am mortified.

Queen Bean comes out of the kitchen, swaying toward us as she takes her fur coat off the banister. "Oh, Henry! I thought you had already left!" she exclaims, handing him her coat. Henry helps her put it on. Once more he opens the front door. She bangs her hip against the door frame, gathers herself, and tips back the to-go cup of Irish coffee that my brother has so graciously provided. "Thank god that's over," Queen Bean says rudely, descending the front steps. Henry notices my hurt expression, and says hurriedly, "It was a very special evening for my son. He had a wonderful time. Thank you so much."

"I didn't mean what I said earlier, Henry, about hardly knowing you. I'm sorry if it hurt your feelings, I just—"

"Oh, don't bother explaining," he interrupts. "It's true. You do hardly know me. I was so wrapped up in finding the puppy and my talks with Brendan, and then our conversation on the phone, that I felt like we had known each other for much longer. It was dumb of me . . . a little foolish . . . I've been out of sorts lately. It isn't your fault. Go back inside and have fun with your guest and wonderful family. Mason seems like a really good guy." Henry shakes my hand abruptly, yanking it up and down. "Merry Christmas," he says finally releasing my hand and fleeing out and across the lawn. Moonboy's luminous eyes stare at me from the back seat of Henry's beat-up old Subaru wagon. I think about Henry's girlfriend. About how lucky she is.

Pip's Departure

My extended brood will be staying over, thanks to alcohol poisoning. Grammy, being the only sober family member, has set to preparing the extra beds. The aunts poke at the fire and cook marshmallows on metal coat hangers with Lucy, whose face is aflame with Moonboy lust. My mother is yet again massaging Yoga Alien, this time, thankfully, in a sitting position. Mason is picking on his mandolin. The tune he's playing is a peaceful one and it has lulled Brendan to sleep. His huge body looks all baby. The puppy is tucked under his arm. I sit down close to Brendan on the soft living room carpet, since he is the safest.

After what seems like a long time, Pip yawns and says, "I should be going." She arches her back and stretches her arms. She is gorgeous. Her shirt rises up, exposing her flat tummy. Mason notices, I am sure.

"Yes, you really should," I say. Even though she is my best friend, it is completely unfair that she is able to carry off short hair plus get all the men. I guide her to the door.

"I should give what's-his-name a jingle before heading off," she says, and I know she means Henry. "My cell phone is dead. Can I use your phone?"

"Don't you think it is a little soon to be calling him? He's probably not even home yet," I say, trying to shove her out the door. "He lives on the other side of town."

"*Numero uno, no,* I don't think it's too soon to be calling him. *Numero dos,* he just gave me his cell number," she says coquettishly.

"He gave you his cell number?" I ask.

"Yeah, I told him I would get him free tickets to go see the Bruins."

"You offered him free tickets to the Bruins?"

"You sound jealous. Are you still interested in him?" Pip asks.

I notice that Mason has stopped playing his mandolin. I whisper, "What are you talking about? Me, *interested* in Henry? Are you joking! He has a girlfriend."

"What if Henry didn't have a girlfriend? Would you be interested in him then?" Pip asks, suddenly serious.

"Not at all," I say, looking around, hoping Mason isn't within earshot. Just in case Mason is lingering in close vicinity and heard Pip's question, I say loudly, "I am interested in the man who is sitting in the next room who just drove all the way from Alaska to see me!"

"Are you sure?" Pip asks.

"Absolutely." I am firm.

"Take off that fucking ring."

"I will."

"Promise?"

"Yes. Now go!"

Bedtime

My family has retired for the evening. I put covers over Brendan and Lucy, who is also now fast asleep on the living room floor. Lucy has marshmallow and dog hair stuck to her face. Brendan snores gently. Sometimes my heart fills with so much love I cannot bear it. I switch to guilt. I think of my selfish antipuppy soul and depressed pre-Christmas self. Thank god they didn't hear my drunken licking statement. Horrible. They deserve so much more. I can't even remember what I got them for Christmas. I didn't even take them to Mass. I'm a shitty mom. Tears well up and I rub my eyes hard. Mason throws another log on the fire. His shirt comes untucked, revealing his tight hips and the gentle slope of his back. He pushes back his hair and looks at me with compassion and concern. Instinctively I reach out my arms. He enfolds me, carrying me to the chair and holding me on his lap. We don't speak. Sometimes we just need hugs and silence. Sometimes this is all we need.

Sleep

Still in his arms, I go to move. He tightens his hold, in sleep. I try to gently extricate myself and he wakes instantly.

"You don't have to get up, I'm fine," he whispers.

"Lucy and Brendan," I whisper back and point.

I leave his warm lap. He pulls down my tiny maternity-like frock and I stumble over to the couch. I grab a throw blanket and hold it out toward him. "I have a sleeping bag in my truck," he says. "I'll go get it." When he returns, he lifts the throw off me, replacing it with his downy sleeping bag. It's slightly chilled but warms instantly.

"You should go upstairs," I remember to tell him through a yawn. "Grammy made your bed."

"I'd rather watch you," he says, and walks back over to the chair, dragging the throw cover. He is illuminated by the glow of embers. I'll have to make him pancakes tomorrow, I think. A tall stack. Lumberjack hotcakes. I feel as though anything is possible, like fresh snow has fallen. Pure, white, and calm.

Crack of Dawn

"Get up, you," Grammy snaps. She flicks on the living room light. Apparently even in Cambridge, there is still milking to be done. I shut my eyes tighter. "You're awake, so stop pretending you don't hear me," she says. I roll over onto my back. Grammy's face looms over the couch, her lips forming a tight buttonhole. Her finger is crooked and pointing, a baton of judgment. She is waving it in the air to me, then to Mason in the armchair, and then to my sleeping children on the floor.

"Oh, get off her, she's a grown woman in her own house," Aunt Mary sirens from somewhere off in the distance. The kids wake momentarily and, realizing who made the racket, fall asleep once more. "He's sleeping in the chair; it's not like he is lying on top of her bare-assed," Aunt Mary adds. Grammy opens her buttonhole mouth and then forms it into a thin, flat line. Her cheeks turn purple. She folds her arms across her chest, turns, and struts into the kitchen, where she slams pots and dishes into cabinets.

She shouts above her own angry noises, "The damn pup did his business right on the floor. You better get your fanny off that couch and tend to it, Missy!" I sit up. My head pulses and whirls from last night's excesses. I lie back down.

"My brain feels like a truck ran over it," Aunt Eve says, as she tiptoes in, rubbing her eyes. Grammy slams another pot. Aunt Eve flinches, comes to a standstill. She looks at us for an explanation.

"The Holy Mother is preparing breakfast for us sinners," Aunt Mary tells her. To me, she says, "Guess I'm cleaning up the puppy shit."

"I'll do it," I say, not moving.

"I've got it," Mason is standing.

Aunt Mary raises her arms skyward. "The messiah has arrived!"

"Ah, that will win her over. Go in there and flirt shamelessly," Aunt Eve says, pushing Mason toward the kitchen and then taking his chair. She places her feet on the ottoman. "Handy little buggers, have to get me one." Aunt Eve says. I look at her in shock. "Not *him*. Don't get your panties into a bunch. I'm talking about this thing, this footrest thingy." She taps her foot up and down on the ottoman. "Mind you, I'd go to church every day if God sent me a young strapping stud like him."

"Amen to that," Aunt Mary says. They stare at each other quietly. I watch them. For an instant they feel like my children. That young and vulnerable. "You only have one life, one life! So you better god-damn live it. Don't end up like us, two dried up old biddies making pies and cleaning up other people's messes." Aunt Mary's tone changes, and now she sounds like a wise old woman. She clasps my hand in hers. "Don't pass this one up. Enjoy it. Do you understand what I'm saying?"

I nod and she pats my hand.

"And make sure you ring us after he leaves and give us every single detail," Aunt Eve says.

Aunt Mary adds gravely, "If you don't, we'll never speak to you again."

Yoga Twists

The house is clean. Beds made. Rugs vacuumed. The children gone with Ex-Rat for the rest of Christmas break. The aunts and Grammy gone, too, after fleshy kisses and long hugs and leftovers, labeled and sealed for Grampa and Uncle Abel, tucked under their arms. My brother gives me a gruff kiss and a big wink and shakes hands with Mason, punching him on the shoulder as well. We get a tight wave from his girlfriend, waiting in the car. My mother still sits at the kitchen table. "I guess we should get going, too," she says.

"Good idea," I say, through locked jaw. It is everything for me not to shove her out the door and throw her cooler after her. Yoga Alien sips soothing herbal tea after a rough morning of interrupted meditation. Margo files her nails.

"How long are the kids gone for?" she asks.

"A week." I pick a grain of nothing from the table, and try to focus so as not to murder her.

"What are you going to do? A week is a long time to be without kids," she says.

"I wonder." I honestly don't know if she takes in Mason, sitting not two feet away from her. The puppy whines and wags his tail at my feet.

"Do you have a crate? I read recently—or maybe I heard it on the radio—that crate training is the best way to housebreak your puppy. They have a natural instinct to keep their 'den' clean," my mother begins. I look at her. It is a look I haven't given her since I was thirteen, I am sure. Like she is the dumbest woman in the entire universe and everything that just came out of her mouth I could not care less about. She either ignores it or has reached new heights of self-love. Either way, she is not budging.

I snatch Yoga Alien's half-full teacup from the table and pour it down the sink. This works. My mother gathers her coat and cooler. Margo stops filing her nails. Yoga Alien does a sun salutation and a series of twists, peels himself off the floor, and clasps his hands in prayer. He bows to me. I take this as good-bye.

"Thank you so much for coming," I say, smiling wide and falsely and grabbing his pressure cooker as I run to open the front door. By the time they both reach it, I am shivering and the temperature of the house has dropped thirty degrees. Once they are outside, I slam the door and lock it and do a little jig. Mason laughs. He picks me up and wraps me in his arms.

"Finally," I say.

"Yes, finally," he breathes. His hair smells of pancakes. I inhale. Inhale. Inhale.

"What would you like to do?" I ask, wanting him to say *Go to bed and never get out of it*. He says, "Go for a long walk and just hold your hand."

"You do?" I ask, disappointed. I pull away, but he grabs my wrist gently and holds it.

"No," he says, letting slip a catlike grin.

"No?" I ask coyly.

"Not even close," he says, leading me upstairs.

six

A Week of Wondering

"So has Mr. Alaskan Wilderness left or what?" Pip asks.

"Yes," I say pathetically, Mason having taken off yesterday in his truck with no heat.

"So how was he?" Pip drawls into phone.

I don't answer. Have yet to admit even to self what a slut I actually am.

"Tell me! Was he as good as he looked—*ssup*?"

"Yes."

"I fucking hate you," Pip whines, then silence, except for the sound of Pip sucking her mints. "Are your brats back yet?"

"If it is my darling children to whom you are referring, no, they are not."

"Then come out with me," she says.

"Where?"

"A party—*ssup*."

"What kind of party?"

"A fucking New Year's party. What other kind of party would it be?"

"I have things to do," I say.

"What things?"

"Things."

"Like sit at home and wait for a call from Mason?" Pip says.

"Please come out with me. I don't want to show up to a New Year's Eve party by myself. C'mon. I'll be over to pick you up at 8 p.m. Wear something besides old maternity clothes." She clicks off. I stare at the receiver, then look at the clock. 7:08 p.m. I don't move.

8:32 p.m.

Pip has yet to arrive, and still no call from Mason. I check the phone. It still works. Am now convinced Mason tried to call from a pay phone while I chatted away with Pip. Curse myself. I feed Darling, let him out into the backyard. I decide to have self-pity party. I grab chocolate cake left over from the aunts' towering pile of Christmas baked goods and nuke it. I watch as the cake spins round in the microwave. Ding. The cake is warm, with drippy icing. I eat it with my fingers. I have eaten almost the entire cake when the doorbell rings.

Pip's nose and face are pressed against one of the door's little window panels. She sticks out her tongue and I let her in. She's dressed in a slip, blond wig, and kitten heels.

"How's my mole?" Pip asks, pointing to what looks to be smeared eyeliner on her face.

"Fine."

"Why the hell aren't you dressed?"

"I'm not feeling well," I say. Which is the truth. Feel vilely ill.

"He hasn't called, has he? He's one of those fuck-'em-and-leave-'em types. Those politically correct assholes always are. They pretend they're so evolved and act like the mother you never had until they've gotten enough pussy and then they PC their way out the door. Look at Martin. Perfect example. Wouldn't fry an egg—" Pip fumes intensely then stops, wig cocked to one side, and says, "What are you doing? Go get fucking dressed."

I'm in too over my head to argue. As I run upstairs, the phone rings. I rush to the bedroom to answer it but realize I left the portable receiver downstairs with Pip. I fly back downstairs, where Pip sits on the couch. She presses the button and places the phone down beside her. I grab it from her. All I hear is a dial tone.

"You hung up!" I yell.

"It was only James, your fucking ex-husband, calling to remind you that he is dropping the kids off tomorrow at 6 p.m."

"Oh," I say, totally disappointed.

"Just call what's his face—Mason—on his cell and get it over with so we can leave," she says.

"He doesn't have a cell phone."

"What do you mean he doesn't have a cell phone? Everyone has a cell phone," Pip says.

"He doesn't believe in cell phones, not regular phones, no computer either, you know, not any sort of technology," I say defensively.

"That's PC for 'I'm a jackass and I love playing hard to get,'" Pip says.

"No it isn't!"

"Whatever. Just put down the phone, wipe that chocolate-looking shit off your face, and let's go."

Party Dress

"You're wearing this," Pip declares, holding up a newspaper-print jumpsuit from the eighties.

"No." I am adamant. She keeps digging. The smell of mothballs makes me gag. She presents a checkered minidress.

"No way. It's freezing," I say.

Pip starts to unzip a hanging garment bag.

"I've never worn those. James bought those for me right before we split," I say, hoping she gets the picture that I have no desire to look at them, let alone wear them. She doesn't.

"Man, that dickhead ex of yours has taste," Pip says, taking out a long velvet burgundy number with a low neckline and velvet cuffs. "Put it on. Now!"

I sigh and step into it. I look like a miniature Morticia, but I don't care. At least it's warm and doesn't smell like mothballs. Once I'm dressed, Pip slicks back my hair with mounds of gel and slathers me with makeup.

"Very fem-butch," she says when she's done.

"I look like a transvestite," I whine, but she ignores me because she is searching through my jewelry box. She finds another Ex-Rat gift, a tenth-anniversary diamond-studded choker, which she straps around my neck.

"I look ridiculous," I say.

"Grown up, yes. Ridiculous, no," Pip says. I put on tights and stand up.

She redoes her mole, smears on lipstick, and looks at herself in the mirror.

"There," she says, straightening her wig.

I follow her downstairs. After securing Darling in his crate with a chew toy, I stuff my feet into my hot pink clogs.

"No fucking way," Pip says, but I refuse to be bullied further. I walk out the door, clogs and all.

The Party

I am so absorbed in my angst about Mason not calling me that I don't notice where we are driving until Pip is parking her car in the circular driveway of one of those expansive Victorians on Brattle Street in Cambridge. We are only a few blocks from my house.

"Why are we parking here?" I ask.

"This is where the party is," Pip says, lighting a cigarette. I buzz down the window. The icy breeze clears my foggy mental processes.

"What party?" I say. I had assumed we were just going to some party at a bar. I have a strong urge to twirl my hair but can't. My hair has turned to plaster due to a gallon of gel.

"That guy invited me."

"What guy?" I ask, with an inkling of doom.

"That guy at your bomb of a Christmas party, the one who gave me his digits," Pip starts.

"Henry?"

"Yeah."

"Henry invited you to this party?"

"Yes. *Henry*," Pip says.

"Henry should not be inviting anyone to a party. He has a girlfriend," I remind her.

"No, he doesn't," she says.

"Yes, he does."

"No, he doesn't. She broke up with him right before Christmas. He's a dumpee just like *moi*," Pip says, and taps the tip of her cigarette in the ashtray.

"No, she did not!" I say.

"Yes, she did," Pip says flatly.

"When did he tell you this?" I ask.

"During or after your party. Whichever. I forget," Pip says, exhaling smoke through her nose as she gets out of the car.

"Why didn't you tell me?" I yell after her.

"I thought I did," she says.

"You didn't!" I say.

"His girlfriend broke up with him before Christmas. There. I told you." She slams the car door and I watch her trot up toward the house. Almost to the steps, she turns, sees I'm not following, and comes back.

"Well, are you coming?" Pip says.

"No. He didn't invite me. He invited you," I say, wanting to cry.

I cannot believe my Perfect Guy no longer has a perfect girlfriend and has invited Pip to a party. I want to run home and finish the chocolate cake.

"Who cares? It's a New Year's Eve party! It's not like it's a candlelit dinner for two. It's a bunch of old Harvard alums and professors. Anyway, you just got seduced by an Alaskan god, so why do you care that Henry has invited me to a party? Now, get out of the car. Don't be such a baby." My lower lip trembles. "Listen, if you're still interested in Henry . . ."

"I'm not interested in Henry!" I yell, utterly confused by my own emotions. How can I be interested in Henry when I just spent a week having glorious sex with Mason?

"Well, then what's wrong?"

"What if Mason doesn't call me?" I ask, relieved. This must be what's bothering me.

"Mason will call. I was being an absolute jerk back at your house. I was just jealous. I'm still really fucked up about Martin. I'm sorry. He'll call. He seemed really into you."

"Really?"

"Really. I mean he must be, because he didn't even notice me!" she says, and winks. I smile meekly.

"But I don't even know these people." I point to the house.

"Neither do I."

"That's the point, Pip. You don't even know them and now you've invited me," I say.

"Get out of the fucking car this minute. If you don't, I'll make a scene. Right here. I swear," she says, her hands on her hips. I crack up. "There, that's better. Let's go have fun."

A big, hulking man holding a drink opens the door. He is wearing a worn-out Harvard T-shirt.

"Invitation?" The man raises his brows and holds out a hand.

I'm going to kill her.

"Just kidding." His face splits into a grin.

"Brian, they're my guests," Henry says, coming into the hall. He is frayed and rumpled, wearing his paint-speckled khakis and an old blue oxford shirt. I am completely overdressed.

"I believe, Professor, the invitation suggests 'a guest,' not 'guests,' but I won't tell if you don't." Brian sniggers but Henry looks at me. There is uncomfortable silence. Henry rocks back and forth on his worn-out loafers.

"I would love something to wet my throat," Pip says, batting her false eyelashes, obviously thrilled there is such a large male looming in front of her.

"Certainly, this way," Brian says. Noises of clinking glasses and the bubble of laughter rise from further inside. Pip takes Brian's waiting elbow. They walk down the vast hallway, Pip's kitten heels clicking.

"So I gather your guest has gone back home," Henry says to me. Suddenly I'm dizzy and cannot breathe. I start to weave. Henry places his hand at the base of my back and his familiarity astonishes me. In this manner he firmly guides me into the kitchen, runs the kitchen tap, and puts my wrists under the water.

"Better?" His face is full of concern. I nod.

"Pip dressed me," I say, able to breathe once more.

"Well, you do look a little like something out of the *Addams Family*."

"I really do look awful, don't I?" I say, my voice cracking.

"*That* is not possible. I'm just partial to striped tights and piggy slippers," Henry says, smiling.

Pip comes bursting into the kitchen, Brian in tow.

"What happened? Are you all right?" she says, rushing over to me.

"I'm fine," I say, not fine at all. I want to go home and get out of these stupid clothes and wash the gel out of my hair. But Henry and

I follow behind Pip and Brian into the library. Intellectual types, drinks in hand, casually sit conversing. They stare at Pip and me with transfixed, overly polite expressions as Pip polishes off a double bourbon in one gulp, wipes her mouth, and yells across the room to me.

"Come on in. The water's fine!" she screams.

I scan the room for a large rock to hide behind. None. Brian heaves with laughter. The rest of the room titters with discomfort. Brian pours drinks and refreshes Pip's glass; he crosses the room back to us.

"Henry, where ever did you find such interesting creatures?" Brian asks Henry, and looks at me as if I am some type of science experiment.

"They're Radcliffe alumnae," Henry says, looking at my very un-Radcliffe-y, far-from-prep appearance and instantly reddening. Brian hands Henry and me our drinks, he hoots and slaps Henry on the back. I shove the drink back into Brian's hand, glare at Henry, then walk away from them both. Henry is quick at my heels.

"I'm so sorry. It was a dumb thing to say," he says urgently, pulling at my arm. I shove him away.

"Don't touch me," I seethe. Henry drops his arm. Tears sting my eyes. I wipe them furiously away, trip on my stupid dress, and find the front door, through which I ungracefully exit.

All by Myself

Waiting for the ball to drop.

First New Year's Resolution

Make New Year's resolution to never speak to Henry Bannister again for the rest of my life.

Second New Year's Resolution

Make second resolution to never have sex again with a guy who doesn't believe in phones, doesn't own a phone, and lives in Alaska.

Closet Party

Have moved the pity party to the closet. I've finished off the chocolate cake and am licking crumbs from my fingers when the phone rings. I leap out of the closet and jump on the phone.

"Collect call from . . ." robot operator voice says. My heart starts to race—Mason finally calling me, thank god I left the New Year's party—and then Pip's voice.

"Pip."

"Will you accept this call?" robot operator drones.

"Yes," I say, crushed.

"You've gotta come get me," Pip slurs into the pay phone.

"Where are you?" I ask, now concerned. I remember Pip is wearing only a slip.

"Police station," Pip slurs.

"Why are you at the police station?"

"Never fucking mind. Are you going to come get me or what?" she says hostilely. I make her hand the phone to the cop, who gives me the precinct and directions. I am fortunate to have someone to save beside myself.

I run around the bedroom, throw on a pajama top and striped maternity pants with a stretchy waist, and search for some boots in the closet. I find a pair of Brendan's from years ago. They have soft fur on top. A little big, but much warmer than clogs. I also find one of his old winter coats to match, with fur-laden hood. I feel like an Eskimo. Makes me feel closer to Mason. Must start wearing furry apparel every day. Less fattening than chocolate cake.

Police Station

In the police station, I see Pip in her kitten heels and blond wig talking to a cop. Now I am highly annoyed at having had to drive all the way to the station, in trafficy New Year's Eve conditions, to pick up my tramp friend.

"What happened?" I ask the police officer.

"She violated her restraining order," he says. Pip looks away. She starts chewing her nails.

"What restraining order?" I ask, totally confused. The police officer looks at Pip, who releases a breath.

"Martin got a restraining order," Pip says.

"Why?" I ask, trying to make sense of this information.

"Why the hell do you think?" Pip looks wrecked under the fluorescent lights. "What *is* that thing you are wearing? I've never seen a hood that big. You look like you should be ice fishing," Pip says. I notice she has bitten her nails to nubs. I ignore her coat comment and turn to the cop.

"But she was at a party in Cambridge. She wasn't anywhere near Martin," I tell the officer, certain there has been some mistake. Pip slumps in her chair.

"Apparently she had a change of plans," he says.

"You drove all the way to Martin's?" I ask Pip.

"No," Pip says, then makes a motion on her lips for me to zip it.

"She better not have been driving," the cop bristles.

"I took a cab," Pip says. I know she is lying.

"Where was Henry during all of this?"

Pip shrugs. "He didn't take your keys or offer you a lift home?" I ask.

Pip shrugs again.

Finally, the cop has Pip sign papers and I lift her up to her feet and drag her out the door.

"My car is parked in front of Martin's apartment building," Pip says when we reach the parking lot.

"I guess you'll just have to get a tow truck to pick it up for you, then," I say airily.

Pip screws up her face and mimics me.

"Real nice, Pip. Next time you don't have a ride home, call a cab!" I growl.

"You know I hate cabs," Pip sulks.

Henry's Abode

I make Pip wait in the idling car while I bang on Henry's door, then ring the bell. Bang. Ring. Bang. Ring. Until Henry opens the door. He is shirtless, wearing plaid flannel pajama bottoms and I can't help but marvel at his perfect chest. I remind myself that I'm furious at him.

"Are you all right?" Henry asks, his eyes anxious.

"*I* am fine," I say haughtily.

"Do you have any idea what time it is?" Henry asks.

"Yes, they had a big clock on the wall at the police station."

"Police station?"

"Yes, the police station where I was collecting Pip. Apparently you didn't take her keys or give her a lift home, even though she was completely inebriated. Instead, you let her just drive off wearing nothing but a slip, drunk off her ass, without any thought about her well-being."

"I did no such thing. I left shortly after *your* premature exit," Henry says defensively.

"Because you made a horrible, vile joke at my expense!" I say, incensed.

"I said I was sorry. And I am sorry. Very sorry. I have a knack for saying the dumbest things. It was a bad joke. I was only trying to lighten up the whole stuffy situation and I did tell Pip I was going home. She chose to stay there. Quite adamantly, I might add."

"So you just left her there?"

"What else could I do? Throw her over my shoulder and carry her out?" Henry says, exasperated and, I sense, losing his patience. Well, how dare he! He should be glad I'm even speaking to him!

He rubs his arms hard, then flexes them. I am sure he is doing this for my benefit. "Are you finished with your interrogation?" he asks. "I'm freezing and I want to go back to bed."

"No, I don't think I am. No . . . I'm not," I ramble on. His arms and chest are too distracting and I have no idea what I am saying. I zip up my hood and try to disappear.

"Well, what else are you raving angry at me about? Maybe you should come in and have some coffee. You can go on and on until dawn proclaiming why I am such an awful person even though you hardly know me," Henry says, reminding me that I am more than capable of saying insensitive things myself. Hmff.

"No need. I have only one thing left to say." I try to think of something. Can't.

"Then go on and say it, so I can shut the door," Henry shouts.

"Forget it," I say, going back down the front steps. Great recovery. Excellent.

"Fine, I will!" Henry yells after me.

Large Mitt

New Year's Day and still no word from Mason. The priest is talking about Jesus's journey into the darkness and wilderness, alone and struggling. Afterward we bow our heads and say the Lord's Prayer. I place my hands on the pew in front of me, putting my whole weight on it. I lift myself up, then lower myself. My furry boots catch on the kneeling bar and I slam hard onto my butt. I let out a slight yelp. Everyone turns. At least, thank goodness, I haven't seen Henry in the congregation today. He must be done researching Catholic Mass for his new book about the American Revolution. I stand back up, wave, and then whisper loudly, "Sorry." Everyone turns back around.

I rub my tailbone, search my huge bag for Rescue Remedy or arnica, but find only cantaloupe lip balm, which I smear over my lips. I lick it off. Smear more on. Repeat. This keeps me occupied until we are within peace offerings. I shake the hands of an elderly couple in front of me. Their hands are cool and paperlike. When I turn around, I am face to face with Henry. He holds out his huge mitt. I put forth my tiny one.

"Quite a show of acrobatics," Henry smiles.

"It's a talent I usually confine to the bedroom," I slap my hand over my mouth. The old people in front of me tsk-tsk, and Henry laughs. It booms and echoes.

Coffee and Doughnuts

To avoid Henry, I brave doughnut time without my kids. The basement of the parish has a cold and cranky feel. Little round tables are covered in yellow-and-white-checked plastic tablecloths. Families sit together. My anxiety rises as I scan the room for a place to sit then get in line for coffee. I dump too much creamer in the styrofoam cup. My coffee is light tan. I fill a tiny paper plate with chocolate doughnut holes that roll back and forth as I walk to an empty table.

I sit there alone for one second then, when no one is looking, I get up and throw everything in the garbage and run out the door. As I come around to the front of the church, I see Henry, who sees me too. He points across the street to the coffee shop. "They have much better coffee and pastry," he remarks.

"Mmm, yes," I say.

"Well?" he asks.

"Well?" I ask back.

"Would you like to join me for a cup of coffee?" Seeing my expression change, he adds, "As friends, a show of peace—leave the whole holiday mess behind us—your licking and my leaving," Henry says, obviously tickled with his own clever wordage.

"Why not," I say, shrugging my shoulders.

"My thought exactly."

A Friend

We sit down at a table. It's quiet. Boobies No. 1 and No. 2 put down their playing cards, warm up our cheese danish, and make froth. Henry is wearing a black V-neck wool sweater over a worn-out white T-shirt. I'm very much a one-man girl. I shouldn't be admiring Henry's deep-sea watch and perfect, long fingers. Henry sips his double espresso with lemon-peel twist and I drink my bowl of cappuccino with almond syrup. Booby No. 2 brings my danish on a blue plate. It is the perfect temperature. I eat it quickly. It is nice to have a possible boyfriend who lives in Alaska. It eliminates the need to impress anyone. You can be yourself at all times. Even if Mason never calls, I will pretend he is still my boyfriend—it works well when having coffee with highly desirable men.

"Do you play Scrabble?" Henry asks.

"No," I respond. He sets his espresso cup on its saucer, clasps his hand under his chin.

"Cards?" he asks.

"Uh-huh," I say, sipping sweet almond goodness.

"Rummy?" I shake my head again.

"How about you tell me," he says smiling.

"Go Fish or War. Not very Radcliffe alum, I am afraid," I say.

"Very funny. Well, we could play both," he says.

"When?" I ask.

"After you finish daintily slurping your cappuccino," he smiles.

"Where?" I ask.

"My house?"

I shake my head.

"A walk then?" I nod.

A Windy Walk

Our eyes tear as we walk against the subzero wind. Henry turns and says, "I want to show you something I think you'll like." I follow him across Harvard Yard, my face numb from cold. Finally, he stops in front of an academic-looking building, takes off his gloves, reaches into his pocket, and pulls out a bundle of keys.

Inside, it is dark and too quiet. Henry touches my shoulder and I jump. He turns on the light. "Is that better?"

"Yes," I say. He leads me to a back room where there are three mud huts. Each has a little door and windows. They are just my size.

"These were made by one of my more exuberant students; they were a part of her thesis project." He crawls into the first hut; I bend only slightly and walk in also.

"I know *all about* your exuberant students," I say without thinking.

"What was that?" Henry says distractedly, watching me unzip my coat.

"Oh, nothing," I say. I don't want Henry to find out that I was stalking him for months prior to taking care of his son.

"No, really. What did you mean? What do you know about my exuberant students?" Henry presses.

"Oh, it was a long time ago, in a bookstore, you were there reading and a bunch of your female students were tittering about how you were ruining their GPAs—"

"Ruining their GPAs? How am I ruining their GPAs?"

"I think they were just talking about how good-looking you are—I mean . . ."

"You think I'm good-looking?" Henry asks, delighted.

"No, no. Your students think you're good-looking."

"Oh," Henry says. He looks at the ceiling of the little mud hut.

"So did you give her an A?" I ask, trying to change the subject.

"Who?" Henry asks.

"The student who made this little hut."

"Unfortunately I'm not as exuberant about her writing skills as I am about her art. I gave her a C."

"Well, the only thing I seem to be able to do with the slightest success is to be a stay-at-home-mom. Pretty pathetic, huh?" I'm not sure why I tell Henry this.

"It's not pathetic in the least and nor is it a small achievement. It is a very brave thing to allow others to be dependent on you," Henry says. He looks at my ring, which I resumed wearing again after Mason's departure.

"I think it's *me* who is dependent on *them*." I twirl my hair.

"Are you still in love with him? Is that why you wear it?" Henry wants to know. He takes out a deck of cards and begins to shuffle.

"No," I say.

"Then why *do* you still wear your wedding ring?"

"Where did you get those?" I point to the cards.

"I stole them from the coffee shop," he says.

I look at him in shock.

"Don't worry, I asked if I could borrow them for the day while you were using the restroom. Scouts' honor."

"If you knew they had a deck of cards, then why didn't we just play there?"

"That's privileged information." Henry grins. "I think we should play Go Fish, since War is now out of the question." He deals and then asks, "Do you have the king of hearts?"

"No," I say.

"That's right, I forgot, he's in Alaska—hiking a mountain, chopping wood, reading my newest book," he teases.

"Actually, he's still driving to Alaska," I correct him.

"Oh, yes, in his truck with no heat," Henry laughs.

"Go fish," I warn, taking off my coat.

Questions

"So why did your girlfriend break it off with you?" I ask Henry.

"Who said she broke it off with me?"

"Pip did," I say.

Henry frowns. "Well?" I press.

Henry shifts uncomfortably. He pauses.

"Kate didn't break it off with me. I broke it off with her."

"Oh," I say. "Why did you break it off with her, then?"

"Because . . ." Henry stops. Puts his cards down. Clears his throat. "Let's talk about something else." He picks up his cards again. "And you never did tell me why you still wear your wedding ring."

I squirm.

"Your turn," he reminds me, pointing to my cards. I sigh and place a pair of kings down.

"You had the king of hearts all along!" Henry says.

"I did?" I ask, innocently.

"It's right there in front of you! You just put it down."

"Oh, look, I did," I say, pretending to be surprised.

A Snack

"I'm hungry," Henry says, as we are walking outside again.

"We just ate."

"You ate and I watched," Henry says.

"Oh, right," I blush.

"Now it's your turn," Henry says, as he opens an ornate door. I timidly approach. Unsure. The chichi hostess looks me over. She looks at my furry beat-up boots. She looks at Brendan's old coat with the huge hood. She looks at my unbrushed and grown-out mess of a bob, held back with three barrettes of Day-Glo substance. She notes my chipped pink nail polish.

"Can I take your coat?" she asks.

"No," I state flatly. Henry hands his over. An old mothball-smelling cashmere. The type everyone wears here—pure WASP. The hostess seats us in a cozy nook. There are very few tables, and they are covered in antique linen. Henry orders a bottle of wine, which I drink most of as he goes on at length about its vineyard and its year. I smile, twirl my hair. He continues about the "process" and "art" of making fine wine. I pretend to be fascinated. I'm brilliant at this. It's my special talent. When he finally pauses I interject, "What restaurant is this?"

"Chez Henri," Henry says.

"You're kidding."

"I kid you not, Madame." Seeing my discomfort, he leans across the table. "Don't worry, you look far more fetching than any Radcliffe girl. That furry hood around your adorable face walking over here was about to make me swoon." I break into a giggle.

"Why are you doing this?" The "as friends" feeling is replaced by something more vast and wonderful.

"To be *nice*," Henry says. "Actually, I wanted to lure you back to do a bit of cleaning. My mother is driving me crazy," he adds, like a stupid sack of rocks.

"So you thought this would do it? By taking me out for a whirlwind tour of art and wine tasting, you thought that would seduce me into coming back to do your dishes?" I feel like a dimwit for thinking he might possibly want me.

"Hold on—it was a joke—I thought we were kidding around," Henry stammers. "I'm not doing these things so that you'll clean my house. I'm doing these things because I want us to be friends."

Friends.

This makes me no less flawed, in my thinking.

Henry continues, "The only thing I might be guilty of today is trying to make peace so that my son's connection with you will continue. You're the first person he's allowed in, you know, since his mother died."

"Henry, I am more than happy to continue to care for your son. I *want* and *cherish* him in my life. But have you ever considered that if your mother was a little gentler toward—"

"I know how it must look," Henry interrupts. He takes off his glasses and rubs his eyes. "My mother is not known for her love of small children. But in her mind she believes she is helping me move on with my life by insuring the house is clean, the dog is walked, and my son is taken care of."

"But she seems miserable doing those things."

"I realize that. Believe me. If I could get her to stop, I would. I just put an ad in the paper in hopes of finding a housekeeper."

"So there was truth in what you said before!" I throw my napkin on the table.

"What do you want me to say—that I don't want you back? Of course I want you back. Is that such a horrible thing? It was nice having you take care of things. You made everything cozy and clean. The house really felt like a home again." Henry sucks in a breath and continues, "I mean I do get the picture. I know you didn't do it for the money. And now that this man you just barely met—Mason—is in your life, you probably—"

"I've known Mason since I was sixteen."

"Oh, that's bullcrap!" Henry says. The couple sitting near us clear their throats. "I heard the whole story, you watched him jump off a rope swing when he was, what, ten? Then years later he shows up at your doorstep and you've known him all your life!"

"Look at you! After meeting Pip once, you invited her to a New Year's Eve party. At least Mason and I have some history!" I retort.

"I was being nice. Pip called me four times that day!"

"Yeah, sure." I roll my eyes.

"Are you jealous?" Henry says.

"Why on earth would I be jealous? I have a boyfriend. With whom I just spent a marvelous week. What do I care if you invited Pip to some snooty party," I insist, trying very hard not to sound jealous in the least.

"Oh, I see," Henry says, deadpan. His face set, he looks over my head to the waitress and waves to the waiter, "Check, please!"

A Message

The house is strewn with chewed bits of wood, cloth, and garbage. Puddles of pee and poop cover the kitchen floor. I am wracked with gut-wrenching shame over my own stupidity: Thinking Henry might me interested in me! Me! A stay-at-home single mother with no job skills other than washing his dishes and cleaning his toilets! I scream a slow scream. Like being torn from the womb. "I hate my stupid life," I shout, and throw my library bag down, take off my boots, and throw those as well. I curl up in a ball on the hallway floor. I could stay here for a lifetime.

I hear the phone ringing and the machine pick up. A voice crackles and snaps. Mason is telling me he misses me. His voice fills the house. He is telling me to come visit him. He'll buy the plane ticket. He is thinking of me lots, lots, lots. "Thought for sure you would be there on a Sunday night. I really need to hear your voice. I'll try back in fifteen minutes. Maybe you're in the bath or something. I hope you haven't given up on me. My truck broke down. I'll tell you all about it later. I miss you. I miss you so, so much. Bye. I'll try later. Bye."

I feel the floor's coolness on my hot cheeks. I stand up slowly, legs shaky. Darling whines and drops the clog he has been gnawing. He follows me into the kitchen. I fill his bowl with fresh water and food then clean up the mess. "I'll never do that again, Darling," I promise. I take off my furry coat and hang it outside on a hook by the back porch door. It needs air, I think. Lots of fresh air. When the phone rings, I go inside and pick it up.

Kids Come Back

In the foyer, Ex-Rat brushes off the snow from his trendy yellow Crocs. Sailing footwear goes perfectly with his new tan. Hate him. He is always on the upside of hot new trends.

"Is that guy still here?" Ex-Rat asks after the kids have disappeared into the house.

"You mean Mason? No. Why?"

"I don't want some strange guy moving in and disrupting my kids' lives. The divorce is a hard enough transition for them to deal with," he says, all self-righteous.

"That's a little hypocritical, considering you presently live with your fiancée."

"I broke up with her. She moved out while the kids and I were in Florida," Ex-Rat says.

"What a thoughtful holiday gift. I'm sure she was thrilled."

Ex-Rat, ignoring my comment, points his finger in my face, "I don't want him moving in here. Got it? I'm still the one paying the mortgage on this place. Remember that." He walks his Croc-laden feet to his car. I quake with fear, terrified by the thought of further court processes.

Institution

Sun-kissed Lucy gallops around the house in her new bathing suit with her ear glued to sand-encrusted shells. I try to vacuum behind her. "I can't hear the ocean!" she screams in my face and Brendan yells up the stairs, "I'm trying to talk to Sophie on the phone!" I think of committing myself to an institution. I think better of it. Decide to become nun instead.

My Birthday

Huge fantasy about being a nun: I see a little room with white walls and one very narrow bed. I see myself scrubbing floors and peeling potatoes, spinning wool, possibly knitting. Praying and chatting away with God every day—day in, day out. If I have to be divorced, my second marriage might as well be to God. Much more stable. And wonderfully clean. No more mountaineer men who leave for the opposite end of the world after five days of passionate sex, making you insane with heartbreak on your birthday. A nun is definitely a far better way to go, safely wearing chastity threads every day without fear of further court processes.

Birthday Wishes

"I'm calling to remind you that Lucy and Brendan have a dentist appointment at 9:00 a.m. for a cleaning," Ex-Rat says.

"Is that it?" I ask.

"Yep."

"Are you sure?" I ask.

"Yep," he says again, and hangs up. I cannot believe he forgot my birthday. I think of fifteen years wasted in a dead-end relationship. Throw half-eaten toast in the garbage. Ponder calling 911 for nearest nunnery to commit myself. Birthday off to wonderful start.

Reality Check

"I've decided to become a nun," I tell Lucy, handing her buttered toast with raspberry preserves for breakfast.

"Can I come watch?" Lucy asks, still wearing her bathing suit and jumping up and down. She grabs the end of my bathrobe and covers her head with it like a veil. I look at her dewy eyes and jam-covered face. All Mary goodness.

More Birthday Wishes

"He's left. He *called from the airport.* Can you believe it? He called from the airport to tell me he is going to Nepal. 'Hello! On my way to Nepal. Sorry I didn't tell you!' I can't understand why he would do such a thing!" my mother screams hysterically to the answering machine. I put the car keys and the kids' new toothbrushes on the kitchen counter, pick up the phone, click the on button, tuck it under my chin.

"Mom," I say.

"Oh, you're there. Why didn't you pick up earlier?" she asks.

"I just got back from dropping the kids at school. They had dentist appointments this morning."

"He went to Nepal!" she shouts. I cringe and turn the volume down on the phone.

"Who?" I ask.

"Mark! The guy I brought to your house for Christmas." I cringe again. Don't need to be reminded of turnip-birthing Yoga Alien on my birthday.

"We just went shopping yesterday and bought you a pressure cooker for your birthday! Now he's on a plane for Nepal!" I feel overwhelming un-joy about birthday purchase. Hate pressure cookers: Don't like explosions.

"What made you buy me a pressure cooker?" I ask, dismally.

"It was Mark's idea. He noticed you didn't have one. Actually, it was very thoughtful of him," my mother says, tearfully. The fact that my mother is calling me on my birthday to boo-hoo about being dumped, then going on about how thoughtful the guy is, causes nun impulse to grow by the nanosecond. It's on the verge of blossoming into a full-fledged plan.

Card and Small Package

The mail arrives as I am deep in my abandonment issues. There is a card and a small package for me. Neither of them is from Mason. I open the little yellow card with Grammy's handwriting on it. It's a single-parent birthday prayer. Where does she find these things? Next I open the small package from my father. Inside is a birthday card with a scratch-and-sniff strawberry birthday cake on it. My father knows I love, love, love scratch-and-sniffs. Inside it reads: "Have a Berry Great Birthday!" I scratch the birthday cake. I sniff. A little present, wrapped in white sparkly tissue, contains mittens, perfect little white mittens. Attached is a note in my father's perfect script. "I knit these for you." I rub the softy mittens against my nose and sniff these as well. They smell like love—berry, berry sweet love.

Monkey Clip

Lucy and I are ogling bags of Dum Dum lollipops in très early Valentine's display. I grab two packs. Lucy claps her approval and then rips the bags from my hand. We are in one of those drugstores that have soda fountains. It's old-fashioned and famous, right on Brattle Street. I hardly ever go in here because I have not honed the look of high society slumming it in blue-collar digs. However, I bribed Demon Princess that if she stopped screaming and pulling her hair at the dentist's office this morning, I'd buy her the monkey clip in the drugstore window that she has been coveting for weeks.

Taking back the lollipops, I put them on the counter along with the monkey clip. Brendan adds a big bag of salt-and-vinegar potato chips. I say nothing, because for reasons I can't decipher, we are no longer on speaking terms. Am hoping purchase of chips will earn at least a grunt. I proudly refrain from pointing out that we are on our way to my birthday dinner. He doesn't notice or appreciate, just tears open the bag and begins to munch.

Birthday Dinner

Having no desire to find another parking space, I make the kids walk to the nearby restaurant known for its blues. Perfect for my mood. We have to wait outside in a slow-moving line for a table. Lucy starts spinning and banging into me on purpose. I hand her the bag of lollipops and she crunches one with her newly cleaned teeth. I pocket the wrapper, which carries a message promising love forever and a day.

Brendan strolls over to a college-age-looking girl, who is leaning against the wall in front of us, and says hello. She smiles sly and serpenty. He tosses the bag of chips in a trash can on the curb. Sinks it, then trips. She giggles. "I meant to do that," he says, shrugging his shoulders, not blushing, with a slight smile. His boxers fold out like window dressing, wallet chain hanging past his knee, he has on an old-fashioned paperboy lid. I am watching him become a man. I grasp Dum Dum wrapper tight in my pocket. I won't let go. His skinny arms and chest, yet to fill out with muscle, in his zip-up hoodie. These are still all boy. The boy I love.

Birthday Message

Mason's voice crackles and fades on the answering machine, "Happy birthday to you . . . happy birthday . . ." I hit PLAY again. Again. Then again. Each time his voice seems further away.

Waking

Thank god it is no longer my birthday.

Hearts

Moonboy and Lucy fold red and pink paper and I carefully draw half hearts, which they cut slowly with kid scissors. This is their first real playdate—Lucy's idea. She even called him herself. Lucy also, without my permission, invited Manic Pup so that Darling had someone to play with, too, and wouldn't feel left out. At pickup, Lucy did not complain about afterschool boredom; rather, she leapt into the car in expectation of meeting her moony love.

Moonboy is quietly observing her second Demon meltdown, his inner glow intact. Lucy screams, "We are old enough to have big scissors instead of these stupid ones that stick to our knuckles and *hurt us*!"

I don't cave on the matter of the big scissors. I trust Moonboy, but not Demon. Instead I give them some health nuggets with added protein.

"We want something good, this tastes gross, we hate it!"

I take back the health nuggets with added protein and replace them with yogurt-covered almonds. Moonboy devours several nuts. Must give Lucy credit—she definitely senses his needs. She also pinches him every time he smiles. I tell her to stop. Moonboy just shakes his head and smiles again, loving it.

Darling bites my pant leg and tugs and growls underneath the table, then skitters after Manic Pup. Every shoe, hat, pillow, and toilet brush in the house has teeth marks. Luckily I have kept my supply of hot pink clogs in boxes on high shelves in the closet.

When the mail slot opens, huge amounts of mail tumble and clunk to the floor. I run to look though the pile. Darling and Manic Pup race behind me. Along with the bills and junk mail are three recycled dark-yellow packages, duct-taped. They are from Alaska. They are from Mountain Man. Yes, Mason.

I leave the bills on the floor and run upstairs to hide Mason's packages in my panty drawer. A perfumed paper-lined drawer is the perfect place for love parcels. Maybe Valentines? My heart leaps.

Demon continues to scream and bang below, so I close the panty drawer and run downstairs. I guide stuck scissors over Lucy's knuckles, as Mason's parcels smolder and beckon upstairs. The puppy nips and I don't flinch; Demon thrashes around and I don't flinch. I am well drugged with expectation.

We squeeze glue and sprinkle glitter, lay dozens of hearts out to dry on the dining room table, which is now a shrine of hearts. I light candles and draw the curtains. Demon purrs. Darling barks. Moonboy sighs. The dogs snuggle and are quiet and I reflect. We stare at our magnificent hearts, which glint and glisten.

A Feast

I am happy, so I cook. I force Brendan to snap green beans. He throws ends at Lucy's head. She gathers fallen-bean artillery and hurls them back at him. Moonboy traces his finger in a small puddle of water on the counter, waiting for his weasel of a father to pick him up. The kitchen reeks of fresh paint because I have painted the walls aqua. Am now a junkie for drenched colors, having juiced myself up during postbirthday depression on a documentary about Central American female artists.

The doorbell rings and I lower the flame underneath my minestrone. I tidy my hair and then go answer the door. Henry stands on the steps holding a hot pink balloon.

"Another peace offering?" I ask.

"It's actually an invitation," he says.

"An invitation?"

"An invitation for you to make peace with me," Henry grins.

"To make peace with you?" I ask. Henry gives me a puppy-dog look. "You're incorrigible."

"The smile on your face is *encouraging*," he says, handing me the balloon.

"Come into the kitchen and have some soup, and leave that profound wit of yours outside," I say.

"Does that mean you're inviting me in for supper?"

"The term we use is *dinner*. And yes, I'm inviting you to have dinner with us," I say.

"I don't know if my attire is suitable. I am not wearing anything remotely furry or pink," Henry says, leaning casually against the door frame with his arms folded across his chest, his eyes boyishly mischievous. I notice the curve of his neck, the span of his shoulders. I smell his aftershave. I have a sudden desire to touch him and to draw him close. I think of Mason's letters in my panty drawer and bite my lip.

"Mom, do you want me to put these beans in the soup?" Brendan yells from the kitchen.

"Yes!" I yell back. "Well, are you coming in? I'm sure we can find something furry or pink for you to throw on," I say to Henry. He nods and stands up straight.

Henry follows me down the hall and views the new kitchen decor from the foyer, "I see someone has discovered Frida Kahlo."

"Among others," I say.

"I'm sure she would approve of your new balloon," he says.

"You think?"

"Yes. And I think she would tell you that whoever gave you such a balloon was a very nice friend," Henry says. The dreaded *friend* word again. To soften the blow, I once again think of Mason's letters.

"Really," I sigh.

"Really," Henry says.

"I think you're nice," Lucy chirps. Brendan opens his mouth in shock. Lucy never issues compliments.

"You see?" Henry says, and Moonboy dimples.

"I see. Now be a nice friend and set the table," I say, lifting up my chin. I walk over to the stove and turn the flame back up under the soup and vow to never—under any circumstances, no matter how charming or handsome Henry may be—think of him in any other way except as a friend. A voice somewhere inside my head says, *Never say never*. Must get that wee part of brain matter excised.

Soup

"You're a culinary genius," Henry says, as he ladles soup into his bowl.

"You haven't even tasted it yet," I say, passing the basket of rolls to Moonboy.

"Yes, but it looks far more promising than my fondue. And it has wheely pasta in it."

"Wheely isn't a word," I say.

"Wheely?" Henry says, wrapping his napkin around his neck. He looks completely goofy but no less desirable. *Grrrrrr*. I put my napkin on my lap and plunge my spoon into my soup.

Love Parcels

Henry and Moonboy have gone home. Lucy is sneak-reading in bed with my tiny new book light that I bought myself for my birthday. Even though she's not technically sleeping, at least her bedroom is dark. This is far better than her typical late-night prowling with jab-friendly objects. I hear Brendan laugh and then his voice drop into low murmurs in the den. He is talking on the phone with his beautiful girlfriend Sophie.

I go upstairs to my bedroom and open my panty drawer. I take out Mason's packages, lay them on my bed, remove the tape carefully, and open the first one, which contains a bundle of handwritten letters. I note the dates, then open the second and third parcels, piling the letters according to days. I find rocks, shells, an eagle feather, and a bear claw, each in its own small plastic baggie, carefully labeled, indicating the area where he found it.

I examine the bear claw. It's long and sharp.

. . . .

seven

A Week of Waiting

It's been over three months since I got my period, and I am wondering how to tell Mason. When to tell Mason. I think of how such a letter would look: "Went to garden supply center to buy bulbs. I think I might be pregnant." Later in the letter I mentally include, "I don't know if it is yours or my ex-husband's, but I thought you should know."

This is why it is important not to have postmarital or premarital sex, I suppose: so you don't have to think about writing a letter that contains such sentences.

In the Gym

Pip sweats away like a maniac and swigs spring water from a "deep source." I slowly pedal the bike machine. She isn't talking to me, because she is thinking. She is thinking of every angle. She is going to come up with a plan for me. I watch the news on the TV and think about how stupid and meaningless my life is. This happens a lot in the gym. It has something to do with the gerbil-wheel feel of the place. I begin to actually feel like a gerbil and my self-esteem plummets. Right now I am a pregnant, ill-feeling gerbil with no husband and no plan. Not good. Pip is coming up with a plan. Far worse.

"Get an abortion," Pip says.

"No," I say.

"Don't tell him it might be his, then."

"Which him?" I ask.

"Your ex-husband, dumb-ass."

"What about Mason?"

"Tell him it's his," she says.

"It might not be," I say.

"What he doesn't know won't kill him."

"If the baby is blond and six feet by age three, I think it will be obvious," I say.

"By then you'll be married and you'll hate one another anyway, so you can get a divorce." I look at her. She does have a point. "Anyway, eighty percent of second marriages end in divorce, so what's the difference?" A very good point.

The Purchase

Pip refuses to purchase a pregnancy kit, after having agreed she would. She changes her mind as soon as we get to the correct aisle, near the condoms, which I view with sheepish whorelike guilt. She snaps, "Fuck this shit," pops an antianxiety med, and runs from the store. Asking Pip to escort me to the condom aisle wasn't such a hot idea, since she has yet to find someone to have sex with since Martin broke up with her.

Alone, I bypass the condoms and grab the first pregnancy kit I see. With my last shred of hope, I also grab a box of tampons. On my way to the checkout line, I experience a rising urge to drop everything and follow Pip's lead. Instead, I secure a place in line. My stomach churns. At the register, a pimple-ridden cashier boy blushes as he scans my feminine needs. I notice Pip waving to me outside the drugstore window. I wave back. She smiles and then gives me the finger. I smile and then give her the finger. I feel better. Normal even. Like everything is OK.

The Test

"It's not doing anything." Pip examines my urine on a stick.

"What does that mean?" I ask in an anxious whisper.

She picks up the box, takes out the insert and reads, "Innocent until proven guilty."

"Give it to me!" I yell, grabbing the instructions from her hand. "It means I'm not pregnant, you jerk," I say, relieved.

"Like that's a big fucking surprise considering you're almost forty," Pip says, lighting a cigarette.

"Then why am I not getting my period?" I ask.

"Early menopause." Pip says, exhaling smoke toward bathroom ceiling. I don't question it. Far better than being pregnant.

Ash Wednesday

I'm feeling all holy and good with ashes on my forehead. I've been led away from evil thanks to finally getting my period. I suck on a lollipop and swagger around the kitchen, phone in hand. I'm calling Grammy to ask for some holy water, since I forgot to fill up a jar prior to Lent.

Grammy answers the phone with a brusque, "What?"

"I need some holy water," I say.

"I'll put it in the mail tomorrow," she says, all angry.

"What's wrong?" I ask.

"Don't ask me, ask your grandfather," she says. There is a pause and then Grampa breathes into the phone but she grabs it back.

"On the way home from church today, I asked your grandfather if he loved me and you know what his answer was?"

"What?" I ask.

"'I told you on our wedding day that I loved you and if I ever change my mind I'll be sure to tell you.'"

She hangs up and I humbly place the phone on its stand.

Green Raincoat

It is sunny, yet I wear my kelly green raincoat. I even wear it indoors. It feels safe and snug, like a closet. It's great to cook in. I just wipe it down if I get any food on it. Lucy loves the idea; she has taken to wearing hers indoors as well. We walk to the corner store with Darling, who growls and pulls against the leash. A little old man heading toward us on his walker stops his slow progression and says, "It's always good to be prepared this time of year." I smile. Lucy frowns.

"Where's your smile?" he says to Lucy.

"I left it at home," she answers, tapping her purple clog with hot pink flowers.

"That's a good place to leave it," he says, and moves his walker forward once again.

Pickup

Ex-Rat has taken to remaining in his car and honking for the kids at pickup. He is honking right now. Lucy shoots me a dagger look, since I didn't let her call Moonboy a second time this afternoon. She ignores Ex-Rat's honking, as do I. The honking becomes more frequent, then less frequent, then the sound of his car door slamming. He does not ring the bell but he raps loudly on the door, which I slowly walk to and unlock. I derive pleasure from his annoyance.

I wait.

He raps again.

I open the door.

His face is boiling.

I smile calmly. Very Zen. Must be the raincoat.

"Didn't you hear me honking?" he says through clenched teeth.

"Was that you?" I say.

"Of course it was me. Cut the crap. Is Lucy ready? We have to pick up Brendan at lacrosse practice in fifteen minutes."

He has cut off his ponytail. The short hair suits him.

"No, she's not. She's finishing up an art project. Why don't you call Brendan on his cell and tell him you'll be a few minutes late. He won't mind. That's why you bought it for him, right—for times such as these?" I say with bitchy sweetness, venting my angst over his recent purchasing of the brain-tumor-causing communication device for my only son. Brendan, however, is thrilled and calls all his other cell-connected friends, even if they are only five feet away.

Ex-Rat whips out his cell and yells into it: "Brendan!" He looks up at me with crisp intensity, and asks, "What's with the raincoat?"

I don't respond. I am not a good communicator.

A Movie

I eat a kid-size portion of popcorn with lots of salt and sip sugary coffee between bites. Chocolate chips are warming in my pocket—I like them mushy. I'm in heaven. Usually, I prefer previews to the movie itself, something I have always attributed to my short attention span but now realize is because I have gone only to kids' movies with whining children for the past fifteen years.

This is my way of killing time while waiting for a response to the last letter I sent Mason. Not being pregnant has done wonders for my epistolary skills. I even quoted John Muir. I wrote with lavish passion about nature and how I would love to live on an isolated mountaintop but am jailed within city limits, due to threatened court processes.

The movie makes waiting for Mason's response more bearable. I think I'll go to a movie tomorrow as well. I'll become a moviegoer. I'm thinking of this when I notice the leading lady in the movie is knitting a soft pink scarf. I remember my father knit me mittens for my birthday and I decide that right after the movie is finished I'll head over to his apartment. He is sure to have some yarn.

Knitting

I huff up the stairs to my father's apartment. He looks at me through the peephole, then carefully turns three locks. "I thought for sure an elephant had escaped from the zoo and was stomping up the stairs looking for that travel packet of peanuts I absconded with on my recent flight to Gay Paree," my father says upon opening the door.

"You didn't go anywhere," I say, out of breath. "You never even leave your neighborhood, let alone fly on a plane to Paris."

"It sounded good, though, didn't it?"

"Could you teach me how to knit?" I ask.

My father responds by walking into the living room and turning up the jazz on the stereo. Finally he says, "There is nothing I'd rather *not* do than teach you how to knit." But he does show me a knitting book and his loads of yarn, which are neatly packaged in freezer bags in a sealed plastic box in the guest room closet. I have a fleeting thought that mother issues should take a back burner if I ever find a new therapist. I am just like him. Love, love freezer bags. An insane neat freak as well. Instantly, I am possessed by yarn lust. I gobble up bags and stuff them into my already full tote. My father watches and says dryly, "Maybe I should give you an empty pillowcase."

"Could you?" I smile indulgently and follow him into the kitchen where he makes fresh OJ while I ransack his fridge, finding cold roasted asparagus and risotto. Devouring stolen eats while flipping through the knitting book, I worry because the photos are dead boring. But I refuse to be deterred.

"Shall I grill a side of cattle?" my father asks.

"I don't eat beef anymore after reading a report on mad cow disease. Mom is beside herself with joy," I say. "She sends me loads of literature on it." He smiles. I giggle.

"Lately I miss your mom," he says seriously.

"Really?" I'm surprised.

"I miss her exuberance, her lust for life." What he says is true. My mother is always up, even when in incredible emotional pain. She needs no green raincoat.

"She has never stopped missing you," I say. He touches my hand. We look at each other. That's all. It's enough.

Night

I miss Mason deep. Too deep for such short a time together and such a long time apart. I should know better. He has probably found some wilderness goddess, red hair, great calves. They probably build fires with reckless abandon deep in the woods. I place Lucy's junior sleep sack in the closet and bring in a flashlight. Also some water and Ugly's favorite peanut butter dog bones for Darling. We lie in the dark. I flash the flashlight over and over. My kelly green raincoat squeaks. Darling crunches and snuggles in. I hope Mason gets my signal. I hope he signals back.

Mason Calls

"Got your letter, read it, and drove to the nearest pay phone so I could hear your voice," Mason says all husky and warm. "So when are you going to come visit me?"

"I don't know." Suddenly shy, I twirl my hair. I am afraid of flying just like my father.

"How about May?" he suggests.

"I can't in May, the children are in school," I say.

"Can't their father take them for a spell?" There is no way Ex-Rat could do it then. May is the start of his busy work months.

"I could come the second week in June. That's when their father has them anyway for vacation," I say, bravely.

"Sounds good, I'll take it. I'll buy you a plane ticket for that week. Give me the dates," Mason says. Trembling, I go grab my daybook from my purse.

Easter Eggs

Wearing my yellow flowered dress with pink rosebuds, I am on my way out to buy eggs for decorating. Love, love, love Easter eggs! In the hallway, I put on my new bonnet. Brendan stops me with a horrid look and snatches the hat from my head. "No way," he says. I leave the bonnet on the bench, to be chewed by Darling. Brendan says he'll come along for the ride if he can utilize his new learning permit. I am a desperate woman—I want him to love me again—and I toss him the keys. He bolts out the door, and I follow, carrying assorted cloth bags to look politically correct while shopping at the local co-op. I plan to buy organic eggs and natural dyes. Mother will be well pleased. I'll invite her to an egg soiree since Yoga Alien is now a monk in a Nepal monastery and she is beside herself with rejection. Brendan blasts hardcore and we sail smoothly along. I turn down the music and ask diversified questions and he turns it back up before answering. I give up.

Moonboy and Lucy are on their first field trip with Ex-Rat. He has taken them to view fish tanks large as houses, with miserable creatures swimming in circles. It seemed appropriate for his mood, he said. I gave my blessing and sent Lucy out the door in matching Easter colors, with a bonnet of her own. Moonboy, arriving with Manic Pup in Ex-Rat-mobile, was surely smitten. He handed her a quarter to put in her white purse. She responded by stamping on his toe and exclaiming, "I only take dollars," to which he smiled, shoved the quarter back in his pocket, and opened the car door for her.

"Remember, we have to pick up Pip on the way to the store," I scream over the music. Brendan nods and burns rubber. As we screech up to her apartment building, I am slammed forward and then back against the seat. "Cool it," I warn. "Beep your horn." He beeps. He beeps again. And again.

"You want me to drive?" I ask. He stops beeping.

Pip comes out dressed all in black with a new cat's-eye look achieved with liquid eye pencil. Her midriff is exposed and she has on her thong sandals. Her toes are lipstick red. She is swigging a tiny bottle of liquor, which she holds up, announcing, "I'm going to need a much bigger one."

And we roar away from the curb.

The Market

Brendan waits in the car with the windows down and the music blasting. He has donned shades. Pip has insisted we go to a new gourmet food store, instead of the co-op. Big-deal people shop there, she tells me. Really big-deal people. Pip is now hell-bent on finding a rich gentleman her age or slightly younger. She wants to be courted, which is the reason we are far afield on the other side of town. Thanks to the National Hockey League strike, she is at a loss with her time—she needs help navigating the nothingness of her days—and has become extremely attached to my nothingness. When I suggest that perhaps it is better not to reek of alcohol when seeking gentlemen, she laughs and says, "Big-deal people are big-deal drinkers. It comes with the big-deal territory."

Her tipsy inanity is putting me out of my blissful innocent Easter egg mode. I ditch her by the booze section and go in search of eggs, which I find in tiers, stacked in wooden crates. Like gifts. I'm possessed by egg lust. I breathe deep and focus, lest I break one. The eggs smell like seashells that have been empty for years and bleached by the sun. I spot lovely baskets in different shapes and colors and pick one to match my frock. I fill it with two dozen eggs and am humming a tune when I feel a presence. Henry stands behind me, holding butcher-paper-wrapped packages. I had forgotten this was his neighborhood. Still—Henry grocery shopping on a Saturday? I thought for sure he'd be playing squash at the club.

"What are you doing here?" I ask.

"Grocery shopping. It's my new hobby," Henry smiles. "I know. I know. It's a little boring as hobbies go—nowhere near as interesting as dog walking, for example—but there are a lot of grocery stores in my neighborhood and I meet other people who have just as much passion about expiration dates as I do."

"Very funny," I say.

"And you're very pretty," Henry pauses, looking up and down the length of my body, "in your Easter dress, carrying your baskets of eggs. Don't tell me—you're making mousse, lemon meringue pie, or Easter eggs."

"Easter eggs," I say, noticing that his hair is slightly damp and he looks fresh and sparkling. I stand up straight and think, *He is just a friend, he is just a friend.*

"What is your favorite color for dyeing?" he asks.

"I love all colors." Which is true.

"I instinctively knew this. However, if you could have only one color, just one, what would it be?"

"Orange," I say.

"Einstein's favorite color," he says approvingly.

"And you? What are you doing here, really?" I point to his packages.

"I just finished playing a rather rigorous game of squash and I invited some of my buddies from the club over for a barbeque this afternoon."

"Ah," I say. I knew it!

"I thought having a barbeque would be far easier than making fondue. You just slap the meat down on the grill and violà! It's a one-step process."

"As opposed to *Fondue 1, 2, 3!*" I tease.

Pip rounds the corner and I hurriedly go back to selecting eggs. Pip is carrying gallon bottles of Scotch and gin. She approaches Henry and says in a sultry voice, "Well, I see someone likes his meat." She rubs his packages with a free finger and bangs a bottle of booze against his arm. "Where have you been hiding? I haven't seen you since New Year's. Have you been being naughty?" She sways slightly and falls against him. "Well, you're in good company, because I too have been very, very naughty and I adore the flesh."

I yank Pip off Henry and shoo her toward the cash register. I'm so flustered that I don't notice Pip's former boyfriend, Martin, ahead of us. But Pip does. I hold tight to my basket as she cuts in line and inspects Vegan Boy's groceries.

"What's in them?" she says, too loud. Vegan Boy looks terrified. "What the fuck is in that fucking butcher paper, you vegan fuck-wad!" She slams the booze on the counter and begins unwrapping his butcher paper. A horrible, misshapen blood clot reveals that it is liver. I remember the restraining order and start to sweat.

Pip throws down the package and droplets of blood splatters around it. The manager heads toward us and asks if there is a problem. "The problem is that my bald fuck vegan boyfriend left my meat-eating ass and look what I caught him purchasing this very fucking fucked-up moment!" Pip picks up the liver and shoves it under the manager's nose. He grabs her wrist. Quickly, Henry moves around me. The manager looks at Henry with recognition.

"Forgive me, is this woman with you?" asks the manager, as he removes his hand from Pip's wrist.

"A friend of a friend," he responds evenly. He takes the liver from Pip, hands it to the manager, then puts a finger to his lips to shush Pip and guides her gently through the line. They have blood on their hands. I hope they wash them, I think. I hope they get it all off. Vegan Boy says to me apologetically, "I found out I'm anemic. That's why I was buying the liver."

He is so young. So sad and kept. He pays for the booze Pip left on the counter. He points to it. "Don't tell her I bought it, it will only make her angrier." He gives a short wave and leaves empty-handed.

In the Car

My basket of eggs rests in my lap and Brendan revs the engine in neutral. "What's taking her so long?" he grumbles.

"She had to use the restroom," I say.

"Whatever." He slams his head back against the head rest, folds his arms and continues to rev the engine. Since his fifteenth birthday, he has become vastly more of a jerk. I want to tell him you can be only so cool in a Volvo wagon. But I wisely bite my tongue.

Soon, Pip comes briskly out of the store, having apparently recovered her sobriety. She holds her head high. Henry tags along behind.

"What is Henry doing with Pip?" Brendan says. "She's not his type."

"Henry was helping her clean up a mess. She dropped something in the store," I tell Brendan.

Pip opens her door and plops in, while Henry approaches the car and says, "You have a chauffeur today, I see. Hey, Breno." Brendan grips the steering wheel, arms fully extended like a race-car driver, and revs a warning. Henry ignores hellish teen behavior and leans over Brendan's window. Brendan throws the car in reverse and backs up a few inches.

"Brendan, stop. That is so rude," I say.

"Don't worry, we already said our *fond* farewells in the bathroom." Pip winks and blows Henry a kiss. Brendan looks at Pip with disgust. I count my eggs. I look down. I don't look up.

Flowers

Back home, I busy myself boiling eggs and calling the florist. I order five dozen tulips, all white, and ask to have them delivered right away. When they arrive in full glory, I tip the delivery girl and place the flowers in a large crystal vase. The doorbell rings again and there is another delivery person, who hands me a box. Inside it is an orange egg. I try not to smile. Smile. Can't help myself.

Sleepover

Moonboy and Lucy are having a sleepover. He's wearing Brendan's old PJs, which hang over his feet. Lucy tries to trip him up as he skates around on the hardwood floors.

Brendan is out with his girlfriend. He is driving her around town while Ex-Rat sits in the backseat reading the *New York Times*. Passive-aggressive me bought Brendan a brand-new CD for the ride: Really awful metal music that he loves. Much better sound system in Ex-Rat-mobile.

Coloring Eggs

We are lifting eggs with tiny wire scoops when the doorbell rings. I drop my egg and it splashes purple dye all over my raincoat. I wipe it down and answer the door. Henry has Moonboy's little suitcase.

"I brought over his pajamas and a new toothbrush." He holds up a light purple toothbrush with flowers on it proudly. "It's battery-operated. It does its own little twirly thing, like you do with your hair," he says, pointing to my hand which is currently in my hair, twirling.

"It's lavender," I say.

"Violet," he corrects.

"It has flowers on it," I point out. He adjusts his glasses to give closer inspection.

"Heavens, they are! I thought those were some kind of threatening weeds or deformed snakes. This won't do at all." He is really too cute.

"I'm sure it will be fine," I say, and take the toothbrush. He hands me the suitcase and peers around me into the hall.

"We're just finishing up with the eggs," I say. He has that lonely-without-my-kid look. I know it well.

"May I come in and say goodnight to my son?" he asks. I open the door wider and pad down the hall in my piggy slippers.

The children sit with their faces pressed close to the little cups as they try to scoop their eggs out over and over. Henry sits down next to Moonboy and ruffles his hair. They fish out a blue egg with yellow polka dots and carefully lay it on a paper towel. Henry helps Lucy retrieve her egg, which is red with black Xs. "It's more fun dyeing Easter eggs with other people than dyeing just one Easter egg on your own in an empty house," Henry says shyly.

"Thanks for the egg," I say shyly back. He smiles at me, a really nice smile. "Would you like some tea?" I ask.

"Love some, thanks," he says.

Tea Is Poured

The children are upstairs and quiet for the time being. I bring a tray of tea and scones into the dining room, believing that if I am more formal it will somehow subdue the delicious effect that Henry has on me.

"You really are a great cook. These scones look absolutely delectable," Henry says, taking the tray from me and putting it on the table.

"So how did your barbeque turn out?" I ask.

"I burnt every steak to a crisp," he says.

"You didn't," I laugh.

"I did. I'm a total BBQ failure. I ended up ordering pizzas." He hands me half a scone.

"Well, you buttered this scone flawlessly," I say between bites.

"I'm glad," he says. "You deserve nothing less." He wipes a crumb from the side of my mouth. I stiffen.

"I am just trying to remove a crumb, not your panties," he says.

"Unless, of course, you would like me to," he adds. I get this sick feeling. A bad feeling. Like I just might want him to.

Easter Morning

I tiptoe around in my new bunny slippers—the mail order arrived just in time. I'm hiding Easter eggs, placing them gingerly in their secret spots: in the wheelbarrow, in assorted pots, underneath the porch steps.

All dog poop has been removed from the yard, thanks to last night's clean-up session by flashlight. Very trying, considering the flashlight was hard to hold while shoveling. I was tempted to turn on the back porch light, but I did a brilliant job without it, propelled by my newfound gusto for grim outside activities—I want to be wilderness-ready for the trip to Alaska.

Inside, Darling whines and scratches, so I leash him and take him out front. It's so quiet. No one is on the street. I sing a tune I love, "Amazing Grace."

Easter Service

Brendan, Moonboy, and Lucy flank me in the pew. They are scrubbed and dressed to J. Crew ideal. I asked Henry to meet us at the church with his car, since he made reservations for the five of us for Easter brunch at the Harvard Club. Lucy is on her best behavior. I threatened no more special sleepovers if she pulls any stunts during the service. She clutches Moonboy's hand and tells him what to do in loud whispers: "Stand!" "Sit!" "Kneel!" I'm wearing his mother's seahorse barrette. I pointed this out to Moonboy before the service and he smiled his beautiful smile. He now runs his finger slowly down the spine of the seahorse. I rub my finger over the birthmark on his neck. It tickles and he squirms, suppressing a giggle.

Henry slides into the pew next to me. His body is solid and warm.

Cozy. Remembering that I have a boyfriend in Alaska, I switch seats with Moonboy so he can sit next to his father. Much safer this way.

Moonboy climbs onto his father's lap. Henry gives him a big hug and kisses the top of his head. Lucy, jealous, clambers over them. I try to stop her quietly but Henry waves me away. He shifts Moonboy to one knee, balances Lucy on his other knee. "The barrette looks lovely on you," he whispers to me and we bend our heads in prayer.

A Week of Wonderment

I've just dropped off the Volvo to be serviced and am now at a record-store listening station. I have discovered Dolly Parton. I keep rewinding tracks from her newest album. Surely it is great preparation music for Alaska. She suits my new country smocks, with cotton slips underneath—heavenly. I think about dyeing my hair blond; instead, I purchase every Dolly CD ever made. Also purchase a book about her life. Highly absorbing, I am sure. I dump them on the counter. The guy behind the register is a Dolly fan as well and tells me everything he knows. I ask him if I should dye my hair blond. "No way could you pull that off," he says.

I nod. I'm not hurt. There is something honest and true in his face. I wonder if all Dolly fans are like him. Bet they are.

Headphones

A nasty saleswoman at the electronics store points me toward the CD players. I want a cheap portable one with headphones. Must have Dolly at all times to alleviate nervousness about my trip to Alaska. Dolly makes mountains and fresh air seem easy. I pull out my plane ticket from the pocket of my raincoat and smell it. It smells like raincoat, which is a very good smell.

I buy loads of batteries, which cost more than the CD player, and walk out of the store. I can't open the CD player package. Need a hacksaw. I go back in the store and the same nasty saleswoman tells me, "We don't carry scissors!" She is too happy to tell me this. Luckily, though, I am in the city and not some God-awful wilderness without a store for miles and can easily locate an army surplus store with an assortment of buck knives. I ask to see the smallest one. When I catch the reflection of my lips on the blade, they look dry.

I decide that a knife is too similar to a gun—terrifying. I hand the knife back to the salesman and ask him to open the CD player package for me. He slices like a pro. I purchase some lip balm and a combination nail file/scissors/screwdriver set. When it's all folded down and compact, it looks like a knife. Very practical and not scary at all.

I load the CD player with batteries and put on the headphones, lube lips, place the nail file set in my pocket with the ticket. I feel overheated and snug in my raincoat. Womblike. Dolly's voice is like honey, and as I walk the streets, I observe people. I feel invisible. I feel like myself again.

Irish Pastry

In a new bakery, waiting for a table to open up, I am dizzy with desire. My appetite is beyond reckoning. The pastries have lured half the city. Truly Irish, cream-filled, pale substances beckoning over the edges of puffs. My whole half-Irish being lusts full-tilt.

As I read a few pages of my book about Dolly's life, I understand I am truly lucky to be waiting for a table in a bakery, and not a poor child stuck in Tennessee.

Henry Calls at Home

"What are you doing right now?" Henry asks when I answer the phone.

"Nothing. The kids are at school. Why?"

"Because it is a beautiful spring morning and I want to show you something."

"What?"

"It's a surprise."

"What kind of surprise?"

"A good kind of surprise. I'll be over shortly to pick you up. All right?" Henry says.

"Alllll riiiight," I sing happily. As soon as we say our good-byes, I bolt up the stairs to change into something more appealing than granny pants and an old ripped T-shirt.

Public Garden

Henry opens the passenger-side door of his beat-up Subaru. The passenger seat is covered in crossword puzzles. A pencil jabs my tush. I reach down and try to locate it. Henry motions for me to lean forward and he removes the puzzles and pencils. He also reaches down by my feet and gathers some empty coffee cups. There must be at least a half dozen down there. I lift my feet. His arms brush against my thighs and my body warms. And then he throws everything in the back seat.

Henry drives to the Public Garden, parks the car on Beacon Street, comes to my side, and opens the door. It seems tentative and innocent. "This is the surprise. The garden is just about to burst. I thought you might like to have a look," he says, "since I know you consider yourself—what's the expression you used?—a wood nymph." He grins.

We walk through the park entrance. I haven't been here in forever. Not since Ex-Rat and I first moved to the city. Now I've just gone to the parks near my house. My pace quickens as I see shiny green buds coming forth from the ground, touching the ends of tree branches, and daffodils' yellow crowns. The breeze this morning is soft and gentle. Henry leads me through the garden, over a tiny bridge. The swan boats are below, waiting for summer's steady stream of passengers. At the top of the bridge Henry stops, turns to me. I think he might kiss me. Suddenly the air around us is charged. I step closer. Just a bit. Like a wish.

He towers over me.

"He must have really swept you off your feet in the short time he was here," Henry says, quietly.

"When who was here?" I say, absolutely clueless.

"Mason. I remember the way you looked at him at Christmas . . ." He drifts. I turn away, quickly descending to the bottom of the bridge, feeling guilty that I haven't thought of Mason all morning.

We walk around the vast pond in silence, the air swiftly turning colder. Henry takes off his corduroy jacket and hands it to me.

"I'm fine," I say, and he tucks it under his arm and walks on ahead.

Mother

While I am staring out the kitchen window, drinking black coffee, my mother calls. Her voice is clear and distinct. Thank goodness—it means she is not in Nepal in hot pursuit of Yoga Alien. My fears have not been realized.

"Where are you?" I ask, taking a slurp of coffee. Love slurping while on the phone with her. Drives her nuts.

"That better be tea," she says, irritated.

"Mmm," I breathe, she takes this as a yes.

"Good," she says. "Coffee has lethal oils in it."

"So, are you home?"

"No," she says.

"Then where?" I ask.

"I'm at Grammy's." This is the last place I expected her to be. She must be making Grammy's life a living hell. "I left Nepal a couple of days ago and flew into Montreal. There's this excellent Chinese herbalist up there. He does wonders for menopausal symptoms," she says, too brightly.

"So you went to Nepal," I sigh.

"I had to," she says. "You know me."

"Are you all right?" I ask.

"I'm just sick of being alone," she says.

"I know what you mean," I say. A chickadee lands on a branch outside the kitchen window. I remember as a child at Grammy's lying on the hammock and watching the birds at the birdfeeders: finches, robins, blue jays, shifting and beating their wings.

"Are you still there?" my mother asks.

"Yes, I'm still here," I say.

A Blessing

Another gorgeous day, sunny and bright. The hockey strike still going strong, Pip calls and asks what's on the agenda for this afternoon. I tell her we are planting bulbs. "Fuck me," she says, and hangs up.

I tuck the bottoms of my overalls into my muck boots, and put on my wide-brimmed hat. I bring a wheelbarrow filled with bulbs around to the front yard and start digging in the middle of the lawn. Tough turf. I can barely get the shovel past the grass part. My boots are too big, and they slip off the shovel as I press down. Finally, I manage to dig two very small holes. Maybe a pickax and little hand shovel would be easier. Droplets of sweat gather on my forehead, and I need mega water. At the door, I discover I have locked myself out. The phone is ringing. I pull on the door, jiggle the handle. No point getting furious at the stupid door and phone. Kick the side of the house instead.

I rummage in the garage for a possible hidden key, which I know is not there. No lost or misplaced key either. There is, however, a leftover case of beer dating from Ex-Rat days. I hate the stuff, but if I don't drink something I am sure to die of thirst from shoveling and door-kicking.

I pop one open. Even warm, it tastes like the elixir of gods. Now I know why construction crews are so keen on it. I'm on my third beer when Pip shows up, in a bikini top and capris. She has brought a thermos full of lovely Tom Collinses with lovely glasses that have flamingos on them. Very summer. I continue my haphazard digging as Pip decants an ice-cold Tom Collins for each of us. I take a break and sip lovely lemon tartness. Thank god Darling went with the kids to Ex-Rat's this weekend. Otherwise he'd be locked in the house, pooping all over the floor.

Some days you are just blessed.

A Theory

We've been sitting on the lawn drinking for quite a while, when Pip asks if I'll go with her to a meeting about her drinking problem. She calls it the happy hour meeting. It's her theory that if she goes drunk enough it will not be that bad.

"OK, but no way am I letting you drive," I balk. "And I'm soused, too. We're either walking or taking a cab."

"Fine. Have it your way," she says, and stomps up the sidewalk.

Charles River

Pip and I stumble and zigzag in the direction of Back Bay, stopping periodically to take a few nips from Pip's thermos of Tom Collinses. When we reach Harvard Bridge, Pip leans over the railing, looking down at the Charles River.

"What are you doing?" I ask, nervous.

"I'm wondering whether I should chuck my cell phone in the river."

"Why would you want to do that?"

"Because it's a hot potato of self-loathing. This way, when I get rid of it, I can believe he has called even though he probably hasn't." I gather she is speaking of Vegan Boy.

"You'd go bonkers without a cell. You know you would. And, anyway, it would be copycatting."

"What are you talking about? How am I copycatting?" Pip asks, taking her cell phone out of her purse.

"I threw my cell phone away. Now you're doing it."

"You threw yours in a trash can! I'm throwing mine in a river!"

"Same difference," I say, shrugging.

"No, it's not!"

"Yes, it is."

"Not."

"Is."

"Is not!" Pip screams and hurls her cell phone into the river. We both lean over the rail and watch it go. It doesn't make a ka-plash. It doesn't even make a plunk.

"That was really stupid," Pip says. "Now I have to buy another fucking cell phone."

Happy Hour

The meeting is about to start. There are rows of folding metal chairs arranged in concentric circles. A few people sit right in front. Pip and I take seats far in the back. At our turn, we don't introduce ourselves. Rather, we mumble and moan and others get the point. The next person to talk is a woman who draws out her words slowly. "Let go of your suf-fer-ing," she says.

A fountain of tears begins dripping from Pip's nose but when I offer her my shoulder to wipe on, she shakes her head. I reach around and rub her back.

Refreshments

When the meeting ends, I whisper in Pip's ear, "Did you notice there was only one other woman at that meeting, besides us?"

"Noted," Pip whispers back with a satisfied smile. "I may be a fucking alcoholic, but I'm not blind."

"I need to call Ex-Rat. He has a spare key to the house. And you threw out your cell phone and I don't even have a dime to my name. There has to be a pay phone somewhere around here so I can call collect," I ramble.

Pip opens her change purse and hands me a few coins. "Here's fifty cents—go knock yourself out. I'm going to go take a look-see at the refreshment table." She gets up, runs her fingers through her short hair, pops a mint and starts toward the group of men lingering around a fold-out table, a half-empty bottle of generic ginger ale and some paper cups scattered atop.

"I'll just make my call and meet you back here. All right?" I yell after her anxiously. I don't want to be ditched in Back Bay with zero cash and have to walk home in the dark.

"*Ssup* . . . yeah . . . *sssup* . . . sure, whatever," Pip answers.

Ditched in Back Bay

After losing fifty cents to reach Ex-Rat's voice mail, I schlep back to the church to find Pip so we can just go home to her house. I'm beginning to feel very cranky now that I am sober. When I open the church's basement door, I find only the other woman who was at the meeting. She is folding chairs.

"Where is everyone?" I ask her.

"Oh, they bailed out of here after your friend left with Dicky—you know, the guy with the mustache and the AC/DC T-shirt? I guess she was stranded or something. She said she needed a ride back to her car."

"*Stranded?* Is that the word she used—*stranded*?"

She stops folding chairs and looks up at me. "Yup."

The Key

I keep calling Ex-Rat collect from a payphone at a chain bookstore. Finally he picks up.

"I locked myself out of the house," I tell him, miserably.

"And?" Ex-Rat says.

"And I was hoping you had a spare key."

"Where are you?" Ex-Rat asks.

"In a bookstore near the corner of Clarendon and Berkeley."

"What the hell are you doing in Back Bay?"

"Never mind," I say, ignoring his question. "Can I just pick up the key?"

"We just got out of a movie. I have to drop off Henry's kid, anyway—"

"He came with you to the movies?" I can't imagine Ex-Rat permitting such a thing a second time—he grumbled for weeks about having to take Moonboy along with Lucy to view the fish tanks. I thought I'd never hear the end of it.

"Lucy had a fit and locked herself in the bathroom with the dog and threatened to stay there all night unless we took him with us. The dog was scratching the crap out of the door. I'll pick you up on the way over there. Meet me at the corner in about fifteen," he says in a heroic tone. I am helpless and he makes the most of it.

I feel like a complete mess. My overalls and muck boots look highly illiterate. I go in search of the self-help section of the bookstore but am sidetracked by the magazine section. I thumb through a fashion magazine that promises ten hot secrets for steamy sex. I read and reread the Butterfly Flick Technique, becoming even more depressed, since I have no one with whom to practice this hot secret.

At least no one who lives in close vicinity. My long-distance relationship is starting to feel like no relationship at all.

I walk to the corner and wait for my savior.

New Mercedes

Ex-Rat pulls up in his sleek new Mercedes, which goes well with his new short hair. I climb into the passenger seat. Brendan doesn't have his usual sour teenage look, and I wonder what this means. I find out when he confesses, "Dad gave me his old Mercedes."

I try not to lash out. Instead, I take deep rhythmic breaths, as during labor, inhaling through my nostrils, then hissing out. This has a surprising side effect: everyone's mouths tighten and their brows furrow. Ex-Rat jiggles his leg nervously and pulls away from the curb. He clutches the tan leather of the steering wheel.

I labor all the way to the stoplight.

"I have to wait another year before I can drive it on my own," Brendan concedes timidly.

I let out one long hiss. Thank goodness Ex-Rat hasn't completely lost his mind.

"I want to go to the bun shop in Chinatown," Lucy says.

"No," Ex-Rat says with a no-argument tone.

"Let's," I say, gathering bounce. "I'm starved and I love buns this time of the evening."

Ex-Rat gives me a soft look. I'm mystified, since my statement does not have intended anger-inducing effect.

"OK, then, why not?" he says.

A Quick Call

Ex-Rat makes a call to Henry on his cell about the delayed drop-off. When Lucy asks if Moonboy can spend the night, Ex-Rat waves his hand back and forth like he's swatting a fly. "We are doing a quick stop into Chinatown," Ex-Rat says into the phone, "because a certain weary mommy who was locked out of our—I mean, her—house today desires buns." He smiles and nods over to me. My toes curl in my muck boots. "No later than ten. Great. See you then," he says and snaps the cell phone shut.

Buns

Ex-Rat idles in an illegal parking spot while the children and I dive into the bun shop, like sharks to blood. We buy loads. I get sweet coffee and eat a whole bun before we get back in the car. Yum. I'm instantly revived, hangover gone. "Did you buy them out?" Ex-Rat asks, as I heft two large bags onto my lap. I can't answer—bun in my mouth—and pass a bag back to the kids.

"Wait until we get home. Absolutely no eating in this car," Ex-Rat barks. I wave my hand in swatting-fly fashion. Moonboy and Lucy—who have not been promised ownership of an old Mercedes—dig and munch.

Ex-Rat peels out from the curb. I am beside myself with normalcy. Cross myself. Spill coffee. Hallelujah.

A Sighting

Pip's car is parked in front of Henry's and I'm aghast.

Ex-Rat laughs and says, "Looks like Pip has found herself a new man. Henry's quite a step up from that weirdo she was seeing for months. He's around her age, too! Will wonders never cease?" I lose my appetite for buns and hand my bag to Moonboy as he opens the door to leave Ex-Rat's crumb-ridden tan leather interior. We watch as he walks up to the front door and rings the bell. Henry lets him in and walks out onto the stoop, wearing what must be his squash uniform. Pip doesn't emerge. She's probably frying up a bunless burger.

"Make sure Pip gets one of those buns," I yell out the window. "She loves buns."

Henry reddens and, ignoring my comment, addresses Ex-Rat. "Thanks so much for allowing my son to tag along for the evening. The squash tournaments tend to get carried away."

"Couldn't be helped," Ex-Rat responds rudely.

Home

As soon as I get home, I go onto the porch and put a spare key under the mat, then change my mind because of its obvious location, then change my mind again, figuring the location is so obvious that no one will look there. I decide to call Henry and apologize for Ex-Rat's evil comment. I also want to tell him I'm sorry for making the bun remark.

"Hello," Henry answers. Suddenly, I have no idea what to say or how to say it. I hear Moonboy talking in the background about the movie he just went to with Lucy, and Pip pretending to be interested.

"Really, wow, how cool!" Pip says in exaggerated tones.

"Hello? Hello?" Henry repeats.

I bite down on my lip and hang up.

nine

A Week of Reckoning

After a dismal night of bad dreams, I thank God it's morning. The phone rings and I leap for it, trailing my long nightgown. I trip and recover. "Thanks for sending your only mother a card," my mother says in her manic chirp. I've completely forgotten Mother's Day, the newly single mother's most dreaded holiday. Must have subconsciously blocked it out.

"I was going to call," I say guiltily.

"Sure," she says.

Without thinking, I spew, "I made reservations for all of us at this new restaurant in town, I was really just about to call you."

"Really?" she says, sounding genuinely surprised and happy.

"Really," I lie boldly, and cross myself three times for good measure. Surely there is nothing wrong with a white lie when truth-telling might prompt one's mother to commit suicide.

"What should I wear?" she asks. "Is it really fancy?"

"Totally. Dress to the hilt." For her this means a hippie hand-painted dress.

"What time?" she asks.

"Seven," I say.

"Seven is the number for life in—"

"Mom, I don't have time, I have to head to the gym," I lie once more. Actually, I'm heading to Mass. My mother can't stand the thought of me going to Mass because it makes her feel like a failure of a New Age mom.

I hang up and wonder how I will pull off a fancy-restaurant reservation last minute on Mother's Day.

Mary

I've been in love with Mary ever since I can remember. She is all beauty and calm. I light a candle at her station before Mass and ask her for a reservation at a fancy restaurant. I tell her I know it's a ridiculous request and I'm sure she has much better prayers to answer. I also pray for more patience with my children and vow to take them to Mass next Sunday if my restaurant prayer is answered. Then I pray to be forgiven for being so demanding and conditional.

An old woman taps me on the shoulder. I look up. "You can't kneel there praying all day with the rest of us waiting here," she says. Behind me is a line of old women in plastic bonnets and gray trench coats. They are not happy. I speculate that self-absorbed children and no cards are in their prayers. I know their children's children photos are tucked in their wallets, which are in purses that smell like rose talc and peppermints.

A Mother's Day Surprise

I return home with a frothy soy mocha for me and a gerbera daisy plant for my mother. Booby No. 1 told me about some great chi-chi macrobiotic restaurant near the artsy side of Cambridge. Surely it's not a popular place to take one's mother on Mama's Day, so I'm hopeful. I whip out the phone book but realize I have no chance of finding a nameless restaurant in the city. I instinctively call Pip. Her cell phone is ringing . . . at the bottom of murky river. Her land line rings once and then a recording: "The number of the person you are trying to reach is no longer in service. No further information is available at this time." Gasp. When I dial 411, the operator informs me that Pip has switched to an unlisted number. Gasp again. I cannot believe Pip hasn't called to give me her new unlisted number.

I try Ex-Rat—he eats in restaurants all the time—but get his voice mail. I call the coffee shop and ask the Boobies to think harder about the name. They have no clue what the restaurant is called, but they assure me it is really, really, really rockin' in the food department. I pray Lucy goes to Smith College, which has reputation for teaching girls how to think coherently. Don't want her to suffer same brain fate as Boobies.

The macro joint is in Henry's neighborhood. He may have an inkling of the location and maybe the name. I remember from my cleaning days that he has a large assortment of restaurant guidebooks with menus, since he never cooks. I dread calling him. Dread it so much that I consider cooking a fancy meal at my house. Visualizing my mother's crestfallen expression as she stands there in her hippie dress, absorbing the news, I pick up the phone and dial. Henry answers in a deep voice. He sounds different. It unnerves me. "I need to ask a favor," I say bluntly.

"Yes?"

"I forgot to reserve a table at this restaurant in your neighborhood for Mother's Day," I say.

"And?"

"Well, I was just wondering if you could look it up in one of those foodie field guides of yours," I say.

"Foodie field guides?" he asks. I hear a raspy laugh. A familiar raspy laugh: Pip's.

"Is that Pip?" I ask. "She's hanging out at your house again?"

"Yes, but it's not—"

I hang up. I picture the phone in his hand, his puzzled expression. Pip's summary.

I'm the odd person out. Odd indeed.

A Manic Moment

I call Information. A computer voice recites the drill, "What city and state?"

"Tongass, Alaska," I say, louder than necessary for voice recognition.

"What listing?" it drones.

"Mason . . ." I have actually forgotten Mason's last name. The computer waits. There is dead air. A real voice comes on the phone: a woman in a cranky mood.

"What listing?" she asks.

"Mason, um, just, can you hold a sec, I just need to run up to the closet."

"Ma'am?" she says.

"Yes," I say.

"Why don't you call back when you have the full name, just so we don't waste each other's time."

"Okie dokie," I say. Bet she always remembers Mother's Day. Why am I never on the ball? I put the phone back in its cradle and decide not to look for Mason's last name. I know he cannot be reached. He is in his cabin somewhere in the mountains. His oil lamp lit, his well-defined muscular body in boots and work pants, his feet up in a rocker, reading. I rummage in my raincoat for the plane ticket, inspect its crumpled markings. Departure. Destination. I imagine the plane landing. Me in that plane. I try to make it real, but it's a blur, too distant. Instead, I see city streets and fancy restaurants. My real life.

Treadmill

After three hours spent trying to locate the restaurant, I find it, then decide to hit the gym to relieve stress before mother and children descend. Pip enters the workout machine area during my cooldown.

She glides over in a thong leotard and tight black leggings. Thong-wearing must be encoded in Pip's DNA. I can't help but smile.

"Why the hell are you wearing a tracksuit? It's so damn grandma-looking," Pip says. "And why haven't you fucking called me?" She pauses. "You're pissed at me, aren't you, for hanging out with Henry?"

"No," I say, trying to sound casual.

"Yes, you sure as hell are. I don't see why, it's not like you were interested in him anymore after Mr. Alaska swooped in and—"

"I repeat: *I don't care that you're hanging out with Henry,*" I interrupt, in a less casual tone. Thank god everyone else in close proximity has earphones strapped to their heads. "Maybe if you hadn't ditched me in Back Bay and had given me your new *unlisted* telephone number I would have called you."

"Shit, I forgot to give you my new digits!" Pip says, slapping her forehead. "All this time I thought you were pissed at me for hanging out with Henry." She laughs and gets on a stationary bike. I get off the treadmill, far from cooled down, and go to the locker room. I don't care to hear *hanging out with Henry* one more time. I've heard enough.

Macro Moments

My mother is in a full Nepalese sari. I am horrified. The kids are equally disgusted with my prairie dress and muck boots. But still. I mean, really.

It takes forever to find a parking space. I slam into the bumper of the car behind me and park a foot and a half from the curb. Parallel parking is not my strength. We teeter out of the car and my mother walks about three feet before noticing that the sari has unraveled and is stuck in the car door. I see skin. More than I wish to see. She is still in the sixties mode of no underwear or bra. Lucy thinks this is hilarious. She skips around and laughs. My mother rewraps herself and I unlock the door.

"Not even a tear! It's beautiful *and* durable!" my mother exclaims. Lucy grabs her hand and they skip up the sidewalk. Brendan, too embarrassed to be seen with us, sits in the car. I tell him to roll down the window.

"You have to be nice to me! It's Mother's Day!" I hiss. He resentfully joins us, dragging his feet and slumping his shoulders until his head is almost touching his navel. Lucy and my mother skip past the restaurant. I whistle badly and they come back.

Inside, my mother is swept away by a hostess like Mother Mary herself. Turns out that a sari is an excellent choice for fine macrobiotic dining. The hostess seats my mother at the Lotus Table, a squat board on the floor with a bunch of cushions around it. Brendan finally relaxes, sensing that no one he knows is likely to see him with either me or my mother. He smiles and nods to the waitress, who is svelte and wearing false eyelashes. No bra. Not that she needs one. I try to sit with my muck boots on. No go. I take them off. A faint mildewy odor is released, since I never wear socks with them. The waitress, attentive to my mother's displeasure and her loud comment about mildew toxins, takes away the boots. My mother has assumed the lotus position and begins to chant in a tantric way. She is in her element, very in control. I marvel. She lights the incense on the table, pours us tea. I am upset I did not wear geisha threads and very pale foundation.

My mother orders for us. The waitress is delighted with our order and snaps her little book closed, beaming at my mother. I start tapping my chopstick on my teacup. Tap. Tap. Tap. Lucy follows suit. Tap. Tap. "Stop that this instant!" my mother bellows. Lucy and I stop mid-tap. The waitress turns. My mother smiles calmly and runs her hands over the tabletop. "I took some herbs this morning to balance my *pietà* energy. Maybe I antidoted too much and it has swung in the opposite direction," she says to the waitress. "Forgive me. I must talk to my Chinese herbalist."

The waitress smiles and nods. "I know what you mean," she says, "the same thing happened to me last week. Total unbalance. Awful energy rush from Vitex."

"That's what *I* am taking!" my mother squeals.

"Oh, my god, how weird!" the waitress says and bats her false eyelashes.

I wonder if maybe we should switch positions—she can take my place as daughter and I'll be the waitress. But then I would have to be nice to people like my mother, if I wanted tips. Would rather slit my wrists.

Therapist Thoughts

The kids are reading quietly in their rooms after our macrobiotic meal with no sugar. I take note and plan to hide all sugar products. I watch my favorite single-gals-in-city show in blissful peace. It is all about therapy. It makes me ache. I love therapy! Must find a new therapist immediately. I make another note in my new little pad with my new little pencil that hangs on a shoelace around my neck, the very thoughtful Mother's Day present Brendan gave me with the comment, "Now you have no excuse." I write in tiny letters: "therapist," underneath "no more sugar." The show has no commercials so I write it quickly.

Indifference

Demon Princess holds on to the back of my shirt as I try to gather stray socks and pack lunches. Each time I try to shed her, she screams and reattaches. The phone rings and Demon pulls me over to it so she can answer. It's for her. She lets go and chatters away in a giggly soprano. Brendan crunches his cereal louder. I drink more coffee. Demon hands me the phone and reattaches. It's Moonboy. He says "Happy Mother's Day" and then hands the phone to Henry.

"I'm sorry about your phone call yesterday, when Pip was at my house," Henry says gravely. I feel absolutely nothing at all so I say nothing. I am sure he is just making nice since Moonboy and Lucy have a playdate scheduled for today and he needs to work on his precious manuscript. "You have been such a wonderful asset to my son this year. He is so fond of you and your family and we really wanted to do something special in regards to Mother's Day—and then Pip stopped by." He stops, then adds, "I could tell that you were upset on the phone."

"I was not."

"But you were."

"Listen, Henry, if you want to keep chasing all these women who dislike children because of your own screwed-up mother issues, it's your problem, not mine."

"All these women? Screwed up mother issues? What in God's name are you talking about? You really must have a dismal perception of my character—"

"I'm in such a rush to get the kids out the door right now," I cut him off smoothly. "Can we talk another time?"

"No. I would rather we discuss this right now," Henry says, furious.

"Wonderful! All right, then. Talk to you later. Have a great day!" I bleat falsely and hang up. Must avoid that discussion at all costs, since I have no idea what I actually mean. I hastily stuff a peanut butter and banana sandwich in a baggy, gather speed, head out the door, dragging Demon behind me.

Brendan leaps into the driver's seat and starts the engine. I haul Demon into the backseat and sit next to her. I look like a very young Miss Daisy but with a bad attitude and no class.

Children have taken over self. Self is gone. Death music blares. I vow to find a new therapist. IMMEDIATELY.

• • •

A Good Find

There is only one therapist in the Cambridge yellow pages who has an opening for a new patient. The secretary asks me if I can come in at 11:00 today, as there has just been a cancellation. It is 10:32. I jump in the car and park downtown, still gripping the therapist's address, torn out of the phone book, and walk down the street, stopping and looking for the right building. Stop. Look. Stop. Look. I feel manic. Finally see it. A sign directs me to the fifth floor, where the elevator opens and an arrow points me to a reception room. The reception room is empty.

"Hello?" my voice echoes.

"Hello?" A female voice echoes back from behind one of the closed doors.

"Are you the therapist?" I ask.

"Of sorts," comes the voice.

"Does that mean of all sorts?" I ask, and hear her chuckle.

"My secretary took an early lunch. Have a seat. I'll be with you shortly. "

On an end table is a beautiful bowl, which I touch.

"From my trip to Japan this past fall." The therapist appears in the now open door of her office. She looks older than Grammy. She has thick, frizzy hair, which she wears in a bun. Her reading glasses hang from a chain. Her lips are painted mauve.

"I've never traveled anywhere. I'm terrified of flying."

She nods. "Come into my office, we need to do an intake form." The office has big windows, lots of light, loads of plants, vases of lilacs, roses, lavender, and daisies. Botanical photographs cover every inch of wall space. She pats the seat across from her by the windows. I sit. She holds up her pen, asks me the usual questions: married, divorced, children, and so on and so forth. As she is talking and writing, I notice our hands are the same size and shape. Our big toes graze the floor. Her eyes curve at the corners just like mine. And they are brown, like mine. I touch my face.

"We look the same," I say, the hairs on my neck rising.

"There *is* a similarity between us," she says, and stops writing. "I noticed that. Except that I am more than a lifetime older." She smiles warmly. "So now that we are done with the paperwork, tell me why you decided to seek therapy."

"I want to be invisible," I say.

"How come?"

"I suppose because it's better than if you're visible, and feel like no one ever really sees you at all."

"Do you really believe that no one has ever really seen you for whom and for what you are?"

"Yes."

"Even yourself?" she asks.

"I'm not counting myself," I say.

"But who else could?" she asks.

"There has to be someone other than yourself," I say.

"I don't agree," she says. "People might have an idea of who you might be, but they can't know the exact essence that makes up your entire being. They can only know aspects of it."

"What about a husband? Can't he ever really know his own wife?" I ask.

"That's exactly what I mean," she says.

"Well, what's the point of love and marriage, then, if it isn't to fully understand another person other than yourself, to be really seen by that other person?" I have slipped into a slightly argumentative tone.

"That's the mystery," she says.

I shake my head.

"For example, do you feel like you knew your husband?" she asks. Her eyes loom like moist globes, waiting.

"Yes," I answer, uncertainly.

"Think," she says gently. She taps her notepad with her pen.

"I thought I did," I say, sliding my ring up and down my finger.

"Exactly," she says. "That's different. Did he think he knew you?"

I recall how he used to gently tug on my T-shirt at night, waking me just enough to let me know he had come home, that he was there.

"Yes," I say quietly, all traces of defensiveness having melted away.

"Did he?" she asks.

I would lie there in the stillness, feeling the tug, pretending not to care.

"No," I say. After a moment of silence, I ask, "But what if you don't really know who you really are—or what it is that you want?"

She points to a photo on the wall of a bee gathering pollen from a flower and says, "Then you have to be both the bee *and* the flower." I look at her confused. She tries again.

"What do you like to do?"

"Well, I spend a lot of time in cafés drinking coffee," I say.

"That's a start. What else?"

"Sometimes I like to get biscotti or something to nibble on."

". . . and," she probes.

". . . and?" I respond, still confused.

"Any other interests?"

"What do you mean?"

"Like fishing, bird watching, drawing—those sorts of things," she says.

I stare at her blankly.

"If you would like to make another appointment, maybe we should come up with a list of things that you would like to accomplish, then."

"I love lists," I say, excited.

Post-Therapy

I am carrying a therapy-inspired to-do list and feel important. Why this is, I have no clue. I plan to make many lists in the coming days and weeks. Lists of lists. It's quite amazing that my therapist is on the same track as Brendan was when he gave me my little notebook necklace for Mother's Day. Hmmm.

I drive fast to Lucy's school. Important feelings cause lead foot on the accelerator and I arrive early and wait in the car for dismissal. I study my to-do list. I turn on the radio to a classical station and find I don't mind it too much. I cross out #10 on list: "Listen to something other than Dolly."

Lucy hops into the backseat.

"Ahoy!" I exclaim.

She shoots me a piercing look. Assessing. Judging. "You've changed," she says.

"How have I changed?" I ask.

"You're smiling," she says. She buckles her seatbelt and I pull away from the curb. I turn up the music and conduct as I drive. Cheesy, I know. But why not? Our eyes meet in the rearview mirror.

"I like you this way," Lucy says.

ten

A Week of Preparation

At breakfast I tell Lucy and Brendan I'm going to Alaska. It's #1 on my to-do list.

"Today?" Brendan asks.

"Of course not today!"

"I was just asking. How would I know?" he shrugs and pours his cereal.

"I wouldn't just leave on the same day I told you," I say. I think guiltily of the tickets in my raincoat pocket.

"When?" Brendan asks.

"In June," I answer.

"Cool," Brendan says, obviously thrilled to get rid of me. I look at Lucy. She has fallen asleep. Head on arm. Arm on table. Spoon in hand.

My Father

I call my father. He picks up midmessage. He screens his calls.

"Hello, pet," he coos.

"Hi, Daddy."

"What's my little girl up to today?" he asks.

"I have to go buy hiking stuff for Tongass."

"Tongass, Alaska?" he says, surprised.

"Yes," I say.

"Why on earth are you going there?"

"My boyfriend lives there," I say.

"When did you get a boyfriend?" he asks, sounding tickled.

"Around Christmas."

"And you didn't tell me? What does he look like?" he asks. "No, wait, don't tell me. Being an Alaskan native, he must be hairy and huge."

"He's not hairy. He is, however, a rather big and strong mountain-man type." I let a giggle escape.

"How is his brain? Functional?"

"Very. He's also well read," I say.

"A well-read Tongass native. Curious." He turns on the blender for a second. He always is turning the blender on and off while we're on the phone. Very rude. Very me. "Why doesn't he visit you? Forget I said that—with those hellish children of yours, it would send him packing."

His tone is gentle so I don't scream at him yet delight in responding, "He already has visited me here and he loved Lucy and Brendan." I'm exaggerating a tad bit, since Mason hung out with them for only one night when he came to visit.

"Some people are born tolerant," he says. "Yet, my pet, I do not see you hiking all over the tundra."

"How's your mental health?" I ask in a warning voice. I refuse to be terrified into staying within walls.

"My mental health? Why would it be anything but good?" he says. I don't press. Subject closed. He blends again.

"Daddy, I have to go," I yell over the sound of the blender.

"What?" he yells back.

"I have to go."

"Well, I'm not stopping you!" he yells, and hangs up.

Map

I've found a nice librarian, a volunteer named Phil, who has a sharp mind and takes slow steps. Just right. I show him my list, point to #2: "Study map of Tongass, Alaska."

"Follow me," he says. I like him immediately for not telling me to look it up on the reference computer. I get impatient with those things. Hate them, actually. Typically I meander and happen upon things. But not today. Today I am doing hard research and Phil is helping.

"Wonderful," I say. Phil leads me to the elevator and we go up to the second level. He bends down in front of a shelf of oversized books and grabs one. He moistens his fingertip. Love that. He finds the index and scans up and down, head cocked to one side, glasses down on the very tip of his nose. Suddenly he shakes his head, slams the book shut, and shoves it back on the shelf. He goes to another row and opens another thick book, finds what he's looking for and hands me the book, opened to a large map. He points to Tongass and slowly draws a circle with his finger, showing me the measure of the area. "It's expansive," he says, and gives the page a final tap. "All set?" he asks.

"I think so. Thank you," I say.

"You're welcome," he nods.

I go to a large table and sit down with several very academic-looking folks who have made the table their home. Papers and pens cover the surface. No one looks up at me. They are all deep in thought.

I examine the map. Imprint it in my memory. Its costal ridges, waterways, looming mountains. Somewhere in that forest is Mason. I kiss the map's cool, mildew-smelling paper. "Hi, baby," I breathe.

Camping Store

In the chain camping store in the heart of Harvard Square, I fondle the merchandise: headlamps like the ones miners wear, fluffy sleeping bags, soft little pillows that squish down to the size of a golf ball. My clogs make a big noise on the wood floors. I try to shuffle. No go. A salesman in a neon yellow fleece vest with the store logo on it races over and offers his help. I cannot take seriously men wearing vests if they are not fishing or working in a hardware store. Those are the only times when little vests work. As he approaches I come to a standstill, waiting for the vest to land. *Come on, just land,* I think. Instead he flutters around me. Maybe I am overreacting. No, the vest is ridiculous.

"What can I help you with today?" he says, all aflutter.

"Nothing really, I'm just looking," I say.

"Going on a trip?"

"Kind of," I say and try to walk away. Can't. Am trapped by fluttering vest.

"Canoeing, biking, hiking?" he asks. *Flutter, flutter, flutter.*

"A little of each, I guess," I say, squeezing and unsqueezing the pillow.

"Great! I have just the thing." He takes the pillow from my hands. "There's a sale on these great fanny packs."

"Oh?" I loathe fanny packs.

He leads me to the fanny packs and presents me with one that is large enough to hold a small child. He straps it around my waist. It is red. The buckle alone is a monster. "I don't know about the color," he says, grabbing a black one. "That's better," he says. "These things make everything so accessible. It's perfect on you. What do think? Can I ring it up for you now?"

I nod. Anything to be out of vest vision. He trots over to the register. I trot behind.

"OK, that's $103.78," he says firmly. Very cut-to-the-chase. I look at him and realize that the vest has its benefits. I take my miserable fanny pack and myself out the door.

• • •

Fanny Pack

I cut through Harvard Yard to find a used camping-goods store, which should certainly have backpacks cheaper than my fanny pack. I sip VitaWater with my newly freed-up hands. The fanny pack holds Dolly and the headphones snake out of the zip pouch. It also holds my very important list. I marvel at its true convenience. I'm in fanny-pack bliss when I scope out Henry crossing the green over to me.

"Wait!" he shouts and I stop. Henry is in disrepair. His hair sticks up all over the place. There is a big stain on his white shirt and his arms are a jumble of papers, cell phone, briefcase, and paper coffee cup. He really should get a fanny pack. It would do him a world of good, I think as he runs up to me panting. "I would like to have a word with you, please," Henry says, as if I am one of his students. This instantly puts me out of fanny-pack heaven.

"A word about what?" I ask.

"About our recent chat on the phone, about me chasing women—"

"But that was *over a week ago*," I interrupt. Groan. I thought I had safely avoided any "discussion" about it.

"But we haven't seen each other at all since that conversation, have we? It seems you've been hiding," Henry says, accusingly.

"I haven't been hiding. I've been busy."

"Busy doing what? Walking in a cloud, drinking assorted liquids, and buying whatever that *thing* is that you have attached to your person?"

I take a sip of VitaWater, unzip my fanny pack, take out my list. "Do you have a pen I can borrow?" I ask. Henry puts all his stuff on the ground, rummages in his briefcase, and then hands me a slightly chewed pencil. I cross out #3: "Drink something other than coffee."

I turn to Henry. "I've been preparing for my trip to Tongass—as in *Alaska*—to see Mason, for your information." I pat my fanny pack. "This is for day hiking." I wave my to-do list, fold it, and put it back in my fanny pack, along with Henry's pencil. "These are all the things I still need to do to get ready for my trip. It's called setting goals."

"Oh, I see," he sighs. "When are you leaving?"

"In June."

"A bit far off, isn't it, to be packing?"

"It's only three weeks away, and I'm *preparing,* not packing. Big difference," I correct him.

"Oh, I see. Very well, then, if you can't talk, I won't interfere with your *preparations,*" Henry says, picking up his briefcase and walking away from me.

"How's Pip?" I call after him, because I just can't resist.

"Why don't *you* ask her—she's your friend."

Boots

The used camping-gear store is small and filled to capacity. I can barely get around the goods. Used backpacks, tents, stoves, pots, pans, water filters, everything anyone would need. I stand in the middle of the store and tuck my hair behind my ears over and over. I take out my list and Henry's stolen pencil and cross out #4: "Stop twirling hair."

There are no salespeople, just oodles of stuff. On the counter is a big jar of lollipops and a can that reads, GOLDENSEAL POPS, 25 CENTS, then underneath in smaller letters, ALL PROCEEDS FROM LOLLIPOP SALES WILL GO TOWARD SAVING GOLDENSEAL. SAVE THE GOLDENSEAL! Had no idea Goldenseal was on the endangered species list. I grab a lollipop and deposit a quarter in the can.

Suddenly, an earthy woman emerges from the book section. Her arms are like barrels, her shoulders like a bull's. She has no neck. Or patience.

"Earl!" she yells. "Customer." Earl comes in from the back, taking his time. Clearly, the salt of the earth.

"What can I do you for?" Earl growls at me.

"I am going to Tongass and I need some gear." I unwrap the lollipop and suck. Earl looks me over carefully. His neck veins pulse.

"By yourself?" he rasps. "Or with a group?"

"With my boyfriend," I say. "He's a guide there."

"Sounds about right," Earl says with a laugh, hard and mean. He sizes up my thighs, breasts, and face. "I'll see what I have in your size." He pulls out lots of gear, creating a pile at my feet. There is a steel-framed backpack, a harness, and a helmet.

I stop sucking and ask, "What's the helmet for?"

"For your pretty little head," he snarls. I shut up. He hands me a book called *Wilderness Survival Guide*. "This is your bible," he says. He points to the steel-framed pack. "And this is your ark." I strap my ark onto my back. Rather, Earl straps the ark to my back, then unstraps it. He sits me down on the floor. "What's your shoe size?" he asks, removing my clogs.

"Five," I say, flexing my perfect toes. I feel all toe-proud as he examines my feet.

"Soft feet, you are going to have some big-ass blisters," he mumbles and disappears into the back, returning with a box marked Kids' Everest.

"I am *women's* size five," I say, jutting forth my chin.

"We have nothing that small in adult sizes, but these should work." The boots are dark pink leather. I raise my brow.

"I assume the color at least is to your liking," he says. He laces up the boots so tight I feel my circulation slow, but I'm afraid to breathe a word. He pulls me up to my feet and tests the fit with his thumb, then he straps the ark back on my back. "You should walk around in the boots with at least twenty pounds in your pack to get used to the pack and wear in the boots."

"What about the helmet?" I ask. He rolls his eyes and slams my clogs in the pack. I almost fall backward. He places my helmet in my hands. I put it on. He takes it off. I get the point. I'm not stupid.

Off the Beaten Path

I walk down the sidewalk, fanny pack in front, ark on my back, boots on my feet. People give me wide berth. I catch my reflection in a window. Love the ark. It is very un-citified. Thrilling. Can't wait to do this again tomorrow, and the next day and the next. Maybe I'll bring it to the gym and do the StairMaster. Surely that's close to real mountain climbing.

Later in the Day with Moonboy

When Lucy, Darling, and I arrive to pick up Moonboy, he is digging small tunnels in the lawn and pouring glasses of water into them. The water seeps into the earth. Lucy gives him a steely look and says, "That is the stupidest thing I've seen all day."

Moonboy shrugs and smiles and climbs into the car. His pants are mucky at the cuffs and I notice he is barefoot.

Queen Bean comes out onto the porch, brandishing Moonboy's worn-out sneakers. I tell Moonboy to jump out and get the sneakers. Sensing his reluctance, Lucy volunteers to go instead.

She hops up the walk.

Hop. Hop. Hop.

Darling barks from the car. Whines and wags his tail. He hates being left behind.

Queen Bean declares, "I can't stand children who hop!" The comment is directed at a large woman who is standing behind Queen Bean. The woman looks too terrified to answer but she nods. Lucy grabs the sneakers and accidentally hops on Queen Bean's foot. "Ow! You see that? That is why I hate hopping!" she screams. "You forgot the dog!" she reminds Lucy. Lucy hops over to the screen door and whistles loudly. Manic Dog smashes into the screen door, which Lucy opens, and he flies off the porch and runs over and puts his paws up on Darling's window. Both dogs bark excitedly as Lucy hops back to the car.

Hop. Hop. Hop.

"This is Maria," Queen Bean says, introducing the woman behind her. "She has taken over the housecleaning. It was an absolute disaster after you left us high and dry."

"I hope you're paying her a lot!" I yell out the window and we're off.

Lacrosse Game

We've arrived in time for the game. The fanny pack has done wonders for my organizational skills. I've even remembered my new folding chair that seats two. I drag the chair behind me because it is taller than I am. Lucy and Moonboy carry between them a cooler filled with ice and juice boxes. We pick a spot to settle in and unfold the large canvas loveseat. The cooler makes a great ottoman. The dogs are happy and content with their tennis balls and bowls of water. I think we look very well put together.

Brendan comes running over, all suited up in his bulky gear. The mouth guard is too cute. I beam and smile triumphantly. He whips off his helmet, puts it under his arm, and takes out his mouth guard. "Mom, you're on the wrong side," he says. "This is the away team's side."

I almost get up but think twice. My legs are tired from shopping for my own gear all day.

"Don't you play both sides of the field?" I ask. "Don't you switch?" He nods.

"Well, then won't everyone be moving over here eventually?"

He nods.

"Don't you play forward?"

He nods.

"Then I think we'll be just fine over here," I say. "We know what side we're on, so what does it matter?"

He shrugs. I cannot believe it is so easy. I whip out my list and check off "saying no." Then in parentheses, I add, "Almost."

Henry

Henry, still in his stained shirt, his briefcase beside him, plus books in a small stack, and a red pen behind ear, is sitting on his porch steps when we pull up to the house. He walks over to the car and peers inside, notices Lucy and Moonboy asleep, and opens the door quietly so as not to wake either of them. He disentangles Moonboy from the dogs and lacrosse equipment and lifts his son into his arms. I smile at the sight of such a large dark boy in Henry's lithe white arms. He shuts the car door with his hip, walks around to my driver's-side open window and whispers, "You're wrong about me, you know." He turns and carries Moonboy swiftly toward his house. I look over at Brendan, who is tapping his thigh to a tune on his iPod, then back toward Henry, holding Moonboy now in one arm, as he opens his screen door and Manic Dog skitters inside the house.

Ex-Rat

The doorbell rings at 10:30 on a school night. Ex-Rat stands outside full of rage.

"Do you know what time it is?" I ask.

"So when were you going to tell me?" he fumes.

"Tell you what?" I say.

"That you're going to fucking Alaska to see your goddamn boyfriend," he whispers. How thoughtful of him to spare the children's sleeping ears.

"You have them for summer vacation during that time anyway," I respond with forced nonchalance. Brendan must have let it slip that I was going. Now I can cross the last item out on this week's to-do list.

"That's up for debate. I have a big job coming up, and you didn't answer my damn question. When were you going to tell me?"

"I wasn't planning on telling you, because it is none of your business what I do with my free time," I say.

"All your time is fucking free time," he says. "I pay for it. I think I have a right to know that you're leaving the state on my dime."

Pure evil. I slam the door in his face and lock it. I wait for the pounding. It doesn't come. I peer through the peephole and see him driving away.

The phone starts ringing almost immediately. I let it ring. He doesn't leave a message.

eleven

A Week of Regression

I've put on pants for Sunday Mass. I adjust the belt and tuck in my shirt. I look like a miniature president of the United States. I head downstairs to make a fresh batch of iced tea. I wear the pants for exactly fifteen minutes, then reconsider, since it is sweltering out, already 89 degrees. I jet back upstairs and take them off, then cross off "wear pants" on my newest to-do list from latest therapy session. Not a worthy goal.

I regress and put on a frock. It's far too long, so I cut off six inches from the bottom and tape up the hem, then put on my clogs and fanny pack. Now I look like a nerdy Himalayan. I stuff all fanny-pack articles into my big straw tote. I fold up my raincoat, shove it under the bed, and put the muck boots in the closet, so as not to be tempted further. I inspect myself in the mirror. The straw tote transforms nerdy Himalayan into virtuous Swiss Miss. When I put my hair into braids for good measure, I'm pleased as punch. Surely my therapist would approve.

I fill my new travel mug with iced tea, toss my tote over my shoulder, and set off for church.

Rainbow Sherbet

As I round the corner near my favorite coffee shop, I sneak in and order a demitasse of coffee. I'm a list defiler, but it takes care of my need to feel shame at all times. I cross the street to the parish and sense someone following me. Look to and fro. No one. Continue onward. Sense it again. Stop. Look behind me. No one. Continue.

Stop and this time, turn quickly, and glimpse a head ducking back into the doorway of an ice cream shop up the street.

"I see you," I call.

Moonboy slinks out shyly. He is wearing shorts and no shirt. His chest is covered in rainbow sherbet.

"What are you doing here? What are you smiling about?" I say, and walk over to Moonboy.

"Where's your father?" I ask. He points in the direction of Harvard Yard. Maria, the new housecleaner, comes out of the ice cream shop. I'm instantly relieved. She hands me wet paper towels and I wipe off the sherbet. Moonboy is wearing sandals, and I can see that the toenails of his chubby feet are still painted black, thanks to Lucy, who after reading the first Lemony Snicket book is creating her own series of Unfortunate Events.

Sweat trickles down my back. Moonboy takes my hand and pulls me toward the entrance to Harvard Yard. I leave the thought of a peaceful, air-conditioned Mass behind and walk with him and Maria. Past Japanese tourists snapping pictures of their children rubbing John Harvard's shiny shoe. Past students studying on the grass. We exit the Yard by Cambridge Common, cross the muddled intersection, and enter the park. Once in the park, we stop. Moonboy beckons us to sit down in the grass and points to a small group of men dressed all in white. I spot Henry, tall and pale, holding a weird bat. A ball is pitched and Henry clocks it, causing a loud popping noise. He runs back and forth, his movement liquid—like a poem.

"What sport is this?" I ask.

"Cricket, it's an English sport." Maria explains.

"Oh, *hooow loooverly*!" I quip in an Eliza Doolittle English accent. Maria laughs. Moonboy scrambles onto my lap and I wrap my arms tight around him. I smell his hair—all earth and goodness, always.

"You take such good care of him," Maria says, pointing to Moonboy. "You must love him very much."

Luck

Henry mops his brow and I offer him a swig of my iced tea. "Thanks," he says, handing it back to me. He lies on his stomach and joins us in our four-leaf clover hunt. Maria finds one and hands it to Moonboy, who then hands it to me. Maria smiles, gets up, and brushes off. Henry, screening the bright sun with his hand, looks up at Maria. "Are you off?" he asks.

"Yes."

"Well, have a great day, then. Thanks for helping me out," Henry says. As Maria leaves, Moonboy bats the cricket ball like he is playing croquet and runs after it.

I can't stop myself from asking Henry, "So you have Maria doing the child care as well as the housecleaning now?"

"Only this once. She has children of her own and made it very clear she needs her weekends." I'm envious. Wish I was the sort of person who knew my own needs and could state them clearly. "So did you finish your long list of preparations for your trip to Alaska?"

"Yes. I'm onto my second list."

"There's a second list? Does it say to dress in overly adorable fashion and put your hair in braids?"

"No." I blush.

"It should," Henry says. I accidentally drop my four-leaf clover in the grass and desperately search the area. Henry helps. He finds it, plucks it out of the verdant lawn, and keeps it.

"Hey! Your son gave that to me. It's good luck," I say.

"It's mine now. Finders, keepers, etc.," Henry says, grinning. I try to grab it. He holds his hand up high, then gets up, snatches my straw bag as well, and runs across the park. Moonboy sees our new game and joins my team. We both chase after Henry. We reach the baseball diamond and lose our breath. Henry prances around us in his cricket whites. He opens my purse and snoops. "Ah, a dainty hanky fringed in lace. Just the ticket." He pretends to wipe his forehead; I recover my breath and tackle him, pinning down his arms. He relinquishes my hanky and purse but still holds tight to the clover. I can't unfurl his fingers.

"Tell me you're sorry for saying all those nasty things on the phone and I'll give you your clover back," Henry says, very serious.

"What things?" I play, innocent, knowing he is still sore about my "chasing women who dislike children" quip.

"You know exactly what things. They were mean and horrible—and absolutely false."

"OK, OK, I'm sorry."

"Truce?"

"Truce."

"Look at your charming dress! It's all dirty!" Henry exclaims. I release his arms and look at my frock.

Henry eats the clover.

"You ate my luck!" I gasp.

"I have to say, as far as luck goes, yours is quite tasty," Henry says, and Moonboy collapses on top of us in a fit of giggles.

A Run-in with Pip

"Isn't this a quaint picture," Pip says, as she walks over to Moonboy, Henry, and me. We are batting around the cricket ball. "Hey, Henry, I stopped by your house this morning and Maria told me I could find you here playing in a cricket match."

"It ended a while ago. I was just showing my newest fan a few sports moves," Henry says, nodding toward me.

"Isn't that sweet!" Pip says, unnerved. I begin hair twirling but catch myself immediately.

"I was just about to leave," I say quickly and grab my straw purse off the ground.

"Oh, don't leave on my account," Pip says evenly to me.

"No, no. I have to get back home. The kids are being dropped off soon." I say good-bye and start walking out of the park. Henry calls after me. I don't turn around, though.

"Hold up!" Henry says, now right behind me. "You forgot this." He presents my hanky. I see Pip and Moonboy waiting in the distance. "Pip and I are just friends. That's all." He looks at me sincerely.

"I think you should tell *her* that. Not me," I say, and rush out of the park, forgetting my hanky.

Confrontation

I'm loaded with gear and climbing what certainly must be Everest. I am on the StairMaster. My legs are not long enough. One pedal goes way down and thumps on the floor, the other goes way up. I feel like I'm plunging into quicksand and am all contorted when Pip bustles in. She is wearing a T-shirt that covers her breasts and tummy, and her legs are even covered, too. I am so surprised that my hands release from the support bars and I tumble off. "Are you *sure* you're not interested in Henry?" Pip asks, as if we have been talking for hours. I climb back on the machine and switch the program to desert mode. Much better.

"What are you talking about?"

"I'm talking about that little powwow in the park. It looked like you three were having a family outing," Pip says.

"I just bumped into Maria and Henry's son on my way to church. It wasn't planned."

"*Right*," Pip says. I stop treading, letting the pedals sink down and hit the ground. My feet feel rubbed raw.

"I'm not interested in Henry," I say.

"Then stop running around taking care of his son and dog," Pip says, following me toward the locker room. Automatically, I think of Moonboy.

"No," I say.

"No?" Pip asks, shocked.

"No," I repeat.

"Why not?" Pip says. "I would do it for you." There is truth in this.

"Pip, this is bigger than you or me or Henry. His son needs Lucy, he needs us—me, whatever—he lost his mother—don't you understand?"

"I lost my mother when I was around his age, and I'm fine," Pip says. Her face snaps shut.

"No you're not, Pip," I say gently.

"And you are? At least I finished college and have a career."

"I have a job. I'm a wife and—" I falter.

"You are no longer a wife," Pip reminds me.

I open and close my mouth, confused by my own mistake.

"That's it, isn't it?" Pip says. "I get it now. I get it. Now that you're divorced and you finally have the chance to do something other than be a wife, you don't. You can't even imagine something else. Or who you were before. Can you? That's why you don't take off that ring, isn't it? Isn't it?"

"I meant I am a mother."

"Wife, mother—it's the same thing, an excuse to hide behind. You gave up a full scholarship to college, a full scholarship! To marry that asshole of an ex-husband and all he did was cheat on you over and over while I watched and waited for you to leave. But you never did. He had to leave *you*! When is it your turn, huh? When are you going to wake up and realize you deserve a life for yourself, without a man to tell you who you are? Now you want Henry because Mr. Fucking Alaska lives too far away to be husband material."

I feel her breath on my cheek. We are that close. If I could concentrate on something, it would be Pip's chin. She has a beautiful, strong chin. But her words unravel me. I look away. I watch the people running on treadmills. Patting their faces with towels. Running, running. Going nowhere at all.

Tubbie

Band-Aids float to the surface of the tub. My feet are now riddled with blisters of every shape and size. I think about what Pip said in the gym and I think about college, my one year, when I was so focused on becoming a kindergarten teacher. I remember how, between classes, I used to ride around campus really fast on my three-speed bike because I loved the feeling of wind in my hair. And how Pip use to pore over two-bedroom apartment listings in the *Boston Globe* and I would study the Sears catalog and make an elaborate detailed list of what we would need for our new pad once we were moved out of the dorm. We didn't consider our differences then—Pip's Bette Midler–meets–Howard Stern personality versus my Betty Crocker–meets–Dr. Seuss mentality. We just knew we could tell each other anything.

I've never really thought about how abandoned Pip must have felt when I called her up that summer before our sophomore year and asked her to be the maid of honor at my wedding. Even though I knew Pip thought James wasn't the right guy for me, I'm just now remembering she had said only, "I'm not wearing anything fucking peach or that has any big-ass bows on it."

I scoop out the Band-Aids, place them neatly on the side of the tub, and climb out of the bath carefully. In my robe, with socks pulled over my blistered feet, I go into the closet and search through boxes of baby clothes, finger paintings, old journals. And then I find it, mixed in a box of old pens and papers from college, in between badly written poetry and doodles on papers: an old photo that my mother took of Pip and me. It was the day she dropped me off at college to start my freshman year. In the picture, Pip and I are in our dorm room, goofy faces filled with laughter, arms thrown around each other's shoulders—friends at first sight.

An Awakening

My mother calls to tell me she is having a Memorial Day barbecue at her house next weekend. I shiver at the thought of barbecued tofu and my extended family's reaction.

"Do you realize it's five in the morning?" I ask.

She says, "I wanted to call you before I forgot," and hangs up.

I curse her, then cross myself. Now fully awake and fully aware of the throbbing in blistered agony of my feet, I move them delicately so as to avoid the pain of the sheets against my blisters. The blisters seem to have grown during the night. I must stay in bed all day. The thought is comforting since I have nothing else to do. I hobble downstairs to the kitchen to feed Darling, who will not eat because it's too early. I urge him out into the yard but he won't go. He runs in circles around me, stepping on my bunny-slipper-clad blistered feet, and I yelp. I grab his leash and totter out the front door. Thank god no one is out and about, since I am wearing an old "Baby on Board!" T-shirt my aunts gave me when I was pregnant with Brendan. It is size XXL and is threadbare and completely comfy. My fave.

Darling sniffs garbage bags, runs up and down the neighbors' steps, and finally poops by a small tree. I am bending over to scoop up Darling's mess when Henry jogs by.

"What are you doing over on this side of town so early in the morning?" I ask accusingly, poop bag in hand.

"This is my new loop," he says, breathing hard. He jogs in place.

"New?" I ask.

"Yes, in hopes of seeing you in your oversized nightie with your doggie bag, so I can give you this." He holds out my hanky. He has a ridiculous bandanna on his head.

I wobble back toward the house. He jogs next to me.

"You're walking as though you're in pain."

"That's because I am," I say, trying to tiptoe.

"Let me look," he says.

"Thanks, but I'd rather you didn't," I say severely.

"Is it infected?"

"No," I say.

"Just let me have a look. I'm a doctor," he says.

"You are not!"

"You're right, I'm not a doctor," he says. "Now sit." I obey and let him take off my slipper, slowly, delicately.

"This could actually become quite serious," he says. I see that he isn't kidding. "You should avoid walking, in case the blisters rupture, like this one." He points to a menacing one on my heel. "The liquid actually prevents infection. How did you manage to do this to yourself?" he asks, removing my other slipper. Again slowly, delicately.

"I'm trying to break in my new hiking boots for my trip to Tongass," I say, blushing bright red in total foot-humility. Henry frowns, then shakes his head.

"Give me your house key," he says.

"Why?" I am wary.

"Come on. I'll let the dog in and then come back for you," he says, like he's some kind of firefighter.

"Look, I'll be fine," I say, my resolve weakening. I've always wanted to be rescued by a firefighter, and Henry really looks the part.

"It's only up the steps," he says, holding out his hand.

"I didn't bring a key. It's not locked," I admit.

He leads Darling inside and comes back. He lifts me up, carries me across the threshold, and then goes to the kitchen, where he takes me over to the garbage so I can deposit the poop bag, then over to the sink so I can rinse my hands next, and then up to my bedroom, where he gently places me down on the bed.

"That's one way to get you in bed," he says.

"Mmmm," I say. Then I suddenly remember Moonboy and sit up, "Who's watching your son?"

"He's staying with his grandparents at the Four Seasons; they flew in yesterday afternoon from Philadelphia."

"Oh, that's right," I say, lying back down. I had overheard Moonboy telling Lucy about his mother's parents coming.

"Speaking of children, where are Brendan and Lucy, are they sleeping? Don't they usually come back on Sunday?"

"James had to work late on Friday, so he took them on Sunday instead and they slept there," I explain. "I have to pick them up later, though, after school."

"Then there's nothing stopping us from hanging out most of the day. We've never really had the chance to do that. You know? And the kids hang out all the time." His face brightens, "How about I go rent us a couple of movies and get some snacks?"

"I have a boyfriend," I say, out of my own need to convince myself of the fact. Right now—with Henry sitting on the edge of my bed—the thought of us innocently chomping bonbons and watching a few films together is the last thing on my mind.

"So? It's just hanging out and watching movies. Besides, after giving it a great deal of thought I've come to the conclusion—and I say this as a friend—your boyfriend is all the way in Alaska and the relationship is not sustainable. Long-distance relationships never are. It won't last. Trust me. You'll visit him, it will be great for a few days, until you realize he isn't ever going to live here and you can never live there. It just doesn't work. It comes down to geography."

"You don't know that," I say, suddenly exceedingly confident I have a boyfriend since Henry used the *friend* word instead of climbing under the sheets with me. "In fact, after giving it a great deal of thought, I think we really love each other."

"You don't even know each other!" He almost laughs.

"I know Mason," I say, with a lot less bravado. I twirl my hair.

"I don't believe you. I think you have created a character. Pure fantasy. Because the reality of the situation dictates that there is no future for you two. He lives in the wilderness and you live in the city." Henry points to my ring. "For Christ's sake, you're still wearing your wedding ring! Doesn't that say something to you? Perhaps you aren't ready. Perhaps—"

"Don't say 'Christ's sake,'" I interrupt, and he grins.

"I'm warm, aren't I? Maybe even hot?"

"Just because I'm wearing my wedding ring does not mean I am not ready for a relationship," I say. Henry raises his eyebrows. "I'll take it off. See." I slap my wedding ring on the bedside table.

His expression doesn't change. "It still doesn't alter the fact that your life is here and his life is—" he pauses. "Is that you and Pip?" he asks, pointing to the photograph on the table next to my ring.

"Uh-huh. It was taken our first day in college." I hold my tongue for a tenth of a second and then out it comes, "By the way, where is your friend Pip?" The truth is I haven't been thinking about Pip and I should be. I gave her my word that I wasn't interested in Henry.

"Not this again," Henry sighs. "I have to run home and take a shower. I'll be back with the movies. OK?"

"OK." I watch as he leaves the bedroom, then I slip the ring back on.

Morning Nap

I maneuver my way downstairs to the couch and put my feet up and the blanket over my head. As I wait for Henry to return with the movies, I listen to the morning begin: car engines start, doors open and close, garbage trucks beep, my newspaper comes through the mail slot. My body loosens . . .

Cheese Danish

I wake in a darkened living room. The curtains have been drawn. The air conditioner is turned on. Another blanket has been placed over me. A pillow is under my head. On the coffee table is a cheese danish and a latte. I smell almond.

He remembered.

I call out but Henry doesn't respond. Darling pads over, licks my face. I reach for the latte, which is lukewarm.

I limp into the kitchen, then upstairs. The bed is rumpled. A stack of movies are on the bedside table. And a note with only one word: "Enjoy."

Want of Henry

There's a tightness in my chest. I take short and quick breaths. Like steps. One, two, three. Going up. Up to his steps. Up his steps. To his doorbell. Ding dong. No answer. I stand outside in my sandals, toes bandaged. I ring again. Ding dong. No one's home. Back down the steps. The tightness in my chest increases even as I pick up the kids from school.

Waiting

I am too frenzied about Henry to think straight. Brendan takes advantage by inviting Sophie over—on a school night!—and ordering five pizzas. As soon as she and the pizzas arrive, Brendan tries to lead her and all five pies up the stairs.

"Where do you think you're going?" I ask Brendan.

"Upstairs to my room to do homework," Brendan says, without batting an eye.

"I don't think so, Mister." I'm not *that* out of it.

Sophie and Brendan recline on the couch without a textbook or mathematical equation between them. There are half-full pizza boxes splayed all over the monstrous coffee table and MTV's *Real World* is on the boob tube. Lucy runs into the living room and shoots spitballs at the teenage lovebirds and then runs out. For Sophie's benefit, Brendan pretends to be amused by his little sister's antics. I'm keeping a watchful eye on them, or really just distractedly peeking in on them because I keep checking out the foyer window every time a car goes by—it could be Henry. I need to get out of the house or I will start climbing the walls. I ask Sophie and the kids if they would like to go out for ice cream and a movie. Lucy jumps for ice cream and Brendan jumps for a dark movie theater. Sophie says, "I have to ask my mom, she usually doesn't let me stay out past nine on weeknights, you know, because of school."

Sustenance

Just as we are about to leave, the doorbell rings. When I open the door, Manic Dog flies into the house and finds Darling. Henry and Moonboy stand holding take-out bags from an Indian restaurant in his neighborhood. Henry cocks his head, grins, and says, "Hi."

"Hi," I say, taking the bag of food from Moonboy's outstretched hands.

"I brought dinner," Henry says. "Thought you could use more sustenance than a cheese danish." I hear Brendan and Sophie titter behind me as Lucy squeezes past and tackles Moonboy.

Movie

Henry flips up the jump seat in the back of my Volvo and we all pile into the car. I drive, despite the pain. Brendan is furious because he is not in the driver's seat, and I tell him he can skip the movie if he wants. He slams the backseat passenger side door. In the rear-view mirror I see Lucy take aim with her spitball straw and a little white piece of chewed up paper flies out, landing in Brendan's hair.

"Cut it out, you brat! I mean it!" Brendan screams at Lucy. I'm relieved Brendan is being a bit more real in front of Sophie—if she sees him for who he really is, perhaps she'll stop sucking on his neck with such fervor. Then I notice Sophie smile and quickly peck Brendan on the cheek, and there goes that happy thought.

We pay ten dollars to park three blocks from the theater and are late for the first showing of the dumb action thriller. During the movie, my feet start to throb. "My feet really hurt," I whisper to Henry.

"Let's go have a look." Henry takes my hand and leads me to a bench by the concession stand. He peeks under my socks. "I think we should have them looked at," he says, with huge concern.

Emergency Room

Ex-Rat cannot be reached; I've been trying him for over an hour. Henry volunteers to chaperone Brendan driving Sophie home. Lucy raids vending machines and Moonboy watches TV with me from the waiting room's hard orange seats. Henry returns with a hickey-free Brendan in tow. I give Henry a thumbs up for being an A-class hanky-panky protector.

It's almost eleven at night when my name is finally called. Henry helps me over to the nurses' station. "So you have some blisters, I hear," the nurse says, rolling down my socks. "Those do look bad. You have a bit of a line running up your leg." She clucks and then points, "You see, here. We'll take you back into a room and have the doctor take a look at that."

"I'll go tell the kids to stay in the waiting room until the doctor has had a chance to see you. I'll be right back," Henry says, as the nurse wheels me into a room. She tells me to hop up on the bed. I lie down in fetal position, with my knees tucked up to my chin. Feels good. I close my eyes. Even better.

Henry's Ex-Girlfriend

The doctor walks in. She grabs the clipboard off the wall, snaps open her pen, and looks at her beeper. She is the very idea of precision and importance. I feel trivial just looking at her.

"Hi, Kate," says Henry, who's just returned from the waiting room. When he says her name I somehow know that this power-house of a woman is Henry's ex-girlfriend. My only way out of this wretched situation is immediate sedation.

"Henry." She nods but doesn't smile.

She walks over to me in quick steps, flashing a light in my eyes, opening my mouth, checking my feet and running a black marker across my leg to show where the red line caused by an infected blister ends. It reminds me of when I used to let Lucy draw on me. She was about one, plump and still nursing. She would draw with washable marker up and down my legs and arms, with the same determined look that Henry's ex-girlfriend has now.

"What's her temp?" Henry's ex-girlfriend asks the nurse.

"Normal."

"Good." With her cool hands, she feels the glands in my groin, armpits and then my neck. Henry's ex-girlfriend looks at me, but she reveals nothing.

Henry and Children

Ex-Rat is still nowhere to be found. Lucy jumps on my bed, almost toppling over my antibiotic IV. Henry and his ex-girlfriend speak about the weather. The kids finally sit, squeezing into the only chair in the room. I can tell they are overtired. Brendan looms over the head of the bed, arms held tight against his chest, except when he occasionally bites his nails.

"You should take them home to my house or your house, so they can sleep," I say to Henry.

"I can watch Lucy," Brendan says.

I shake my head. I can't stand the thought of my kids being alone in the house for possibly all night.

"But who will stay with you, then?" Henry asks.

"Call Pip," I say. She's the only one I can think of.

"Are you sure the kids will be all right with Pip for the night?"

"No, you put the kids to bed and Pip will stay with me," I say.

"Right," Henry says, embarrassed but still reluctant. "It probably would be better for them—it's been a long night."

"I don't want to go home," Lucy says.

"Let's go, Lucy," Brendan says sternly. He turns to Henry, "I think we should go to our house, because of the dogs. They've probably torn up the whole house by now."

"Oh, god," I groan. "I forgot about the dogs!"

"Right, all right, I'll call Pip." Henry says. He rounds up the children. They kiss me. Moonboy hugs me tightly, so tightly I gasp.

After they've all left, the emptiness disturbs me. Henry pops back in. "Pip is on her way." He tucks a stray piece of hair behind my ear and kisses my forehead. "Well, OK then, see you when you get home."

Pip Arrives

I hear the *flap-flap* of Pip's thong sandals in the hall. She scopes out the room. Sunglasses up. "I guess a bender is out of the question," she smirks. I smile meekly. "I'm sorry I was such a dumb-ass," she says, and her eyes fill with tears.

"It's all right," I say. We hug, wrapping our arms through all the tubes.

Questions

Pip runs out to the soda machine for a Diet Coke. Henry's ex-girlfriend, my doctor, comes back into the room to check on the red line running up my leg.

"Good. It's going down. The antibiotics seem to be working." She marks my leg again, this time further down the calf, and caps the black marker. "How is it that you know Henry?" she asks.

Bile rises to my throat. "I used to clean his house and walk the dog." I hate myself as soon as I say it.

"Yes, I remember him mentioning someone doing that. Did you take care of his son as well?" she pries, digging her hands into my glands.

"Not anymore," I mumble. "Now he just comes for playdates with my daughter."

"Is that right," she says, deadpan.

Home

At almost 2:00 a.m., Pip drops me off at my house. Ex-Rat's car is parked in the driveway. Henry's is gone. I give Pip a quick hug, put her unlisted phone number in my pocket, and gingerly walk up the steps as fast as I am able. The house is quiet. The light is on in the kitchen. I open the kitchen door. Ex-Rat sits at the table.

"What are you doing here?" I look around desperately. "Where's Henry?"

"He went home," Ex-Rat says, self-satisfied.

"Why?" I ask. "What did you say to him?"

"Stuff," Ex-Rat says.

"What stuff?" I ask.

"You know—*stuff*."

"What did you say to Henry?" I say, my voice rising.

"Keep it down, you'll wake the kids. I told Henry about you and me, you know, what happened over Christmas—how we slept—"

"You didn't," I interrupt. I touch my forehead, remembering Henry's kiss.

"Come on. You're not fooling anyone. This whole Mason thing is just to get back at me," Ex-Rat says, and I can see he believes it. "Haven't you proved your point? I get it already."

Sedation

"What are you doing, Mommy?" Lucy asks sleepily, standing at the threshold of the closet door, looking in.

"Did you have a bad dream, Lucy?" I tiptoe over to her, brush back her hair. She nods and I take her hand and lead her to her bedroom. She gets into her bed. I fold the covers over her then kiss her on her flushed cheek. I shut off the light and rub her back. When I think she's back to sleep, I begin to make my way out of her bedroom.

"Mommy!" she yells.

I freeze.

"What, bug?"

"Don't go back in the closet. I don't like you in there."

Pip's Gift

The kids finish eating breakfast and take their dishes to the sink without being prompted, then disappear out the door when they hear Ex-Rat honk his horn to take them to school. The phone rings and I hobble quickly over, hoping it is Henry.

"I'm coming over," Pip says and hangs up.

As I place the phone back on the receiver the doorbell rings, and I yell, "It's open!"

Pip comes into the kitchen carrying an assortment of black shopping bags with gold lettering. "I bought you some necessities for your trip. I thought, even though I'm not getting laid, I figured I could at least shop like I was. Open them," Pip says, putting the bags down in front of me. In the first bag is a black lacy slut suit with a matching thong. "It has a built-in padded bra so your tits look bigger. Open the other one." More thongs.

"Pip, you didn't have to do this—"

Pip interrupts. "No, I wanted to. I feel like such a bitch. Here I was thinking the whole time that Henry was into you and it turns out he was trying to get back together with his girlfriend."

"What?" I ask.

"Henry is back with his girlfriend. His mother informed me this morning," Pip says.

"You can close your mouth now." I close my mouth and place the undergarments back in their bags. Pip takes out a fresh pack of cigarettes and a new lighter.

"I thought you quit," I say distractedly.

"Well, it looks like I started again, doesn't it?" Pip says, getting up and going out on my back porch to smoke.

Memorial Day BBQ

Uncomfortable with our estrogen-beset Memorial Fest, Grampa, Cain, and my brother have disappeared in search of beer. Grammy crochets. My brother's girlfriend shuffles cards. Stoned Trollop Wife takes out her Mary Kay demo kit and prepares personal trays for our facials. Margo and the aunts paint their nails. Even outdoors, where we are, the smell is lethal. My mother is having trouble lighting the organic, nontoxic, all-natural BBQ bricks that look like Dead Sea sponges.

"Why don't you throw a little of this on it?" Aunt Mary says, holding up a bottle of nail polish remover. My mother goes into the garage, comes back out with a small torch, and tries to light them once more. I lie on a blanket with my still-tender feet splayed out in front of me. Between the scent of whatever it is that my mother is trying to burn and the nail polish remover, I have lost my appetite. I get up, limp toward the far corner of the yard, and dump my watermelon in the compost, then limp back.

"All because of some blisters. I never," Grammy grumbles.

"Better be healed before you get on that plane to go visit Mason," Aunt Mary says, blowing on her nails. Aunt Eve nods.

"She's not leaving for another two weeks. Her feet will be fine by then," my mother says, fanning a tiny ember.

"How you managed to get that many blisters in the first place is what I'd like to know," Grammy says, putting down her crochet needles.

"I was trying to break in my boots," I explain.

"It seems like you are trying to break something else as well," Grammy says under her breath.

"What is that supposed to mean?" Aunt Mary asks, holding the nail polish wand above her pinky. My brother's girlfriend stops playing solitaire and looks up.

"She's flying all the way to Alaska to visit a man she hasn't seen since Christmas is all I'm saying. How does she know what's waiting for her?" Grammy says and returns to crocheting, needles flying furiously now. "It's foolishness. If you're going to go about this dating business, why don't you date a nice fellow nearby? At least you wouldn't be covered in blisters, have to hop on a plane when we all know you're scared to death of flying, and you'd know what you're in for."

I look down. Grammy's right. I am terrified of flying, have been since I was a child. Derek has suggested loads of times that I fly with him on some of his shorter commuter flights to help me deal with this, and have I? No. Even having a pilot for a brother, I've never faced this fear.

"Don't listen to her. She's just trying to ruin your fun, as always. God forbid anyone has any happiness," Aunt Mary says to me.

"You see, that's the problem with you young folks today, it is all about fun, until you get your heart broken," Grammy says.

"Her heart's already broken!" my mother says.

"What is that supposed to mean?" Grammy snaps.

"James broke her heart a long time ago. Now she's *trying to mend it*." My mother defends me. For this, I love her past reckoning. She is once again the mother of my childhood, secure, loving, and wise. The aunts nod in affirmation.

"Well, what about that man with the boy you take care of? The one who was at your house this past Christmas. He seemed very nice, and he doesn't live in Alaska. What's his name?" Grammy asks.

"Henry," I tell her miserably.

"Yes, Henry. What about him?"

"He got back together with his girlfriend," I say, starting to cry.

"You see what you did? Are you proud of yourself?" Aunt Mary says to Grammy.

"Anyone for a facial?" Stoned Trollop Wife intervenes. The aunts and Margo screw the caps back on their nail polish. My mother stops fanning the ember. Grammy puts away her crochet project. My brother's girlfriend packs up her cards. I wipe my eyes. And we all have our facials.

Mason Calls

Back home, the kids are stuffed and sleeping. I mark my page in *Fear of Flying* (which my mother has insisted I read) and shut off the light. I close my eyes and visualize Henry and his girlfriend back together. They're in his bed, both wearing reading glasses. Henry's hand holds a chewed pencil over a crossword puzzle. "What is a five-letter word for a myopic nerve, last letter ending in *x*?" he asks her, and she knows it—of course she does, she's a doctor.

I roll onto my stomach and put the pillow over my head. The phone rings. My head still under the pillow, I locate the receiver with my fingers, then pull it under and place it to my ear. "Hi," comes a distant voice that I don't recognize.

"Who is this?" I ask.

"Mason," he says.

"Mason?"

"Yes," he says.

"It's so good to hear your voice," I say, although somehow it isn't.

"Are you still coming to visit?" he asks.

"Oh, yes!" I say, my voice high and false.

"Thank god," Mason releases his breath, "I thought you might not—"

The phone goes dead, cutting him off midsentence.

twelve

A Week of Traveling

Ex-Rat pulls into the driveway. I yank open the front door and yell, "You're late! I'll miss my plane!"

"Relax. You have over three hours until your plane leaves. That's if you even board it. I have my doubts." He looks up at the roof. "With all your newfound independence, did you perchance call the roofing company?"

"Yes."

"No, you didn't," he says, looking me over. He sees: my newly broken-in boots; my monstrous fanny pack; my enormous back-pack, with sleeping bag dangling off the bottom; my ringless finger. "When are you going to stop this charade? You look ridiculous." I know this to be true. I'm not a mountain woman. I am a homeless dwarf. Or worse—a child playing make-believe.

Taxi

When the taxi arrives, the kids are playing Sims Online and barely say good-bye. Ex-Rat is sipping a cup of coffee, his feet up on the ottoman. He has reclaimed his throne. I curse myself for suggesting he stay here so I didn't have to kennel Darling. The taxi horn blares.

"Just go," Ex-Rat says, noting my hesitance. "See you in about an hour, or however long it takes to go to the airport and come right back home."

I yell good-bye to the kids once more but don't get even a grunt in return. I teeter out the door, feeling beyond rejected, and wedge myself in the cab, which smells like disinfectant mixed with piss. Attached to my backpack, sitting sideways on the seat, sleeping bag under my butt, I try to find a comfortable position while the cabbie pulls away and barrels down the road at 100 miles per hour. I cannot fasten my seatbelt, so I lie down atop my backpack. I don't visualize what will happen if we crash.

The cabbie comes to an overzealous halt at the airport and my body is flung forward. I am now stuck between the front and back seats. Really stuck. I whimper. I try to remember survival skills from the wilderness handbook. An image of a climber trapped in an ice vortex comes to mind, and bits of wording: Don't panic. Don't move.

Check-In

"The sleeping bag is going to have to be put in the knapsack, Ma'am," the check-in person says listlessly. She checks her watch. I look at my pack, which is already stuffed to the brim.

"You're joking, right?" I ask.

"Wish I was, Ma'am. Regulations," she sighs.

I open my pack and try to stuff in my sleeping bag. Makeup, thong panties, a bikini, and padded lacy bras pop out and spill all over the floor.

"I am going to Alaska to visit my boyfriend," I say, loud enough for all to hear so I won't be pegged as a hopeful hussy with frilly undergarments and no man.

Emergency Phone Call

I shove two quarters into the pay-phone change slot and dial my father's number. I know he'll let me off the hook since he's even more terrified of flying than I am. When he picks up the phone, I cry, "Daddy!" and immediately burst into tears.

"*Sweetie?* Is this you?" he says.

"I'm at the airport . . . I can't do this . . . I just can't . . . I can't get on the plane . . . I can't fly . . . I can't get on the plane!" I say, like the hysteric I am.

"Sweetie, slow down and take a deep breath," my father says calmly. I take a tiny gasp of air. Then he says, "Now, tell me what's wrong."

I tell him everything. I tell him about how Henry is back with his girlfriend. I tell him about what Grammy said to me at Mom's Memorial Day BBQ. I tell him about Mason calling and how I didn't feel excited. I tell him how the kids barely said two words to me before I left the house. I go on and on. My father doesn't interrupt or turn on the blender like he usually does. He just listens.

When my sobs subside, I say quietly, "James was right, I can't fly, I'm not going to even board the plane. I'm never going to hear the end of this one."

I expect my father to say something to soothe me about going back home and facing Ex-Rat. Instead, he says, in a firm and clear tone, "Then why don't you prove him wrong?"

"What?" I cannot believe he is not letting me off the hook!

"I said, *Why don't you prove your ex-husband wrong?* You're a lot tougher than you think."

"I am?" I ask.

"You're at the airport, aren't you?"

"Yes . . . ," I say, looking around at the vast ceilings and the people rushing to departure gates.

"Well, that's a lot more than I could do. I'm proud of you. Now, just hang up the phone, put one foot in front of the other, and board the plane."

"Is this something you heard on Dr. Phil?" I ask.

"Sweetie, I'm hanging up now. I know you can do this," he says, and I hear a click.

Runway

I boarded the plane to prove Ex-Rat wrong.

The flight attendant stands in front of me while a chipper re-corded voice comes from the cabin speaker about oxygen masks. The attendant identifies the emergency exit, the flotation cushions beneath our seats, the no smoking signs, and then sits down in a seat facing us and buckles her own seatbelt. The engine gives a high whine as the plane gathers speed down the runway. I do eight Hail Marys and cross myself numerous times. I think of Brendan and Lucy and Ex-Rat gleefully hearing the news that I actually got up in the air—finally, unfettered hours of computer games and an un-challenged throne! It is everything for me not to scream for them to stop the plane at once.

Luckily, I have an unholy terror of embarrassing myself and look-ing like an idiot. I would rather die.

"My arm," the elderly man next to me says, pointing.

"Oh, so sorry!" I say, releasing my grip on his forearm.

Little Bottles

By the time the flight attendant is carting little bottles of divine grace down the aisle, I have returned to my normal, merely high-grade anxiety. I zip open my fanny pack, grab gum and a lollipop, take my raincoat down from the overhead compartment, and put it on before she reaches me. I order two drinks. For me and me.

"It's my first time flying alone," I explain. She nods in understand-ing and puts my tray down for me. I love trays. Feel unbelievably safe with a tray. By the second drink I could waltz to the bathroom, or join the mile-high club. Even parachute from the plane if necessary. I see myself calmly opening the emergency exit and directing pas-sengers to a blow-up raft in the middle of the ocean.

Newark

I am marvelous at air travel. Who would have thought? I breeze around Newark Airport during the layover, buying fat magazines and Godiva chocolate, then decide to have a little nip at the bar. After the third nip, I exercise influence to call Ex-Rat and rummage in my fanny pack for my calling card (travel gift from darling Mama!). When I find a pay phone, I punch in the numbers. Get them wrong. Punch them in again. This time the phone rings through to my answering machine, on which I leave a long message about the effortlessness of air travel. How beautiful Newark is. Blah, blah.

As I saunter over to the departure gate, a flight attendant is speaking into a microphone, "Would the last passenger to board flight 126 to Seattle please come to gate 18?" I give her my ticket. She looks at it, stops talking into the microphone immediately, and hustles me by the arm down the ramp, personally directing me to my seat.

Seattle

With various Seattle men's phone numbers now in my fanny pack, I float onto the connecting flight to Juneau. Now a seasoned air traveler, I consider becoming a pilot. Like Amelia Earhart. Why not? Plus, I'd get to wear a lovely little leather jacket and goggles. Very sexy.

Descent

Thanks to the "no drinks" rule enforced during incessant turbulence, I am no longer a seasoned flier or rational passenger. The plane circles the Juneau airport for what seems like eternity while "they" decide if it's safe for the plane to land or if we should be rerouted to Canada. When the pilot is finally given the go-ahead to land, the plane bucks and heaves as though it's about to implode. The upper storage containers fly open. Luggage tumbles out. A red light and a very loud buzzing noise turns on. Passengers scream.

I suddenly remember Amelia Earhart died in a plane crash.

A Full and Complete Stop

The plane has successfully landed and the passengers crawl over one another to get off, myself included. The thought of having to board another plane a week from now and fly home is the worst feeling possible. I button up my raincoat till it strangles my throat, putting up the hood, pulling the strings down hard.

Mason

I see Mason first. He stands a little apart from the crowd, with his baseball hat on backward, scanning the passengers filtering through the arrival gate. He looks better than I remember him, with his tan skin and snug Levis and tight-fitting T-shirt over hard muscles. I forget all about the plane's turbulent landing. I push back my hood and sprint right up to him.

"You made it!" Mason says, and scoops me up into his arms.

The Kiss

"Well," I say, finally coming up for air. My lips are burning and my knees are knocking.

Ferry

"I still can't believe you're here," Mason says, squeezing me. I smile shyly. "Let's go grab your pack, OK? The ferry leaves in about forty minutes."

"Ferry?" I might faint.

Mason leans down, nuzzles and kisses my neck. "I know you've been traveling—*kiss*—all day and must be beat—*nuzzle*—but once we ferry across—*kiss, kiss*—it's only a short hike up to my cabin."

"I think I may need some coffee," I whisper meekly.

Hike

We hike up to Mason's cabin in the dark. I have a light strapped to my head and my bladder is about to burst from the three cups of coffee I drank on the ferry. Even though Mason is carrying my pack, I discover hiking on a StairMaster is nothing compared to the real thing. When we reach his cabin, I am swallowing air like a guppy. Mason hasn't even broken a sweat. Inside, he immediately lights a kerosene lamp.

"So what do you think?" Mason asks. I look around: metal wash-basin; two enamel mugs; a pot; a kettle; a twin bed with a stack of books next to it; a tiny writing desk with an old Band-Aid box holding pens; a towel on a hook.

I look around for a missing couch, an easy chair, or a simple rocker. None.

"Is something wrong?" Mason asks.

"No! No! Not at all! I'm fine!" I say too enthusiastically.

"It's not what you expected, is it?"

"No, it's nice, really—quaint, rustic, charming—" I am babbling.

"Are you sure? I know it's a lot different from what you're used to."

"I'm fine, *really*," I say. I twirl my hair. "Um, where's your restroom?"

"The outhouse is out back, let me show you."

Twin Bed

"You're so quiet. Are you sure you're OK?" Mason asks, climbing into the twin bed, spooning me. I nod. My nose brushes against the wall. He turns me around.

"What's going on in your head right now?"

"I was just thinking about Lucy and Brendan, you know, what they're doing right now." I was also thinking of Henry and Moon-boy, but I don't share this.

"And what do you think they're doing?" he asks, gently pushing my hair back.

"Probably playing on the computer," I say, becoming teary. "It's just that they feel so far away and you don't have a phone."

"Shhhh," Mason whispers. "It's all right. They're with their dad. They're safe." He gently strokes my skin. It feels so nice to be touched after months of sleeping alone that my body yields and relaxes. Mason removes my panties, lifts me on top of him, hikes up my frock and pushes his penis into me. He moves me up and down, faster and faster, then stops, flips us around, brings up my legs, and moves more slowly. He tosses back the covers, still moving inside me. The kerosene light burns softly. He looks into my eyes, searching.

I bury my face into his hair and neck, wrapping my legs around his waist. He moans, trying to move away. "I'm going to come," he says. I move faster. Trying to grab hold of something, anything to remember my want, my love for him. To remember why I have come here, to this cabin, these woods. I clamp down hard. Mason's body shakes and he collapses on my chest, then rolls to his side and throws his arm over me. We stare at each other across the pillow.

"Hi," Mason says.

"Hi," I say back.

Henry's Book

Mason snores lightly into my hair. I am wide awake, so I carefully remove his arm from my waist and creep out of the bed. The temperature has dropped in the cabin. I rustle through my pack, find nothing warm, and finally put on Mason's flannel shirt, which hangs on a nail by the fireplace. It smells of mosquito repellent and wood smoke.

I pace around the tiny cabin, then sit down at Mason's desk, looking through the stack of books and nature magazines piled on its surface. And there in front of me is a familiar name: *Henry C. Bannister.* I open the book to the photograph of Henry on the inside flap. I touch his face and I feel something I don't want to feel. I snap the book shut.

Cabinet

After reading a lengthy essay about the migration patterns of geese, I still can't sleep. I have no clue what time it is, since Mason doesn't seem to have a clock. I guess it's around twelve, since I have a hankering for a midnight snack and I curse myself for leaving my Godiva and fashion magazines on the plane. Quietly, I open the only cabinet above Mason's hand-pump sink. There is a jar of natural peanut butter, rye crackers, three blue potatoes, a container of oatmeal, chamomile tea, and a carrot. I root around for a dusty chocolate chip, cookie crumb, or even a raisin. Nada. The hairs on the back of my neck rise. Suddenly I'm having déjà vu. I know I have seen this cabinet before. Where, where, where? And then it comes to me: in my mother's pantry.

The wind echoes eerily down the chimney, a wolf howls in the distance, and the kerosene light flickers, creating shadows on the wall. "Oh, my god!" I whisper out loud.

I bang the cabinet shut, whip across the room, and dive on top of Mason.

Tongass Morning

I wake to Mason throwing more wood onto the fire. His chest is bare and his white carpenter pants hang just right. The big cast-iron kettle is releasing steam, his one pot bubbles with oatmeal. It reminds me of Grammy's house. Very cozy. Light streams through the cabin window, making everything more cheery and less daunting.

"Hey, gorgeous," Mason says. Yes, morning is off to a wonderful start. Maybe the food cabinet was just a bad dream. I snuggle further down under the covers. Mason brings me oatmeal in bed, handing it to me, then sliding in next to me. I look at the gray mass of oatmeal.

"Do you have any sugar?" I ask coyly, even though I know he doesn't. He takes the bowl out of my hand and puts it on the floor.

Read and Cuddle

After having sex for three hours (I looked at Mason's watch), I entertain myself by making paper-chain dolls with my compact scissor set while Mason reads. I put down my scissors on the desk and take a sip of my unsweetened chamomile tea. Revolting. "So what do you do all day out here when you're not working?" I ask Mason. He looks up from the page that he is reading.

"Relax, pick a little at my mandolin, carve wood, but mainly I just read. Why? Are you bored?" I twirl my hair and slowly shake my head. Mason pats the covers. "Come cuddle and read on the bed with me."

I find a magazine that at least has a cute-n-fluffy owl on the front and try to squish into bed next to Mason. We become a mass of body parts banging against the cabin wall. When we finally find a comfortable position in which to both read and cuddle, Mason says, "I should probably get a bigger bed for the next time you visit."

The idea of coming back here in another six months or so makes me think of what Henry said about long-distance relationships not working. I try to put Henry's words out of my mind and flip through my magazine. I find the article on owls and begin to read. A few paragraphs in, I learn that it's all about species that mate for life.

• • •

Bath

Mason pumps a bucket of cold water, pours it into the metal tub, takes the kettle off the woodstove, and dumps in boiling water as well.

"All set," he says. "Come on over and I'll wash your back." I joyfully flit over with my two-pound bag of toiletries and fluffy *Hello Kitty* washcloth that Lucy gave me for Mother's Day until I see there are just two inches of water at the bottom of the metal tub.

Outside Sex

Mason slowly undresses in the high sun and tall grass outside the cabin. His lips flicker in a self-assured smile. He's no longer a gentle mountain man but something other—seductive and alluring, rough and animalistic. My inner thighs tremble. I watch as he takes off his shirt first, slowly pulling it over his head. Flat, muscular stomach. Hair on his chest. All man. Then he unbuckles his belt. Next, socks removed, revealing monstrous feet, weathered and tough. Oh, god. Then and only then the pants: down, to his ankles. His legs are thick and muscular. Smooth calves. Soft hair on his shins. No boxers.

"Now you," he says. It's almost a command, which surprises me. I cross my knees and elbows over my body, suddenly self-conscious. I'm a dark closet kind of girl. I've never had sex outdoors. He moves toward my long-underwear top and tugs it over my head. He lays me face down on the ground. His arms curve around my back and his huge hands close themselves on my breasts as he enters me.

He whispers in my ear, "Do you like this?"

I shiver and a guttural sound issues from the back of my throat.

Magic Words

After over seventy-two hours of amazing sex interspersed with two-inch baths, bland oatmeal, severe fits of boredom, and poor sleep due to the twin bed, I hear Mason say these magic words: "I think we need to take a run to the store."

I scramble out of bed and yank on my clothes.

"Ready?" I ask him.

Country Store

Mason turns into a country store with a single gas pump and we come to a shaky, rattling stop. "I should probably get some gas and stop by the post office while we're here as well," Mason says. As he pumps fuel, I climb down quickly from the truck. My arms scratched and knees scraped from hiking down the mountain to his truck, I look like the escapee I am.

In the store, which seems to sell everything conceivable, from large barrels of pickles and jars of candy to touristy slogan T-shirts, I notice a coffee bar, with three flavors of coffee. Am instantly restored! Yes, yes! I dash over, fill up an extra, extra large cup, pay for it, drink it down, and toss the cup in the trash.

Next item on agenda: bathroom.

It is a real restroom, with indoor plumbing, a large bottle of disinfectant spray, and paper towels on the back of the toilet. I happily spray and wash down all the surfaces, plop my bare fanny on the seat and sigh. It truly is the simpler things in life.

Pay Phone

As I savor a second cup of Java Joe, I tilt the pay phone receiver under my ear and listen to Lucy chatter away about the Sims. After ten minutes of recounting, she takes a big breath, "Daddy wants to talk to you." Before I can protest, she hands the phone to Ex-Rat.

"So are you in Alaska or at some hotel in Newark?" Ex-Rat asks.

"I'm in Alaska," I say, smirking. Finally it is my turn to be smug.

"Well, I wasn't sure. In the message you left on the machine, you seemed to be really enjoying yourself in Newark—something about chocolate, parachuting off the plane, saving passengers—the kids and I could barely understand you. What did you do? Get smashed?" Ex-Rat says.

"Are Lucy and Brendan standing there listening to this?" I ask.

"No," Ex-Rat says.

"Well, I suppose I did have a few too many nips at the bar, but the point is that I *did* board the plane and fly here. You thought I wouldn't be able to," I say. Ex-Rat doesn't respond. There is such a long silence between us that I finally ask, "Are you there?"

"Yes, I'm here."

"Did Lucy get to spend time with Henry's son before he left to see his grandparents in Philadelphia?"

"Yeah, he came over here right after the cab pulled away to take you to the airport. I guess he wanted to give you some drawings before you left," Ex-Rat says.

"Did you see Henry? Did he say anything to you?" I ask.

"No, he waited in the car for pickup and drop-off," Ex-Rat says. "Though his son did ask for your address out there, so I gave it to him—though I *highly* doubt Henry is going to mail the drawings all the way to Alaska since you only plan to be there for—"

"Is Brendan there?" I interrupt. I won't have Ex-Rat killing my coffee buzz.

"He's hanging out with Sophie in the backyard."

"Can you get him?" I ask. I hear the back-porch door open and Ex-Rat telling Brendan I'm on the phone. I wait for Brendan's groan as he takes the phone, but there isn't one.

"Hey, Mom! How are you doing? Are you having fun?" Brendan says.

I almost choke on my coffee. *"Brendan?"*

• • •

A Few Supplies

Between the caffeine and the first real conversation I've had with my son in months, I am full of good cheer. I ask Mason to wait in the car with his brown paper bag of non–junk goods and tell him that I'll only be a couple of minutes.

I jet around the store, throwing sugar, instant coffee, powdered nondairy creamer, a pound of fudge, licorice ropes, and Jiffy Pop into my shopping basket. I also find a rack of mindless magazines. Hooray! I choose three and bring the overflowing basket up to the register.

"I still need a few more items," I tell the cashier. I pile various Alaskan logo T-shirts, sweatpants, caps, snow globes, postcards, and mugs into my arms and unload them onto the counter.

"And one more thing." I run, grab a box of plain yellow pencils for Henry, race back, and put it on top of my mountain of stuff. "There," I say.

Post Office

Mason goes into the post office (or rather post shack), and I sit in the truck nibbling licorice rope, absorbed in a magazine article about a homemaker who is reentering the workforce and needs a makeover. The first photo shows a washed-up mother in her robe and slippers, with frizzy hair and bags under her eyes, looking dismally at her twins who are pouring Cheerios on the floor. Her husband sits reading his *Washington Post,* looking fresh as a daisy in an elegant dark gray suit and burgundy tie. Under the photo, a caption reads *6:15 a.m.* The other photo on the page is of the same woman, still in her robe and fuzzy slippers, looking far more frazzled, cooking dinner. The kitchen floor is covered in Legos, the twins are pulling each other's hair, and her husband isn't anywhere in sight. I imagine he's in the other room smoking a pipe and watching the news with his feet up. Under this photo the caption reads *6:15 p.m.* I can completely relate—I feel like calling her and asking her to be my friend.

I turn the page and gasp. Truly amazing! The team of beauty experts have transformed the fried homemaker into a vamped-out business mogul. The woman sits at a big desk, the city skyline behind her, with a look of completely focused bliss. Her eyes burn right through the page at me. I stop nibbling my licorice and sit up straighter. I catch my reflection in the rear-view mirror. My hair is a barrette-bobbed mess, as always, and my kelly green raincoat looks silly. I don't look any different in Alaska than I do at home. I am not a sophisticated traveler or a wilderness sex deity but a dismantled divorcée in the middle of a nervous breakdown. *How did I become this? How do I change?*

UPS in Alaska

Mason comes out of the post office carrying a large brown box and letters stuffed in each pocket of his coat. As he gets closer to the truck, I see that the box is addressed to me in my father's telltale perfect calligraphy. I am thunderstruck. How did a package arrive all the way out here in three days? I roll down the window.

"I got a package from my father?" I ask, still not believing it. Mason nods. "UPS Next Day Air. You want to open it now or later?"

"Now!" I say, hopping out of the truck. Mason puts it on the ground in the little parking lot, takes out his pocket knife, and carefully slits the top open. Inside is a big picnic basket with gourmet pasta, jarred vodka sauce, Parmesan cheese, my favorite Chianti, cloth napkins, and plastic wineglasses and cutlery. Mason whistles. I sigh. My father knew just what I needed.

"You also got this," Mason says, handing me a battered Federal Express envelope. I notice my name is written in pencil. I take the overnight-express envelope from his outstretched hand.

"Thanks," I say, and tuck it under my arm, avoiding Mason's

questioning eyes. I go back to rummaging through the picnic basket, my chest pounding.

"Aren't you going to open it?"

I nod and open it quickly. It contains two drawings from Moonboy and a long and skinny pad of paper with a heading that reads "Today's List" and a pen with a fluffy, feathery pink end.

"Is it from Lucy?" Mason asks.

"No, it's from Henry's son—it's a joke, I make lists . . ." I say distractedly. I examine the skinny pad and pen. But it had been Henry who had kidded with me about it that day in the park.

"Henry the writer? The one I met at your house on Christmas?" Mason says, his face pensive.

"Uh, yes." I check inside the envelope again in hope of a clue. Nothing.

"And Henry Federal Expressed his son's drawings all the way here? Is he interested in you or something?" Mason asks.

"Who?" I ask, confused.

"Henry."

"Oh, god, no!" I say too loud. "Henry has a girlfriend—she's a *doctor*—we're just friends—or really we're not, anymore, I guess, I don't know—he was interested in Pip and then—"

"Somehow I don't think Pip is Henry's type," Mason interrupts. He hefts the box of goods from my father, opens the back hatch of the truck, then slides the box in.

"How do you know that?" I ask.

"I just know," Mason says, slamming the hatch shut and giving me a measured look.

"What?" I ask.

He shakes his head, takes out his truck keys, and gets in the truck.

"What?" I ask again, opening the passenger side door.

"I just had this crazy thought for a second," Mason says.

"What kind of thought?" I snap on my seat belt.

"It's not important. Let's just forget about it," Mason says. He starts up the truck and grinds it into gear and we bump along the back roads to his cabin in silence.

Dinner by Candlelight

Mason sits on the cabin floor across from me. There is a candle between us. We take bites of pasta and sips of wine from plastic wineglasses. Although my father's gift seemed perfect at the time, it now feels completely forced. The gourmet, citified picnic doesn't belong here, nor does my new heap of Alaska touristy items, my fluffy pen, or my trash magazines. It only amplifies my feeling of being out of place here. Yet, when I think of my house, I know I've never felt comfortable there either. It was always more Ex-Rat's home. And if I'm honest with myself, it was always his life, his dreams that came first, never mine. I just went along. I lost myself in him and the kids, and it's going to take a lot more than a makeover from a bunch of beauty experts to alter that fact.

I put my fork down.

"You don't like the pasta?" Mason asks.

"No, it's good. I'm just not that hungry."

"Missing your kids again?" Mason probes.

"Something like that," I say, twirling my hair.

Mason puts his fork down too. Something has shifted between us. A slight turning. I look down at the floor, afraid that if I meet Mason's gaze, my eyes will reveal too much.

Postcards

I put pink pen to postcard.

Dear Henry, You were right, I begin and then stop. I scribble out his name and the words and take a fresh postcard from the pile. *Hi, Mom! How are you? I'm great! Alaska is beautiful! You would love it here!*

I stop again.

I reread the words, and it reminds me of how I wrote her letters when I went to my first sleepaway camp and I didn't fit in. The other girls in the bunk had called me Linus, and hidden my "fluffy," a ragged piece of blanket that I rubbed between my fingers constantly. I hadn't wanted my mother to know, so I wrote her curly-scripted shallow notes with happy faces lining the edges. When she finally came to pick me up from camp, I held it together until I got into the car and then promptly burst into tears.

The Sweater

Mason throws on a sweater.

"Nice sweater." I touch it. It is soft.

"A girl from work, Becky, knitted for me," he says.

I stop touching it.

"Becky?"

"Yeah, she's a guide on some of the bigger tours with me," he says, as if this explains it. "You'll meet her this morning when we pick up the kayak."

"Pick up the kayak?" I ask, anxiously. Becky is now the furthest thing from my mind.

"Yeah, I wanted to show you my favorite spot before you leave, you know, because—" Mason doesn't finish his sentence.

These past few days leading up to my departure, we have been avoiding any real discussion about me coming back to Alaska. As if we already know there won't be one.

Mountain Woman

"Hey, Mason!" a woman says, running up from the shore. Her hair is long and braided, her body lean and tough. About twenty, if that, she is wearing a life jacket and carrying an oar. She slows down when she sees me, casting her eyes up and down. When Mason introduces us, "You don't look anything like I pictured you," is what she says.

She leaps to help Mason take a double-seated kayak off the rack and carries it toward the beach. They move well together. She holds one end of the kayak, swiftly walking backward and looking at Mason. I can see the spark in her eyes. It's how I look at Henry.

"I'm leaving tomorrow," I call out to her. She gives me a small, fragile smile.

Mama Bear and Cubs

On the inlet to our trail that will lead us to Mason's favorite spot, in which we're going to pitch a tent and sleep for the night, we see a mother bear and two cubs wrestling a distance from her. As soon as she spots our little vessel, she gets up, shakes herself, lifts her muzzle up, makes a high noise, and starts walking toward the edge of the woods.

The cubs unfold and watch us with curiosity. "They'll leave her soon, they're almost fully grown. See how they don't obey her? They're almost ready," Mason says. The mother bear once again cries out.

"Look at them. They're still not listening to her call," I say.

"In a way they're not supposed to. It's the natural process of becoming an adult," Mason says. The cubs finally lazily walk over and follow their mother into the woods.

I think of Lucy and Brendan.

"Why do you look so glum?" Mason asks.

"Because after they both leave, she'll be alone."

Losing It

After hiking for hours up steep glacial terrain in the pouring rain, we start to pitch camp—rather, I chew a soggy Clif Bar and watch Mason pitch camp.

"I want to go home," I hear myself say.

"Now?" Mason asks.

"Yes, right now." I stand.

"The rain will pass."

"I don't care."

"This is crazy," Mason says. "Why do you want to go back to the cabin?"

"I don't want to go back to the cabin. I want to go home."

I stomp over to the trail openings and start descending. I can't seem to stop myself.

"That's the wrong trail," Mason calls after me and I walk back over to him.

"What's going on with Becky?" I ask him.

"What are you talking about?" Mason asks.

"Becky, the girl who knitted you that sweater—did you sleep with her?" I ask.

Mason brushes water from his eyes. "No. I didn't sleep with her. Why would you think that?"

"Because she belongs here and I don't. I just don't fit this place, these woods—I don't seem to fit anywhere."

"Come here," Mason interrupts, but I don't budge. He walks over to me, puts his hands gently on my shoulders. "What's going on?"

"I'm just so confused about everything: my life, my future, my kids getting older, us—you, me—" My voice catches and I pause.

Mason's hands still on my shoulders, I look into his eyes, my voice unsteady, "What happens after this? After I leave?"

"What do you want to happen?" Mason asks.

"I don't know."

Favorite Spot

I'm fast asleep in the tent when Mason wakes me.

"Come on. I want to show you my favorite spot. Here," he says, handing me some clothes from his pack. I lift myself out of the damp sleeping bag. "These are the driest I could find." I pull them on and we both crawl out of the tent.

"The rain stopped," I say, and he nods and takes my hand.

We walk to a small field filled with Alaskan wildflowers, their petals still open in the fading moonlight. He sits down in the grass and pulls me down to his side and we sit together, watching the moon.

"You know, this is how I imagined us. Here. Together."

I see him, here in these woods, this spot. I see him clearly. Mason has found the place where he belongs. I touch his face as if to capture it somehow—to remember the comfort of his soul.

"I even thought of building a house up here and you and the kids could come live with—"

"I can't live here, Mason. Legally, I can't move my kids here. And even if I could, I wouldn't. I'd miss the city too much. I'm a city girl. It's who I am." As I say this, I suddenly know that I have to leave my house and all that it represents to truly change. It's not the city; it's my house in the city. It's not really mine. I am filled with a shrill of fear, which quickly dissipates, replaced with an energetic surety of task. As soon as I get back, I think, I will put the house on the market.

"I know." Mason smiles a sad smile.

"You know what?" I ask, surfacing from my own thoughts.

"I know you are a total city girl. I wish I had a picture of your face when you saw my cabin."

"Was it that obvious?" I ask.

He nods.

"Even with all my months of preparation and my new gear?" I ask.

He nods again. "I knew you were a city girl back when you wore that little polka-dot bathing suit and I was doing spastic jumps off a rope swing."

"Really?"

"Mmmm. Yup." And we both laugh.

Parking Lot

We sit in his truck in the ferry parking lot, both of us staring ahead. We watch cars load. Passengers with cameras and luggage snake up the metal ramp. The deckhand stamps tickets. Mason reaches over and pulls me into his arms, holds me close. The ferry horn blares.

"Go on, then, you better get going," he says. "Your ship is about to sail."

I open the truck door, jump out, and walk hurriedly to the loading dock.

"I'll write you!" Mason yells out the window.

"I'll write you, too!" I yell back, even though I know I probably won't. Mason belongs to Alaska, and my life is in Cambridge. I pause and get one last look at him, in his beat-up truck, his big mountain arm hanging out the window. I wave and think, *I hope Becky tells him she likes him. I hope she finally gets up the nerve.*

Wind in My Hair

Alone on the ferry, I take in Alaska: its rugged beauty, the wildlife on the shore, the stark glacial formations. A tourist offers me her binoculars.

"Breathtaking, isn't it?" the woman says.

"Yes, it is," I agree.

"Traveling alone?" she asks.

I nod and hand back her binoculars, smiling a thank you. It feels so good to smile. I keep smiling. I point my face to the sun, eyes half closed, wind in my hair.

thirteen

A Week of Packing

As I stand in the middle of taped-up boxes, my hair in a sleek pony-tail, the doorbell rings. I kick a box over to the wall and go to answer the door. Henry stands with Moonboy and Manic Dog on the front steps. I haven't seen them since I got back from Alaska over a month ago. I notice Moonboy has sprouted up while visiting his grandparents in Philadelphia for a good chunk of the summer, and Henry—well, Henry looks even more gorgeous than I remember. Crushingly handsome. I know he is back with his also crushingly beautiful doctor girlfriend and I vow to be an unflinching pillar of strength, despite my weak knees.

Lucy clambers into the hallway, dragging Darling by a boa feather leash. Moonboy's face turns into a joyous crinkle and Manic Dog makes feathers fly. Henry and I both fold our arms across our chests.

"Upstairs!" I demand. Children and dogs clomp and clump up the stairs.

Henry frowns at my black sleeveless shirt and straight skirt like I have committed a terrible crime.

"What are you wearing?" he asks.

"It's my new costume. I am trying to look more organized."

"Costume?" A flicker of a smile.

"Yes. When I was in Alaska I read a magazine article about this mother of twins and they gave her this makeover—"

"What are those things on your feet?" he interrupts, unfolding his arms and pointing to my black penny loafers.

"Shoes," I say.

"And what's all this?" He gestures to the boxes in the living room.

"We're moving," I tell him.

"You're moving?" Henry asks, flabbergasted. "But you only just returned from Alaska!"

"Exactly. I figured if I can get on a plane and fly to Alaska, then moving should be a snap." I walk into the living room and start grabbing books from shelves, throwing them into one of the zillion empty U-Haul boxes scattered around the room. Henry follows, watching me. My eye starts to twitch.

"How much coffee have you ingested today?" Henry asks suspiciously.

"None," I answer honestly. I sense he doesn't believe me.

"Are you sure you want to move? Last time—"

"I'm not going to change my mind," I interrupt, staring him down. The box is now full and I search around for tape but can't find my roll and am quickly frustrated.

"Are you all right?" Henry asks.

"I'm peachy." I smack my lips. "Peachy keen." I finally retrieve the roll and start to seal up the box. Love, love, love the ripping sound of the tape! I double tape. Triple tape. Henry's eye is now twitching too.

Brendan appears in the living room. He is growing out his hair. It's shaggy and hangs halfway down his eyes. The effect drives me bonkers. When I suggested he chop it off, he informed me: "I am now hippie prep." Like he just got elected president.

"Hey, Breno," Henry says. Brendan gives Henry the first smile I've seen from him in weeks. "I heard you're moving."

Brendan adjusts his expression to fit his response, "Yeah—looks like it," and keeps walking in the direction of the den, where he turns up MTV until the house vibrates.

"I forgot to ask you where you're moving to!" Henry yells above the din.

"I haven't found a place yet!" I yell back. MTV is so loud that I can no longer hear the tape's lovely ripping noise. I dart around the boxes and into the den, waving the tape dispenser above my head. "Hey, hippie, I'm trying to tape in here!" Brendan gives me a look that says *You're making no sense* but turns off the TV and goes out to the garage. Soon I hear a tennis ball being slammed against the side of the house.

Henry is still standing in the living room with an awful look.

"Don't you have something else to do tonight other than watch me tape boxes?" I ask haughtily.

"Whoever you are, freeze," Henry says. "Stay where you are." He begins frantically looking around the living room, unearthing things.

"What are you doing?" I ask, not moving.

"What have you done with her?" he asks.

"Done with whom?"

"The woman who owns this house. She is about 4′ 11″. She wears lovely flowery dresses and hot pink clogs," he says.

"Very funny." I brush past him to tape another box.

"Seriously, though, are you all right?" he asks. "You haven't even found a place to move into and you're already packing boxes." He touches my shoulder. I melt. I think of him touching her, his girl-friend, in the exact same way.

"I'm fine," I say pulling away.

"Did something happen in Alaska, between you and Mason?" Henry asks.

"Look Henry, I'm *fine*. I was more than fine until you showed up," I say. Which is true. I was feeling divinely together and sure of myself until right now. I should avoid Henry at all costs. I will hide and let Lucy answer the door next time. I will email him the date and time of Moonboy and Lucy's next get-together.

"Yes, well, then," Henry says, putting his hand to his forehead as if he has forgotten something, and then clearing his throat. "I guess I should leave."

I nod, holding steady. When he's gone, I gather myself up once more and start wrapping wineglasses in newspaper, certain that if I just keep moving, everything will be fine.

Ex-Rat Remover

"You're not seriously going through with this?" Ex-Rat asks, his knuckles white as he grips the letter drafted by my new independently-hired lawyer.

"Yes. I am seriously going through with it."

"The kids start school in a little over a month!"

"I know," I say, folding my arms.

"There is no way you're going to find a place by September to move into that's in the kids' school district."

"I will," I answer. Ex-Rat turns a mottled purple. I have never seen him so angry.

"Just because the house is in your name does not make it yours," Ex-Rat says, and then pauses. "I'm the one paying the mortgage."

"You are paying alimony. The mortgage is taken out of my alimony."

Ex-Rat bangs the door frame with his open palm and then points a finger in my face, saying, "If this is another attempt to get even with me, you have gone too far. It's one thing to go off to Alaska for a few days. It is quite another to sell our children's home. If you're going to insist on going ahead with this crazy plan, I am buying this house. I don't want Brendan and Lucy to be victims of your fickleness and have to switch schools."

"Fine," I say.

"Fine?" He's thunderstruck.

"It will make things simpler. I don't have to put the house on the market," I say, hoping he is serious.

"Fine, then. I'll have my lawyer draw up the papers tomorrow." He goes down the steps, opens the driver's side door of his Mercedes, then looks back at me and says, "Don't even think about coming back and crying to me when you realize moving wasn't such a hot idea."

"Don't worry. I won't," I call after him.

The Apartment

Dottie of Dot and Dottie Real Estate screams into my driveway, blasting her horn.

Dottie has big hair, big boobs, and a face just like Loretta Lynn.

It's nice to have a little country in the city.

When I walked into her real estate office and told her that I wanted a nest high above the ground, she batted her luscious lashes and said, "Sure thing, honey." Like finding it would be as easy as pie.

Now, Dottie hollers out the car window. "Get your fanny out here in two shakes. I found an apartment you are going to *loooove*." I hustle Lucy, who is dragging her lime green boa, out the door.

"Brendan, are you coming?" I yell.

"I'm right behind you," Brendan says. If looks could kill, I would be drawn and quartered. Brendan has threatened to just stay living at the house full-time with his father in protest of the move, but he can't resist looking at the possible apartments. I am, though, a wee bit anxious about never seeing my son again. My therapist tells me Brendan's behavior is normal for his age and he'll get over it. I have my doubts.

"Can Darling come, too?" Lucy asks, excitedly. Lucy is all for moving—preferably to a hotel with room service and an indoor pool. Her new favorite book-character obsession, Eloise, has been indulged gruesomely by my father, who is shipping parcels containing assorted Eloise fare daily.

"Not today," I say firmly, guiding her toward Dottie's big, white, air-conditioned Lincoln Continental.

"On the double, gang! This place was just listed!" Dottie says, as we get in. Before we can buckle our seat belts, she's already down the street and turning right toward Cambridge Common. She whips around the rotary, flies down Cambridge Street, hangs a left, then screeches to a halt in front of an elegant prewar apartment building in Henry's neighborhood. Lucy hops out and makes a mad dash for a guy standing in front of the building's double doors. She waits in front of him, saying nothing, nose in the air, her very large foot tapping a very Eloise patent-leather Mary Jane.

"He's not the doorman, Lucy," I say. The guy smiles kindly and opens the door. I nod thanks.

Dottie whisks Lucy, stone-cold Brendan, and me up to the fifth floor. As soon as we enter I know. I know with all my heart that this is where I want to live: cream walls; beautiful tile and wood floors; huge windows with loads of light; high ceilings; porcelain tubs in the bathrooms; a cozy kitchen with fifties fixtures; a tiny balcony overlooking the front gardens.

Even Brendan knows. "I didn't hit the door frame," he says as he goes in and then comes out of one of the bedrooms. "Not bad."

Lucy, barreling out of a bedroom and down the hall, leaps into my arms, almost knocking me over. "There are pigeons outside my window!" she says, already claiming a room of her own.

"We'll take it," I say to Dottie.

"Thought so," Dottie says, showing me the master suite, which is all white. Best, there is no memory of Ex-Rat. Yes! Yes! "The closet isn't very big," Dottie says, showing me its interior.

"Good," I say, as I shut the closet door. "When can we move in?"

"The seller is very motivated. Her company moved her to a position in New York. We can probably wrap this up fairly quick."

"Then let's do it."

Move-in Date

I hang up the phone with Dottie and turn to the kids. "We got the apartment!"

"When do we move in?" Brendan asks.

"September first," I say. Lucy walks slowly over to me, breathes hot into my face, and squeezes my cheeks together, her body trembling with excitement.

Admissions

Apartment hunting out of the way, I apply for college at the Harvard Extension School. Pip, who is finally back at work, has taken an early lunch in order to come with me and scope out the college boys. She carries a look of complete dissatisfaction since the admissions office is void of any male under the age of fifty.

I sit down and fill out my college application. "Are you sure there will be people my age in the class?" I ask the admission's officer for the millionth time.

"Yes. It is the *extended* learning program for *adult* learners," he repeats.

Pip lights a cigarette. "Hey! You can't do that," the officer yells.

"Whatever, Gramps," Pip says under her breath. She stubs out the cigarette on her heel, pops a mint into her mouth, and begins to slurp.

My Calling

"Hello, college girl! Someone in the paper was selling his complete set of encyclopedias," my mother says, hopping out of her minivan and unloading boxes upon boxes. I curse myself for telling her about my big college plans.

"Mom, I am trying to get rid of things, not add more stuff," I say, as neighbors dig through my yard-sale goodies. I try to hide the pressure cooker, which sits obtrusively on the front table. No luck. My mother stomps over and inspects it. Pip, who at 11 a.m. is on her second pack of cigarettes, gives a raspy chuckle.

"Is this the pressure cooker I bought you for your birthday?"

"I thought it would bring up unwanted feelings about—" I almost say *Yoga Alien* but stop myself.

"Mark?"

"Mmm-hmm," I mumble.

"It does," she says, and drops it back on the table. "Get rid of it." She looks over the rest of the inventory. Thank goodness the pressure cooker is the only gift from her out for sale—the rest of her presents to me went to Goodwill. "So where should I put these encyclopedias?" she asks.

"Mom, why did you buy me a set of used encyclopedias? You can look all that stuff up on the Internet now, and I don't have anywhere to put them in the new apartment."

"Who doesn't have bookshelves? You shouldn't spend so much time on the computer, it causes carpal tunnel syndrome." My mother blathers happily, "I thought I'd show my support for your new academic life and buy you some encyclopedias so you didn't have to trolley off to the library every time you needed to look up some, I don't know, some historical fact or what a bison is or something. Is that such a crime? It's what mothers do, darling. We support our daughters' calling."

"Calling?" I ask.

"Yes. Being a kindergarten teacher is *your calling*," she says very proudly for all to hear.

I suddenly remember why I avoided finding any type of professional career and became a homemaker.

New Furniture

Lucy prances around the furniture store with her little yellow Eloise purse. My father follows. Having taken a virtual tour of the apartment online, since it's not within the parameters of his neighborhood, he suggested we go shopping, around the corner from his apartment, of course. We have discovered canopies. Big swooping canopy beds with feather mattresses. Great nest appeal, my father concludes. Lucy and I nod furiously in affirmation. Lucy finds a white princess canopy. My father coos with approval. I find a moss-colored green one tucked in the corner and fall in love. I rush over and hop in.

"It reminds me of *A Midsummer Night's Dream*. We have to add wings. Right here," I say, touching the backboard.

Antique Store

Loaded down with fabric swatches, receipts for delivery, and sample paint chips, we enter an antique store filled to the brim with Fiestaware, Hull vases, and floral curtains. My father and Lucy instantly begin shoving things under my nose that they think I might like.

"I don't want a cluttered nest," I say. "I am thinking Zen, Buddhist shrine, *minimalist*." My father rolls his eyes at Lucy. Lucy places her hands on her hips, stamps her foot, and stares me down. My father finds her a pillbox hat and plops it on her head. She runs to find a mirror.

"Don't even pretend that you have any minimalist genes. You're not fooling me for a second. You said the kitchen was fifties, with porcelain fixtures—these are must-haves," he states firmly. Eyeing a plain white jelly cabinet, I walk over to it and open all its little storage spaces, which are like tiny closets. My father sidles up to me, holding an array of green vases, cups, and plates. "Green and white. That will be the theme—it will bring the whole apartment together," he says, his eyes wide. I think about the apartment, imagining loads of plants, blooming orchids and my newly-framed Beatrix Potter posters on the walls. Green and white would suit the apartment marvelously.

But . . .

I reach up on my tiptoes and place my fingers gently on a pink Hull vase that rests on the top of the jelly cabinet and take it down.

"I think I like this pink, instead—I think *this* should be my theme," I say, holding my chin up.

"OK, I see your point, and you're right, that color is more you." My father understands, and he puts back all the green vases and cups.

Therapist's Office

I run up the steps to my therapist's office. I'm early, so I pace back and forth, picking up magazines, putting them down, picking them up again. When she opens the door, I say, "I'm ready for my next list."

She ushers me in her office, observes me, her eyes hooded, like a cat. I look at her, the clock, her. "All right, it's been five minutes. Can I have my list now?"

She slowly writes something on her little pad of paper, rips it off, and hands it to me.

It reads: *Slow down.*

Trash Bags

The boxes are all packed. The walls are empty and void. The kids and I eat TV dinners with plastic cutlery and watch *The Apprentice*. I'm hoping that frequent viewing of Trumpy comb-over will subconsciously influence Brendan to shear his own mop.

I wear a splendid new dress with three-quarter sleeves. Color: coffee. I've found it's just as exhilarating to wear the color of coffee as it is to drink the substance itself. My wavy dark hair is a bun masterpiece, thanks to my first hair appointment in eight months. I wear black-framed faux eyeglasses that make me look both smart *and* sexy. Very Yoko Ono. I imagine myself zipping to college on a three-speed with a little handlebar basket, loaded with school books. I'm sure to drive the male adult learners mad with desire. I smile to myself, happy as pie.

The doorbell rings and Lucy runs like a bobcat to the door, since she invited Moonboy over for *Apprentice* viewing and fish sticks. She flings open the door and screams, "You're fired!"

"I should hope not!" Queen Bean exclaims from the foyer. I quickly zip to the door to intervene. I haven't seen Queen Bean in quite a while. I notice she looks different, less severe and more . . . *sad*.

"It's a line from a TV show," I explain, ushering in Moonboy. "Where's Henry?" I ask, peeking around her.

"Henry's away at the moment." Her eyes dart toward Moonboy, who is following Lucy into the living room. Then she drops her voice to a whisper and leans toward me, "Henry has been offered a new teaching position in Philadelphia and he's considering it, since you-know-who's grandparents—" she gestures toward Moonboy "—on his mother's side live there. But don't say anything to him. Nothing is final yet." Queen Bean straightens up and smoothes down her shirt. "So Henry will be in Philadelphia the rest of this week and next week as well."

"Oh, my god!" I say, releasing a gush of air, as if I have just been walloped in my stomach.

"Yes, I know, it's quite sudden," Queen Bean says.

"Do you think Henry will take the position?" I ask.

"I'm not sure." She casts her eyes away from mine. "Maybe it's for the best . . . you know, for my grandson to get to know his mother's side of the family. I've never been good . . . I haven't been the most . . ." She stops and clears her throat. "I'm sorry. I'm not myself lately." I notice her eyes are rimmed with tears.

I don't know what to say to soothe her, so I touch her arm instead.

"Ah, well," she says, whipping out a tissue from her purse. She blows her nose, then looks at me with forced brightness. "So I heard you're off the dog walking and onto being a student!"

"You did? From whom?" I can't imagine how Queen Bean could have heard such information. I just applied to college a few days ago.

"Your friend Pip told me. She called Henry's house earlier today when I was there," Queen Bean explains, sensing my confusion.

"Oh, well, yes. Yes, I am," I say.

"I think that is a wise decision," she says, patting my hand. "You wouldn't want to be picking up some canine's excrement for the rest of your life, now, would you dear?"

Morgue

I am now living in a morgue. The house is piled high with box-shaped coffins of all my nothings. I watch as Lucy launches water-balloon grenades over the fence into the neighbor's yard. Moonboy runs around the fence and collects the balloon bits. Brendan leaves the house in his hippie threads. His girlfriend, Sophie, who, unbeknownst to me, turned seventeen six months ago, beeps her car horn, calls his name, then giggles because he is right there. Brendan plants a wet kiss on her full lips and they zoom off. I pick up the phone, dial Pip's office number, then punch in her extension.

"Pip McSweeny . . . *ssup* . . . media relations . . . *ssup*," Pip answers, sucking on a mint as usual.

"Henry was offered a teaching position in Philadelphia," I say.

"I heard," Pip says. "I wonder if his girlfriend is planning to move there with him."

She stops sucking on her mint and considers this. "I bet she will."

"You want to come over after work and tape stuff?" I ask.

"Sure," Pip says, "why the fuck not?"

Flagpole

I watch as Moonboy wraps himself around the flagpole outside the library. He scoots up the pole and I shoo him down. As soon as he is down, Lucy tries the same thing and fails. She slaps the pole, then whimpers. She has managed to grow two inches in a day and is now taller than me. Her toes hang over the edges of her sandals, but she refuses to let me buy her new ones. Between overlapping toes and no T-shirt, we have been cast out of the library, and I am at a loss about what to do. Who will have us? And then, inspiration: we will drive to my grandparents' right after picking up Brendan from his tennis lesson.

After buying the kids large ice cream cones, I scuttle them into the car and we drive home. I insist they stay put as I heft extravagantly-taped boxes of clothes from the living room to the car. When I call Grammy's house, my mother answers.

"What are you doing there?" I ask.

"He has a new girlfriend; I ran into them at the VitaCenter," she says. I know she is referring to Yoga Alien. Makes perfect sense.

"Well, I'm on my way up. We're leaving Cambridge right after I pick up Brendan from tennis," I say.

"All right. Are you still moving into that new apartment?" she asks.

"Yes, yes, yes. Don't worry. I haven't changed my mind. It's just that the movers aren't coming for another two weeks and I've already packed up all our stuff." My mother has been calling me regularly to make sure I am actually "getting out," as she refers to it, as if my prison term is finally ending.

I heave another box down the front steps and into the car. Moonboy and Lucy are silent in the backseat, hyperfocused on finishing their large-size cones. I told them if they didn't finish, I would never order them large ones again. They are both about halfway done and still going strong. I give them credit.

I run back into the house and call Pip at work. "Could you water my plants while I'm gone?" I ask.

"I didn't know you were gone."

"Well, I am."

"I can't take care of anything for a year, it's part of my twelve-step program," she says. "Not even a houseplant."

"You're kidding. I thought it would be just the opposite."

"Nope," Pip says. We grunt our good-byes and I place the phone back in the cradle. I switch off every light in the house and lock up, loading the plants on top of the boxes and then shutting the car hatch.

I turn back to look at the house, holding my hand over my eyes to shield them from the rays of early afternoon sun. The house seems almost skeletal in appearance, as if it's been emptied of both body and spirit. A battered gutter loosened from the underside of the roof bounces slowly in the breeze. I think, *All those years spent in this house.* The images of Brendan and Ex-Rat shooting hoops in the driveway and Lucy racing her Big Wheel up and down the sidewalk come to me. Then further back: Ex-Rat and my friends and their families, us wives with plump babies in our laps watching the men and our older children play horseshoes, the smell of meat on the grill hanging thick. And then still further back: Ex-Rat carrying me over the threshold of our new house and two-year-old Brendan, on my mother's hip, watching us, smiling, his thumb halfway out of his mouth.

I close my eyes and remember that moment—our laughter, the softness of James's lips on mine, his arms firmly holding me aloft. It seems like a lifetime ago.

I open my eyes and let my hand fall to my side, allowing the sun to blind me. "Well, that's it," I say aloud.

As I slowly walk around the car and get into the driver's seat, I check to make sure the kids' belts are buckled. Darling barks and wags his tail in the passenger seat next to me and we pull out of the driveway, the children still crunching on their cones. Eyes on the prize.

Pickup

Brendan is not happy and refuses to get in the car or go at all.

"We always go to Vermont. Why don't we go somewhere else? Like the Cape. It's where *everyone* goes."

"You can drive to Vermont," I offer.

"All the way?" he asks.

"All the way," I say. I think of the interstate and shiver. A reckless gleam fills his right eye and I can tell he has the same thought.

"Cool," he says, popping open his cell phone and pushing a button. "Would you mind if Sophie comes?"

I am beyond thrilled. Finally I will get to spend some real time with Brendan's girlfriend, especially since Grammy is sure to insist Sophie and I share a room and Brendan stay in the spare room next to her and Grandpa. I get into the passenger seat while he speaks into the phone. My excitement diminishes when I realize there's not a chance in hell that her parents will release their beautiful daughter into my insecure hands. Brendan snaps the phone shut.

"All set," he says. I clap. "You're gonna have to get in the back. There's no way Sophie is going to sit with Lucy all the way to Vermont."

I grab Brendan's cell phone and call Queen Bean's abode. She answers in a sultry tone. I look at the phone and then place it back to my ear.

"We have to do drop-off a little early today, there's been a change of plans," I say.

"Oh, it's you!" she says. I wonder who she thought it was? Her knight in shining Mercedes, Sir Bean?

"There's been a change of plans—" I start to repeat.

"Oh dear, that just won't do. My new man-friend is picking me—" Queen Bean says.

"New man-friend?" I gasp out loud. I'm sure my face has fallen off.

"Oh! Hold on. He has just stepped through the door."

Queen Bean must be covering the mouthpiece, because I have to strain to make out her new beau's muffled words. Suddenly she removes her hand and I hear him say using perfect broad *A*s, "No rush, dahling. I'll wait for you in the cah."

"Now, where were we?" she asks, flustered and breathless.

"Well, the kids and I are on our way to Vermont at the moment. I suppose if you want me to take your grandson with us, I'm sure Lucy—"

"Oh, could you? He loved it there last time. It would be a great vacation for him, and Henry isn't back for another few days," she gushes.

"Maybe I should speak with Henry before I do that," I say.

"Oh, I'm sure Henry will be delighted to have a little adult time himself. Once he returns from Philadelphia, that is. If you know what I mean."

I do know what she means. She means that Henry will be able to spend time with his doctor girlfriend, alone. Grrrrr. I hadn't thought of that, and I certainly don't appreciate Queen Bean reminding me of it.

"Did he take the job in Philadelphia?" I ask icily.

"I guess he's still mulling it over. I spoke with him last night and he said he's looking at the housing market, so I'm guessing he will," she says, without a hint of sadness. Obviously now that she has a new man to suffocate, she's perfectly fine with Henry and her grandson relocating. "I'll call Henry on his mobile telephone, though, and I'll pack some things for the trip. Oh, dear, I have to inform Spencer I'll be a few minutes. He's waiting in the car," she adds, and hangs up.

I look back at Moonboy. He shows off his empty hands. As does Lucy. I give them a thumbs-up and decide to forget all about Queen Bean's adult-time comments, Henry's new job offer, and his possible move. None of it will ruin my plans. Excellent decision to go to Vermont. After a little R & R at Grammy's, I'll be ready to move into my new apartment, hit the books, and start a whole new life. What fun.

Fully Loaded

The roof rack is fully loaded with three taped boxes full of clothes and two suitcases, one small and tattered, the other a wheely professional-looking one that belongs to Sophie. The dogs wag their tails in the way back. The plants are gone. I traded Manic Dog for them, finally standing firm with Queen Bean. It wasn't as hard as I imagined it would be. Although, when I suggested the switch-a-roo, I think Queen Bean's "Mmm-hmm" had more to do with her new man-friend's muscular arms straining to tether down the kids and my belongings to the top of my car, rather than the trade itself. It turns out Sir Bean is an absolute whiz with bungee cords. Also, he's pretty good at dealing with hippie-prep teen boy attitude too. In fact, I was so impressed that such a WASPy old codger knew all about iPods, the latest computer games, and the names of every Red Sox player, that I had asked him how he knew more than I did about such things. Sir Bean chuckled and said, "I have three grown boys and two grandsons of my own." I breathed a sigh of relief, because I knew Henry and Moonboy would be safe with him.

Rest Area

Once we're outside the city, I ask Brendan to pull over at a rest area: must make highly desired phone call to Ex-Rat. I forget the password on my phone card, so I have to call collect.

When he picks up, I start, "I'm taking the kids to . . ." I don't want to say *Vermont*. Brendan is right. It sounds limited. It's where we always go. If I can go to Alaska and move, I can certainly take the kids somewhere new. How hard can it be? ". . . the Cape," I finish. I look over at the car and Brendan, thanking him inwardly for his suggestion.

"So," Ex-Rat asks, "how does this affect me—and my moving into *my* house?" He lets loose a big, audible yawn so that I know that he's unfazed by my big news and is utterly bored with this entire conversation.

"It doesn't. Nothing does," I say, and slam down the phone, pissed. Very necessary to add an expensive vacation to newly amended alimony and child support budget.

"You know, Mom, you could have used my cell," Brendan says, as I climb back into the car. He should be the one to read the map and get us to the Cape, since he has a clue.

Bumper-to-Bumper

After sailing past highway signs for Plymouth Rock, we get stuck in godawful traffic. Heat rises from the pavement. The air conditioner barely cools and the car is overheating. Brendan keeps turning the engine off and on.

"Put on the heat," his girlfriend chirps. She sweats delicately, which adds a special glow to her perfect skin.

Brendan snorts rudely and I kick the back of his seat gently.

"What?" he yells, but I make no further comment. Sweat drips down my back. The dogs pant. Moonboy and Lucy are passed out in a sticky mass. I keep checking under their noses to see if they are still breathing, terrified we might all be inhaling carbon monoxide thanks to a million idling cars. "This was a great idea," Brendan says. "Some adventure." Finally the traffic begins to move. Brendan starts the engine and weaves in and out of the lanes until the cars come to a stop again when we reach a rotary.

"Do I take the bridge?" Brendan asks frantically, edging onto the rotary.

"I don't know, you have the map," I say.

"Jesus!" he screams, and throws the map at me. I cannot find the bridge and we have to circle the rotary once, then twice. I throw the map back up front and Sophie takes it, flattens it, scans it with her finger, and says calmly, "Yes, take the bridge."

Brendan takes the bridge. He also turns on the heat and we roll down our windows. The air is cooler. It smells like ocean. We go up, up, up. The view from the bridge is miraculous, like the heavens opening.

A Thought

I am feeling free, alive, independent, mature, and motherly. It's an exhilarating combination of emotions. From now on, I will take the kids on an adventure every summer. I stick my head out the window and feel the rush of wind.

"Get your head back in the window, you're going to get decapitated," Brendan yells.

Further In

As we head further south up Route 6, Sophie shows me the road on the map. We've decided to go as far out as we can go up the Cape in hope of finding shelter for the night, since we're tired of pulling off the main road and finding no vacancies in the motels of the more popular touristy towns. Lucy and Moonboy are up and Mad-Libbing it. They giggle and hoot, filling in sentences with potty words. "Crappy diaper" is their favorite phrase; runner-up is "poop puddle." Brendan asks Sophie to turn on the radio. The static fades in and out as she twists the knob past rap and hardcore and settles on a song to which I know all the lyrics.

"I love this song—it's so old school!" Brendan says. I'm surprised. I didn't even know he knew the song. Sophie turns up "Night Moves" by Bob Seger and I begin to sing softly and then louder and louder as Sophie and Brendan join me in the end chorus: "Oh, sweet summertime, summertime . . ."

Darkness

We have almost reached the end of the road. Still no vacancies, and now it's dark. I try to quell my rising panic. I tell Brendan to pull over at the next exit and we wind and curve our way into a tiny town. The only place open is a snack shack, where people with sandy feet are eating creamies. Suddenly the car dies. Brendan tries to restart it but the engine won't turn over. Brendan and Sophie both flash me anxious expressions.

"Don't worry! It does this all the time. It just needs a rest!" I lie.

I give the kids a fifty-dollar bill to go get some food and ask Brendan for his cell phone. When they're gone, I dial Ex-Rat. His voice mail picks up. I hang up. I dial Henry's cell-phone number. Henry's voice crackles and pops, "Ello." Heart racing, I grip the phone.

"I'm on the Cape," I say. "We have arrived safely."

"Wha . . . hap . . . o . . . pla . . . mont?" Through the dropouts, I can make out nothing, but I fill with shame anyway because I sense by his tone that he's wondering why we are on the Cape and not in Vermont.

"Change of plans," I say, and get out of the car. The connection clears.

"I wish you had informed me," he says. "Where are you staying?" He sounds like he needs to scream.

"Somewhere," I say, trying to conceal my nervousness.

"Where is *somewhere*?" His voice is rising in pitch.

"I don't know yet," I say.

"Everything must be booked. It's the second week of August!" He now screams. "You have to make reservations months in advance!"

"Well, I didn't know that! This is my first time here!" I scream back. "Jesus Christ!"

"The car is dead," I throw in.

"Jesus Christ!" Henry blasts again. "I'm in Philadelphia and I don't fly out for another two days. It's not like I'm in Cambridge and can just come get you!"

"You're not helping!"

"You are never really prepared for anything, are you? Even with all those lists and packing months in advance!" I hang up on him. The poop puddle! I start crying in earnest, because he is absolutely right about me. When the phone vibrates in my hand, I almost drop it but am able to answer it in time.

"I have an uncle—"

"How did you get this number?" I interrupt peevishly.

"It's on my cell phone, right under 'received calls,'" Henry says. "Oh."

"This uncle," he continues, "I haven't seen him in years. He's my mother's brother."

"I didn't know your mother had a brother," I say.

"Well, she does," he says.

"Oh."

"Listen. He lives in a very small town somewhere on the Cape. Jesus, I haven't spoken to him in years. He lives right near the ocean . . . tons of rooms . . . I'm sure it would be fine for you guys to spend the night there. I'm going to make some phone calls. You stay put. It might take a while." He clicks off.

I head over to a picnic table, where the kids join me a few minutes later, loaded down with onion rings, fried clams, and banana splits. Brendan still looks worried.

"Henry found us a place to stay!" I blurt, then realize I may have spoken prematurely and add, "I mean, Henry is calling his uncle and we might have a place to stay for tonight."

Smiles, smiles, and more smiles.

"This is fun," Brendan says, putting the tray of food on the picnic table. He kisses me. I kiss him back. Sophie smiles. He kisses her too.

"I'm glad," I say, and we all dig in.

Backtracking

Miraculously, the car starts and we turn around and head back from whence we came. Sophie has written down all of Henry's directions, taking dictation carefully. She navigates for Brendan, who has the heat turned on high to cool the engine. Combined with the night air flowing in the windows, it gives the feeling that all is well. The dogs, stuffed with snack-shack leftovers, are settled in the far back, farting and dog dreaming. Lucy and Moonboy fade in and out of giggles and potty profanity. Soon their eyelids droop.

We leave Route 6 behind and pass through a beautiful village with quiet tree-lined streets. The town road narrows and we turn into a sandy driveway. The house at the end is not so much a house as a rambling concatenation of New England additive architecture, with sections tacked on here and there. Statues made out of junk metal and driftwood line the driveway. They look like people.

We roll in and Brendan cuts the engine, which has begun to smoke. We can hear the crashing of waves. A door opens and a tall, weathered man emerges from the house and approaches the car. He peers into the front passenger window. He holds a pipe and his eyes shine ghostly blue in the dark.

"Which one of you is my nephew?" he asks playfully, not scary at all. Brendan, Sophie, and I breathe a sigh of relief, and I point to Moonboy.

"What a beaut!" He grins. "By the smell of things, you're going to need a new transmission, water pump, and radiator. Might as well buy a new car. I have some you might like, bought down in Virginia. Things rust around here due to the air—well, forget about that for now. Come in, you must be bone tired."

He opens the door and gently shakes the kids awake, rubbing Moonboy's head several times. "Rise and shine, little fellow. You're at your Great-Uncle William's house." Moonboy smiles sleepily. "Come on, you two, come meet my friends." He takes Lucy's and Moonboy's hands and introduces them to all his statues.

"First," he says, "I made this guy here, and he seemed so lonely I made this girl here to keep him company. Then she needed someone to talk to because he is the silent type, so I made these friends here for her." Lucy and Moonboy soak him in. I see adoration beginning to edge into their eyes. "You like clay?" he asks. "You like making things? Finding things?"

They nod.

"Tomorrow we'll get up real early, before anyone else, and find some really good shells—ones you can put to your ear and listen to. And then we'll dig for clay. I have a kiln, so we can harden the things we make. Maybe we'll make teacups for these guys." He points to the statues. "Would you like that?"

Lucy and Moonboy nod again.

"Good, it's a plan, then," he says. "Right now, though, we'll read a bit of Mark Twain and hit the hay." He leads us into the house and we follow with boxes and bags and dogs. The house has low ceilings and dark wood post and beam. Though odd in shape, there's an element of cottage about the interior, and it's very warm and welcoming.

"This place was an old pub, farm, inn, and everything in between," he tells us, "long, long ago, back in horse-and-buggy days. When you drive in at night you can't tell, but it sits right on the bluff. My daddy's daddy purchased the house for my grandmother. She hated it, though, and wanted him to sell it, but he held onto it and didn't tell her. He hired someone to maintain and repair the place. My grandmother and the rest of us didn't even know about it until he died. So the first time I came out here, I guess I was about your age," he points his pipe toward Brendan. "Maybe a bit older, I don't know. I was supposed to go to college but I couldn't stand the thought."

He stops for a minute and the sounds of crickets and surf rise in the distance.

"Well, I fell in love with the place. Never left. And I mean never. Haven't been back to Cambridge in over forty-five years. And won't ever go back."

"You live here all alone?" I ask.

He takes his pipe out of his mouth and nods gravely. "Of course I only live here when I'm not off being a pirate," he says with a wink.

Missing Cell Phone

"Hey Mom! Have you seen my cell phone?" Brendan says, unloading the boxes from the car roof.

"No. Why?"

"I can't seem to find it, and you were the last one to use it, remember? After Sophie wrote down the directions to William's, Henry asked to speak with you."

"I'm sure it will turn up," I say, waiting for Brendan to freak out. He can't tolerate being without his phone for more than two seconds.

"Yeah, you're probably right. No big deal. I'll ask William if Sophie can use his phone to call her folks," Brendan says, completely mellow. I'm beginning to like this hippie-prep phase.

. . . .

fourteen

A Week of Recovery

Mornings take on a blissful routine. At the crack of dawn I rise, call for the dogs, and we walk. They run after crabs, bark at the waves, nip and kiss each other. Barefoot, I skip and jump, but they pay no attention, entwined as they are. Like my brood: Sophie and Lucy sleep curled on guest beds, and Brendan and Moonboy are on mattresses on the floor, even though there are four other spare bedrooms.

For myself, I've discovered a daybed on the enclosed back porch. I sleep or sometimes stay awake and read, with the tiny reading lamp, or just listen to the waves crash all night. A hollow full sound, if there is such a thing.

Now, William makes his way toward me on the beach. His trousers are rolled up, his long-sleeve shirt whipping hard against his skinny frame. His dark hair is graying at the temples but still thick. He reminds me of Henry without the nervous tension. What Henry could be, if he'd only let himself. William is sure and steady and without reservation.

"You skip well," he says.

I blush.

"I have something to show you," he says. "Follow me." He takes my hand. His own is rough and big. It feels like the hand I imagine a more manly type of father than mine would feel like. He leads me down the beach, and we reach the steep steps that lead up to his house. "Go on," he tells the dogs, and points to the house. They go but soon are back again. "Stay here," he says to me, and leads the dogs up. Light on his feet, he's amazing to watch.

"Come," he says, walking back down the stairs and taking my hand. We round the bluff and the beach opens up, long, flat, and wide. Out in the water, I see three oblong heads peering at us.

"Seals!" I cry happily, and together we watch them play.

A New Car

William shows me his barn full of cars. He has quite a collection, each individually covered. He unveils one perfect vessel after another. "I purchased some of them online," he says. "A hobby." The last one he shows me is a light blue convertible. I'm possessed by an instant urge to drive it fast down the highway with a glamorous scarf à la Katharine Hepburn.

William opens the driver's side door. "Hop in," he says. I slide in and he shuts the door. The seats are creamy and divine, the steering wheel big.

"You look good," he says. "Does it feel right?" he asks.

"Yes," I say.

"Then take it. It's a gift."

"Oh, no!" I am truly shocked.

He looks me hard in the eyes. His eyes are so blue, they are almost white. "For bringing David to me," he says. I sense the weight of his sincerity. He had no idea of Moonboy's perfection, of Moonboy's tide of love.

There is a long pause before I hear myself say, "OK." William smiles, pleased.

"You will stay a while, won't you?" he asks.

"Yes, if you really don't mind," I say. "It's lovely here."

"Indeed it is. Indeed it is." He pushes back his hair. "He's my only great nephew, you know."

"I do," I say, aware that Moonboy has no cousins.

"Henry and David's mother only came out to visit a few times after he was adopted, when he was an infant, before she became ill—she battled cancer for a long time." William sighs, pushes his hair back again. "Then, after she passed on, I sent letters asking Henry to come visit. I know Henry was having a difficult time, and I realize my sister can be a tad controlling."

"Well, recently your sister seems to be letting go a bit," I say.

"Really?" William asks.

"She has a new man-friend," I say.

"I'll be damned." William grins.

"And Henry seems to be doing better now. You know, David really likes it here. He really loves who you are. I'm sure there will be a lot more visits to see Great-Uncle William."

"You think?" he asks, boyish.

"Yes," I say firmly, and then ask, "What was she like? David's mother—Henry's wife?"

"She was a joy to be around. Just like you," William says, opening my car door.

Five Days Pass

We build a fire on the beach. William fixes Moonboy's suspenders, which the two of them purchased in town earlier in the day, along with linen shorts and a white oxford short-sleeved shirt. His feet are bare. Moonboy grows darker every day. In the flame of the bonfire, his eyes are like globes. He is smitten with Tom Sawyer, and William has helped him dress the part. Lucy has cut off her one pair of pants at the bottoms and hiked them up with rope. All Huck. She spits and slicks her hair back, licks her lips, and eyes William, who beckons her. She strolls over, kicking sand along the way. He reties her rope belt in a square knot.

"Tomorrow we'll fish," William announces. "Just us three."

Alone

After days of too many limbs and family smells, it's easier to be alone than I thought. I walk the beach in search of shells. Finding one, I place it in a tin bucket that I found in William's garage. I round the corner to see if the seals are bobbing on the ocean's surface near the shore. They're not. I sit down and watch waves steadily roll in instead.

After a while, I get up and stretch, my arms extended and reaching skyward. I realize I'm content, really content, being alone, without even the dogs for company. For the first time in a long while, my body is emptied of fear, the nugget of anxiety that placed itself in my chest before and after my divorce, the loneliness I tried so hard to relieve myself of by hiding in my dark closet, making my lists upon lists, even flying all the way to Alaska to visit Mason. I think about the manic energy I had while packing my boxes. Here, away from my life, I've managed to let go of all of it.

A Cornerstone

The phone pierces the silence of the house like a bullhorn and I jump. Must have been dozing on the day bed. The phone in the kitchen on the wall is an old rotary with a heavy handle, and picking it up makes me feel like I'm back in the eighties. I want to tease my hair and put on loads of makeup.

"Hello," I breathe saucily. Could be a boyfriend. Who knows? I feel quite loose at the moment.

It's Ex-Rat. His voice is harsh. "Who's this?" he asks.

Flash back to reality. The eighties were my nerdy, braces-filled wonder years, when I couldn't get a date because I looked like a seven-year-old even though I was sixteen. I can't take Ex-Rat now. I hang up the phone quick, dash back to the daybed, crawl right in, and pull the covers over my head.

Waking

I mull about the room, trying to sort things out. Was I just fooling myself back there on the beach? Just one nasty phone call from my ex and I'm rattled. I sigh. No sign of anyone back yet. I brew coffee and drink the whole pot in shame while listening to the news on NPR. Very depressing. I turn to cleaning. I scrub the whole kitchen and move on to the living room. Then I finally get why I'm so up in a heap. I had thought Ex-Rat would treat me better after my decision to move out of the house and become more independent. I thought he would respect me more.

So much for that hope.

I put down my dust rag on the coffee table and spot an old *New Yorker* magazine. I plop my fanny on the couch and start reading. The cartoons make me think of Pip, who's always cutting them out and pasting them on her bathroom wall.

I decide to give Pip a call at work.

"Thank god you woke me," Pip says, in place of hello. "I was on my third desk nap of the day and I still have a shitload of work I need to finish before I leave the office. Shit! All I want to do lately is sleep and sleep. I can't keep my eyes open," Pip says. "I feel like a caterpillar."

"Transformation," I say.

"Withdrawal," she says.

"Withdrawal?" I ask.

"Yes. Withdrawal. I quit smoking because Martin and I are back together."

"*Martin?* What about Henry?" I ask.

"What about Henry?" Pip asks innocently. I want to kill her.

"I thought you still had feelings for him."

"I think I just needed to *believe* I was interested in Henry. When Martin and I took our break from each other, I needed to kind of pass the time, you know."

"Took a break?"

"Give me the benefit of my own delusion, OK? I let you have yours," Pip says.

"What is that supposed to mean?"

"Henry is more your type than mine, that's all I'm saying. I mean, you did see him first, and even though you claimed you were no longer interested in him when I asked you that time right after Christmas, I think you were—and I think you still are."

"What about your remark that I just want a husband? And about how I need to start doing things for myself?"

"You're starting. You flew to Alaska, moved out of your house, and enrolled in college. So now you can go ahead and chase any guy you want. Except your asshole of an ex-husband," Pip drawls, and then begins slurping a mint.

"Thank you so much for your permission," I say.

"You're welcome. Oh, shit! That reminds me . . . *ssup* . . . your asshole ex stopped by my office this morning to get your number to wherever the fuck you took off to. Luckily I didn't have it."

"Why didn't he just call Brendan's cell?"

"I guess it was off or something."

"Oh, my god," I groan, remembering that Brendan's cell phone is still missing. "Brendan let me use it to call Henry when the car broke down. I must have left it on the car roof or something," I tell Pip.

"Your car . . . *ssup* . . . broke down?"

"Long story, I'll tell you all about it when I get back, but then I don't understand how James got my number. He called here earlier and was a complete jerk."

"I haven't a clue. However, the complete jerk did say *before* he slammed the door to my office . . . *ssup* . . . that he was going to track down Henry and see if he knew where you were, since apparently . . . *ssup* . . . your mother had a nervous breakdown. I guess you told her you were going to visit her in Vermont, but you never showed up. Smooth move, Ex-Lax," Pip says.

"I've gotta go," I say, dialing my mother almost before I hang up.

Anger Nirvana

"I wasn't worried," my mother says evenly. "Quite the contrary."

My mother is clearly beyond angry. She has reached anger nirvana. She is so angry, the surface is calm. Not a ripple.

"I'm sorry," I say again and again.

"Why? I can't imagine why you should be sorry. You are free to do whatever possesses you. You're an adult, with two children, one almost grown." Her tone is devastatingly nonchalant, and she knows it.

"Mom, I know you're angry," I say.

"My dear, I was angry when your father left me for a waiter from Miami who just happened to also be a man," she says. "Your little stint of rebellion didn't move a hair on my head. Puh-leeeze."

"Well," I say.

"I should say so," my mother responds to my nonquestion.

" 'I should say so' to what?" I ask.

"Whatever it is that you seem to be insinuating," she says, sounding more righteous. More like herself, thank god.

"Would you like the number here?" I ask timidly.

"That compassionate and thoughtful ex-husband of yours was kind enough to offer it to me after seventeen voice messages hysterically screamed into his machine by yours truly," she says.

"I'm sorry," I say.

"It was humiliating!" she rages now.

"I'm really sorry," I say.

"You should be!" she yells and hangs up. I smile, grateful that she is feeling something. Much better than the awful fake calm. I'll send her a postcard and everything will be fine.

Another Phone Call

The phone rings and I answer it.

"Who is this?" hisses Ex-Rat.

"Me." I quiver. The phone is vibrating with obscene dementia.

"You somehow failed to tell me where the fuck you were going."

"I thought if it didn't affect you, you were not really interested in knowing the specific details of our trip. When I told you our general destination, you stated, and I quote, 'How does this affect me and my move into *my house*?' Quite frankly, it didn't, so I felt no need to barrage you with unwanted information."

"You have become quite full of yourself ever since you came back from Alaska, haven't you?" he says. "So literal. So literally a bitch."

"You can thank yourself for that," I say shakily, and end the conversation.

Another Phone Call

"Maybe we should consider further court processes," Ex-Rat singsongs.

"Be my guest. You foot the bill," I say, and hang up again.

Another Phone Call

"Let me talk to Brendan and Lucy."

"They are out," I say.

"Both of them?" he asks.

"Yes," I say.

"Stop playing games," he sneers.

"I'm not playing games," I say, and this time *he* hangs up.

And Another Phone Call

"I am no longer afraid of you or your court *processes,*" I say and slam down the phone.

A Long Walk

Having resorted to showers instead of baths because of the leaking tub, I am on my third shower of the day. Afterward, I put on a fluffy robe and sit on the porch. I need to get out of the house, but Brendan and Sophie took the car to go play tennis. William is off with Moonboy and Lucy somewhere. But I will not be deterred. I throw on my coffee-colored brown dress, sweep my hair into a messy bun, and put on my Yoko Ono bifocals, and head out of the house with the dogs. The road into town is longer than I remember—of course, I'm on foot this time, and that does make a difference. I amuse myself with images of overturned horse-drawn buggies and fancy myself a humble, smart *and* sexy-looking servant sent to do an errand on foot, under duress, for my lord or lady. Prefer the lord bit. I imagine him looking exactly like Russell Crowe. I imagine this Russell Crowe–looking lord, with a broken leg, on the side of the road, in desperate need of a doctor. Seems to work, because I'm now all sweaty from walking/running and am almost at the edge of town. I hitch the dogs to their leashes, and even with the dogs going in five directions at once and arms being pulled out of their sockets, I am making better time than the cars, which are crammed, bumper-to-bumper, from the outskirts to the inskirts of town. When I arrive at the center, I picture returning to the Russell Crowe–like lord, who furrows his brows in respect and admiration. "You've done it," he whispers. "My love, you have done it!" He leans down toward me, his lips parted . . .

I'm interrupted midsmooch by a loud honking. Actually, more like a tooting. *Toot, toot.* I turn toward the sound, and there are Brendan and Sophie sitting in the convertible that is cooler than coolness itself.

Brendan yells, "You walked all that way?"

"Why, yes, I did!" I yell back.

"What are you going to do while you're in town?" he asks.

"Haven't got a clue," I say, proudly.

"There are loads of stores and stuff," Sophie says.

"You look hot. Do you want us to drive you home?" Brendan says.

"I don't want to go back, I just got into town," I say, wiping my forehead.

"At least let us take the dogs," he says.

"No," I say to the idea of not having the dogs.

"You can't just tie them to a tree, Mom," Brendan snaps. "You won't be able to go into any of the shops."

"We'll come back and pick you up later," Sophie says.

"Yeah, we'll be home, just call the cell—oops, my bad, I don't have my cell," Brendan says.

I bite my lip and wonder how I'm going to break the news to him that I probably left his cell on the roof of the car. Ah! That's what I'll do! I'll buy Brendan a new cell phone in town!

"I suppose the dogs could use some water," I say, walking them around the cars in the traffic jam, then scooting them into the backseat. "I'll call you at William's if I need a ride." I kiss them all. Dogs last. The traffic begins to move and I wave good-bye. I'm off.

A Quiet Church

After shopping for Brendan's cell phone and some postcards in overly crowded stores, I discover a quiet and cool place to rest in the town's Catholic church. It is tiny, like a one-room schoolhouse, with a single stained glass window. I sit down in one of the rustic wooden pews. I open the bag that contains my postcards and take out a postcard that has a photograph of a lighthouse, and I grab a pen from my purse. I scribble down, "I am moving," with my new address underneath, and address the card to Mason. Done. Bending my head, clasping my eyes shut, I say a prayer: "Please help Mason forgive me." I open my eyes, and then shut them again. "And don't let Henry move to Philadelphia."

I leave the church and when I pass the post office, I stop.

I think for a minute, then gently drop the postcard into the box, and walk on.

Phone Call from Mason

The sun is rising. I'm unbearably hot, having slept in my robe. I stumble to the kitchen to make some coffee. The phone rings mid-brew. Who has the nerve to call so early? Surely Ex-Rat. "May I help you?" I ask harshly.

In fact, it's Mason.

"Ah, hi," he says. The connection is crystal clear, as if he is calling from next door. I press my lips to the receiver.

"Where are you?" I whisper.

"Sandwich," he says, "Just over the bridge."

"How did you find me?" I ask.

"I called your aunts, then your mother, then Henry. He gave me the directions from Logan."

"He's thinking about moving," I blurt out.

"Who?"

"Henry. He might take a teaching position in Philadelphia," I say.

"Oh."

"Did he say anything to you?" I ask.

"No. He just gave me directions," Mason says. I twist the phone cord into a knot. There is silence between us.

"You haven't written at all," Mason says.

"Mason—"

"I wanted to make sure you were in before I showed up," he interrupts. "I'll be there in about an hour." He hangs up before I can say whatever it was I was about to say. *What was it?* I wonder.

Mason

Mason stands on William's porch with his baseball hat placed under his armpit, his left leg jutting out ahead of him. His hair is longer. It falls in lopsided waves over his forehead. He brushes it aside with his hand. Just this gesture makes me want to touch him.

He hands me a small box.

"This is yours," he says firmly, and then lets go of his nerve, looks away. I know what it is.

"I can't," I try to hand it back.

"I've already looked into it," he says. "I'll move to the city and be with you and get a job in whatever—I don't care—for a while—there must be lots of carpentry jobs. And when something comes up in the Parks and Rec Department, I'll jump on it."

"You'll be miserable," I say.

"No, I won't be. I'll have *you*," he says without conviction.

"And Brendan and Lucy," I remind him.

"I've loved you since I can remember," he says.

"You'll still be miserable. You told me once, in a letter, that you hate the city," I add. I try again to hand back the box. "You were young," I say practically. "And I had a polka-dot bathing suit."

"You just don't want it," he says, once again firm, able to look in my eyes.

"I'm so . . ." I trail off.

"Don't," he says. "Don't apologize. It makes it worse." He pauses, making a slow circle on the welcome mat with his foot. "It's that guy, isn't it? The writer. Henry. The one who gave me directions here. The one who Federal Expressed his kid's drawings all the way to Alaska. He's in love with you, isn't he?" He looks up. "Isn't he?"

I shake my head.

"Somehow I doubt that," he says, then turns and walks to his rental car, slams the door, and peels out of the driveway. I run after him, and then stop.

I stand still, holding the box in my hand.

William's Words

William does not knock. The door is open.

"So who was that fellow who stopped by? An admirer?"

"Once," I answer.

"Ah," William murmurs. He smoothes his beard over and over. "Hurt your heart?" he pries gently.

"Well, yes and no. I think it was me who ended up hurting him," I say.

"Come now. I can't imagine you hurting a fly, let alone a person."

"I did, though. I didn't mean to. I lied to him. I said I would write, even though I knew I wouldn't. Because he belongs in Alaska and I belong to the city." I pause, taking a deep shaky breath. "Then I came back from visiting him in Alaska, found an apartment, and I just couldn't stop packing, and he kept sending me letters and I kept thinking I would write him after I got done packing, I would write and explain, but I didn't, you know? And then I found out Henry got offered a position in Philadelphia . . . and . . . and . . . he might move and what if he does and . . ."

"And?" William asks.

"And then it would be just awful," I say, starting to cry.

"I see," William says knowingly. He sighs and just holds my hand.

Pretty Flowers

"The kids made you something," William says. I wipe the back of my hand across my puffy, wet face and look up. Moonboy slips shyly around William and Lucy pushes him forward. They both hold mis-shapen clay vases that hold pretty little flowers. Moonboy hands me his and then hugs me. Lucy thrusts hers under my nose.

"Stop crying right now, or I won't let you have it," she says in a threatening tone. I stop crying. She shoves her vase in my hand. "Now go to bed," Lucy says.

Wakey, Wakey

Somehow, Ex-Rat has managed to arrive and place himself comfort-ably at the kitchen table. He is holding a mug of coffee. William and Brendan run from the kitchen when they see me come in. "How did this happen?" I ask.

"I came through that door there," Ex-Rat says. "Nice nightgown. Did Mr. Wilderness give it to you?" Ex-Rat's hands are trembling. The coffee jiggles in the mug.

"No," I answer just as the phone rings.

"'Tis *moi*," my mother says. "Just thought I'd see how you and your surprise visitor are getting on."

"He's here," I say, breathing hard into the phone.

"I knew you'd be thrilled!" My mother drivels on and on. I let her ramble. I can see her waving her hand like a magic wand. I go into the other room, stretching the phone cord tight.

"Not Mason, James," I hiss. "Mom, James is here."

"What is *he* doing there?" she asks.

"You told him Mason was coming, didn't you?" I ask shrilly.

"Do not screech in my ear. He called for directions. I told him you were busy, that you had company, and that the company hap-pened to be Mason—all the way from Alaska, the Alaskan wilder-ness. How was I to know he would crash in on you?"

"You knew, Mom," I say.

"I didn't," she says. "I swear."

I hang up.

She calls right back.

"You'll thank me someday, sweetie. I'd pay to have seen that bastard's face when I told him," she says. The line goes dead. My mother is using me, I realize, to work out her own separation issues. I will address this, at a much later date, with a succession of therapists.

I go into the kitchen to confront the bastard face to face. But he is crying. I've never seen him cry. That's always been my job.

Out the window, I watch Brendan and Sophie grabbing their tennis rackets, and William ushering the kids into the backseat of the car. I wave out the window as they all flee down the driveway.

"I just want to go home," Ex-Rat sobs. I turn to him.

"So go," I say, and point to the door. "You own it now, so what's the problem? It's all yours."

"It's not the same without you and the kids in it," he says soberly, wiping his tears.

"Why are you doing this?" I ask quietly. I swallow, thinking of the months I couldn't even leave the house, full of despair and longing, while he and his new fiancée moved in together before I'd even been handed the divorce papers. "I don't love you in that way anymore."

"No, you hate me," he says. I agree—I hate him, hate him, hate him. But I don't say it.

"So where's Mason? Sleeping in this morning?"

"Why is it that all of a sudden you want me back now that another man showed interest?" I ask bitterly. "Forget I said that. It doesn't matter."

"That's not true," he says. "We made love the night before Mason came into the picture—or have you managed to forget that? Because I sure haven't. I broke it off with my fiancée because I thought there was a hope of reconciliation, a glimmer at least."

"How good of you, how very kind, to break it off with her after fucking the mother of your children," I say.

"Don't say 'fuck,' that was not fucking, we have never fucked," he says. "You're angry. You haven't been yourself since you came back from Alaska. This is cruel."

"Go fuck yourself," I say savagely. "I'm cruel? *I'm* cruel? When you practically crammed down my throat how much you didn't love me, on a weekly basis, by being gone a few nights out of seven. How many fiancées did you have to break it off with then? Or how about dragging my self-esteem around in court? How I was such a loser because I couldn't find a job to save my life? I was the pathetic one? Right? Isn't that right? Aren't those your words?" I've lost control. I am screaming. "Well, OK, you were right. I *was* pathetic, I was a loser—for spending years waiting for you to turn to me and say, 'I love you, I'm sorry.' Even in court, I thought, 'He'll realize he is making a mistake and he loves me.' What a loser, huh? To think that you actually loved me. You just plumb forgot—"

I am growing hoarse. My voice cracks. I feel like I'm in some dumb B movie. Yet I continue, because it feels I am about to finally move—really move—not to some apartment or school—or a one-time walk alone on the beach—but really change—me—finally.

"I am stuck!" I yell. "I am fucking stuck. In this. I loved you so much." I mean this. I loved him like the ocean. Like the heavens. In all his selfishness. All his beauty. All his cowardly ways. How he spit sideways, sweated when he ate, and growled when someone disturbed him while he was reading. How he watched football in his ratty sweatpants and old Peanuts shirt. How he kissed the back of my neck while I washed dishes. How he obsessively fixed everything. How he dragged me into a store to buy something nice. How he bought rotisserie chicken and said, with swelling pride, I didn't have to cook. How he first held Brendan. How he first held Lucy. How he looked at me when he put this ring on my finger. I worshipped him. He was my man. My rock. My cubbyhole. My resting place. My home. It would be so easy to go back. To rest my head upon his shoulder. To laugh. To say how stupid are we to let this chance go by, to not try again.

I slide the wedding band off. I roll it back and forth between my thumb and finger. I look at it. It is just a ring. A band of gold. I lay it on the table.

"You will do it again," I say. "You will take me for granted. And I just can't go back to that. Not ever."

He looks at me. He is about to speak, but I speak first. "You know you will."

Groceries

"Where's Dad?" Brendan asks when he walks in the door carrying grocery bags.

"He went home. To his house," I say. He nods and places the groceries on the counter. Sophie and the children come in and begin unpacking. Me, too. I hand Brendan a gallon of milk to put in the fridge.

Henry Calls

The kids and I are squeezing lemons for lemonade when Henry calls. "Hello," he says.

"Hi," I say, my heart beating like a maniac's.

"Just calling to see how everyone is getting on and if Mason managed to find Uncle William's house," Henry says.

"Mason isn't here," I say. "He left."

"Oh," Henry says. "So you and Mason are not spending some time on the Cape together before your big move?"

"No. Mason and I are not spending some time together on the Cape."

"I see," Henry says, going quiet. With Moonboy in the room, I don't dare ask Henry about Philadelphia.

"Oh! I forgot to congratulate you on finding an apartment. I heard you're buying a really nice place in my neighborhood. Just a block—"

"Who told you?" I interrupt.

"Pip," he says.

"You know, Pip is back together with Martin," I say, in a clear, cold voice.

"Yes, I know. I ran into them at the market—"

"Would you like to speak to your son?" I interrupt again, imagining Henry and his doctor girlfriend Kate running into Pip and Martin in the grocery store. Maybe they planned a cookout together. Isn't that what happily reunited couples do?

"Ah, yes, of course," Henry mumbles, and I hand the phone to Moonboy.

William Extends an Invitation

William points to the phone. "Your mother just rang," he says. "We had a nice chat."

"My mother called?"

"Yes," he says.

"What did she say?" I ask.

"Stuff," he says.

"Stuff?"

"Good stuff. About you, the kids, Henry and David, how you're doing here. Just stuff." His tone is somewhat Brendan-like, adolescent.

"Did you invite her here?" I ask.

"She said she wasn't quite sure if she could manage it, but that she was tickled to be asked." He smiles. Her word *tickled,* coming from William's artistic mouth, is as provocative as a curse. I know she's already packed and on the road and will arrive by midafternoon with bushels of organic produce and maybe even some roadkill. God only knows who she is bringing with her. Probably a whole nudist village with green cotton beach towels and natural sunscreen. Maybe they got hold of a school bus and spray-painted it various Day-Glo colors. I imagine them zooming up the drive, dust all around, like a circus coming to town.

Mother's Arrival

My mother arrives alone. No Day-Glo bus, no bushels of veggies. Just her, in a bathing suit from the fifties, a very yellow towel, a small, round suitcase, a deck of cards, red lipstick in a silver case, Jackie O sunglasses, and her hair in a French twist under a large straw hat. I watch from the porch and pinch myself. It hurts. Yes, I'm very much alive.

She daintily walks up the steps, tilting her head. "Hello, darling," she croons, and waves her hand with the utmost grace. She kisses the air around my face, touches her hat, and dips into her round suitcase, removing another hat. She pulls it down hard on my head and ties the bow tight underneath my chin. "Let's block those cancer-causing rays." She checks her watch. I didn't even know she owned a watch. "I made fabulous time," she says. "Where's Bill?"

"Bill?" I ask.

"The man who owns this property," she says, as if I must live on another planet.

"Oh, you mean *William*," I say. "He's inside."

Just then William bangs open the door. He is wearing a safari-type suit. All wrinkled and just so. I marvel. The old chap is quite handsome. However, he is still wearing flip-flops. I can feel my mother's pulse rising. She holds her hat down as if there are fifty-mile-an-hour winds.

"Well, I say," is all she can manage.

William looks her up and down. I shift, very uncomfortably, as my mother is checked out in her very short swim thingy. His face changes from Sweet William to Bill.

I'm not sure I like Bill at all. He cocks one brow and slicks back his hair, then asks in a husky, thick voice, "Cocktail?"

My mother literally leaps toward him—it's akin to a witch finding her broomstick—confirming a big yes. No formal introduction has yet taken place, but they mush themselves through the door, breasts to chest, giggling and clucking.

"Ladies first," Bill says, with an expansive gesture.

"Oh, my!" my mother coos and steps inside. Bill doesn't hold the door for me, oh no, he just looks down toward the swimsuit's bottom fringe, and further, and smiles a slow smile. He lets the door slam behind him.

Cheese and Crackers

Later, the kids and I wind our way down the stairs to the beach, where William and my mother are reclining. Between them is a bottle of wine in an ice bucket, and a cutting board with cheese and crackers.

My mother stuffs a cracker in her mouth.

"You are eating cheese?" I ask in a shocked tone. "I thought you didn't eat wheat or dairy."

"Oh, lighten up. Life is too short to be so uptight. You have to learn to let go and just enjoy the good things. Am I right?" she coos in Bill's direction.

"Mmmm," Bill murmurs. He looks like he's preparing to breast-feed, since my mother's rather large breasts have flung themselves toward his face.

She spreads brie on another cracker and takes a bite. "Scrumptious!"

Thick in Sand

I walk forever. The ocean rushes back and forth over my bare feet and the salty breeze feels so good.

When the wind picks up, I slow to a stop and tie the straw hat my mother gave me more securely under my chin. I stand, watching as people collect their umbrellas and towels and start to leave the beach. A hard drop of rain hits my arm, and another. I turn and walk rapidly back toward William's house, staying along the shoreline, until waves crash so fiercely they frighten me. I sprint up the beach's width and move past the staircases, my feet thick in sand, the rain whipping sideways against my body.

A Lone Figure

Out of the sheet of rain, someone walks toward me. He is tall and angular and wears a rain poncho.

"Hey!" he calls, moving still closer. "I thought that was you," says Henry. "You had just gone off when I arrived. When the wind started up and then the rain, I got worried about how far you'd made it down the beach." He holds out another rain poncho. My tank top is soaked and my breasts show through the thin material. Henry looks at my breasts and then looks away quickly. As I untie my now soaking straw hat in order to pull the poncho over my head, it blows away, rolling like a wheel across the beach. Henry takes off after it, fast as fury, his poncho flapping wildly behind him. He grabs the hat and collapses it against his chest, then waves it in the air, showing me he has retrieved it successfully. He is so unbelievably handsome.

"So you have finally decided to grace us with your presence," I say, as he returns, hat in hand.

"I risk life and limb to bring you a rain slicker, and I've just retrieved your sun hat, and this is how you say 'Hello, Henry,'" he says, flirting shamelessly.

"Hello, Henry. I'm so glad I could give you and your girlfriend some adult time before you up and move to Philadelphia." And before tears start to fall, I turn on my heels and run.

• • •

Rain Stops

By the time I reach William's steps, I am panting and the rain has stopped.

"Please wait, please!" Henry calls from behind, having run after me. "My god, for such a tiny thing you run like a racehorse."

My mother and Bill are at the top of the stairs, bearing more sundries. They sway merrily as they descend. What looks like a joint hangs from Bill's mouth.

"Henry, you have found our lost sheep," my mother squeals in her old peasant cackle, then loses her balance and grabs on to Bill to steady herself. She takes what is indeed a joint from his mouth and inhales deeply.

"It would seem we are the sheep, my dear, and she is Bo Peep," Bill solemnly notes.

"Were you crying, sweetheart?" my mother asks, suddenly serious. I rush past her, embarrassed. I need to get away from Henry—he is too wonderful and too unavailable. In the house, I hunt for the keys to the car, but can't find them, so I go out to the garage and look for a bike.

I find a frame, without wheels, in a dusty corner. Then I spot another, complete with wheels and a basket. It squeaks as I roll it out onto the driveway, hop on, and start pedaling.

"Where are you going?" Henry shouts. As I turn to look, I lose my balance and crash to the ground. "Are you all right?" Henry asks in alarm.

"No, I'm not all right!" I say.

"I'll get some ice," Henry says, and runs back into the house, returning with what looks to be a white cotton cloth.

"This is not ice," I say, feeling it.

"No. It's what you would call a frock. I couldn't find any ice. I thought this might do instead."

"You bought me a frock?" I unfold it. It has a little lace collar and tiny roses embroidered on it. It's beautiful. I put it to my face.

"I bought it when I was in Philadelphia."

"Oh," I say. "So this is a good-bye present, then?"

"No," Henry says.

"No?"

"I'm not moving."

"You're not?"

"No," he says, sitting down in the grass, "and I do *not* have a girlfriend."

"But your mother told Pip—"

"I know, I know. I ran into Pip and Martin at the market around the corner from my house. You remember that store, don't you? The big gourmet one, where Pip threw the liver?"

"How could I forget?" I say.

"I tried to tell you the day I called you here—that was the same day Pip told me about your new apartment and I learned that you and I would soon be neighbors. Well, Pip also asked me where my girlfriend was. I didn't have a clue what she was talking about and said as much. Pip said my mother had told her I was back with Kate. I couldn't think of why in the world my mother would say such a thing but when I asked her if she had, she said yes! Can you believe it? She claimed she had done it so Pip would stop calling. I had no idea. It was an awful thing to do. I was furious at my mother."

"So you're not back with Kate? And you don't have a girlfriend?" I take in this information slowly.

"No, I'm not back with Kate. And yes, I do not have a girlfriend."

"Oh."

After a long pause, he leans into my ear and whispers, "Unless you were willing. Will you be my girlfriend?"

"What do you think?" I whisper back.

We look at each other shyly and then Henry leans forward, his lips touch mine, and then—

"Honey, are you all right?" my mother hollers, as she opens the door. My eyes fly open. Henry and I withdraw from our almost-kiss. "You rushed right past us and then we heard a little yelp." Now, William and the kids come out as well. My mother looks at my knee, presses her iced bourbon to the scrape.

"I think she's fine," William says to my mother, noticing Henry's and my ruined expressions.

"Yes, Mom, I'm fine," I say.

"Funny, I am, too. Even after eating a dead animal." She pats my back. "You're all wet, dear. You should change."

"I'll go and put this on," I tell Henry as I hold up my new dress. Brendan looks at me. Then Henry. Then back at me, getting it. Brendan taps Lucy's head. "You're it!" he says, and pulls up Sophie. Together they dash into the house, laughing. Lucy and Moonboy take off after them.

"After you change, maybe we can take another walk on the beach now that it is no longer raining." He leans in so close to me I almost swoon. He adds, "So we might have some time alone."

"Yes," I say. "I would like that."

"We'll stay here and hold down the fort," William says.

"Forts are meant to be pillaged, Bill, not held down," says my mother.

"I know," Bill says, joining her on the grass.

Love's Beginnings

My frock fits me perfectly.

I open the porch door a little. Then a little more. Then a bit further. Henry stands outside, holding out his hand. "You look beautiful," he says. I place my small hand in his.

At Last

We walk on the empty beach. The surf is quiet now, and the full moon hangs over the ocean. Henry stops and looks up at the clear night sky, then draws me close. With my head on his chest, I can hear the rhythm of his heart beating slow and steady.

"I think I'm going to like having you for my neighbor, Gracie," he breathes softly into my hair. "I think I will like it very, very much."

Acknowledgments

My tremendous gratitude to my mother who, while battling breast cancer, drummed up the energy to read a very lengthy excerpt of this novel to her women friends at her annual Solstice party. To my writing pals Daphne, Julie, and Nina, who were my hot-pink-clog cheerleaders from the beginning. To my early fans Elise, Scudder, and Angie, who convinced me years ago that it was just a matter of time before I was a *real* writer. To Rob, who said, "Send it out." To my agent, Albert La Farge, who opened my first overstuffed envelope containing my inklings and had enough faith in my work to put it out into the world. To my husband, David, my own Perfect Guy, who supported my writer's fantasy life. And loads of thanks to my editor, Amy Gash (the most fabulous editor on the planet), who taught me how to write a novel (*wink*). And of course to my children, Iris and Oskar, and my stepchildren, Rachel, Meghan, and Jeremy, who showed me that life can be a wonderful, thrilling adventure every day—except, maybe, if you're an adult.

OXOXOX, Me